YO-CAF-159

THE MYSTERY. THE LIFE. THE LOVE. THE LEGEND.

DRAGON

THE BRUCE LEE STORY

UNIVERSAL PICTURES PRESENTS

A RAFFAELLA DE LAURENTIIS PRODUCTION A ROB COHEN FILM

JASON SCOTT LEE · LAUREN HOLLY

"DRAGON: THE BRUCE LEE STORY"

NANCY KWAN AND ROBERT WAGNER MUSIC BY RANDY EDELMAN COSTUME DESIGNER CAROL RAMSEY

CO-PRODUCER DICK NATHANSON EDITED BY PETER AMUNDSON PRODUCTION DESIGNER ROBERT ZIEMBICKI

DIRECTOR OF PHOTOGRAPHY DAVID EGGBY EXECUTIVE PRODUCER DAN YORK BASED ON THE BOOK "BRUCE LEE: THE MAN ONLY I KNEW" BY LINDA LEE CADWELL

SCREENPLAY BY EDWARD KHMARA AND JOHN RAFFO AND ROB COHEN

PRODUCED BY RAFFAELLA DE LAURENTIIS DIRECTED BY ROB COHEN

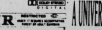

A UNIVERSAL RELEASE

DOLBY STEREO DIGITAL

R RESTRICTED
UNDER 17 REQUIRES ACCOMPANYING
PARENT OR ADULT GUARDIAN

UNIVERSAL.
AN MCA COMPANY

1993 UNIVERSAL CITY STUDIOS INC

DRAGON

THE BRUCE LEE STORY

A novel by Michael Jahn.
Based on a screenplay
by Edward Khmara and
John Raffo and Rob Cohen.

JOVE BOOKS, NEW YORK

To Ellen Jahn

DRAGON

A Jove Book / published by arrangement with
MCA Publishing Rights, a Division of MCA, Inc.

PRINTING HISTORY
Jove edition / June 1993

ISBN: 0-515-11171-6

Jove Books are published by The Berkley Publishing Group,
200 Madison Avenue, New York, New York 10016.
The name "JOVE" and the "J" logo
are trademarks belonging to Jove Publications, Inc.

PRINTED IN THE UNITED STATES OF AMERICA

10 9 8 7 6 5 4 3 2 1

1

1949

THE SHRAPNEL AND THE SCARS FROM THE FRAGMENTATION BOMBS that the Allies had dropped in a fury of vengeance against Hong Kong's Japanese occupiers were still evident four years after the fighting stopped.

It was 1949 and the city was still rebuilding what it had lost in the devastation of World War II. The people of Hong Kong—especially the common men, women, and children—already suffered from living in the most densely packed city on earth. Imagine the entire city of New York packed into the confines of Central Park. Into that steamy mass of humanity, sweltering much of the year or pummeled by furious typhoons, had come four years of brutal Japanese conquest and occupation. That nightmare had been ended only by the terror of Allied day-and-night bombing.

When the Japanese were driven out at last, there came beating at the door a new threat—Communism. The Red hordes of Mao Tse-Tung rampaged across the vast Chinese mainland in 1949, bringing their own brand of horror. They stopped at the outskirts of Hong Kong, halted by a threatened confrontation with Great Britain, the city's founder and overseer, but their presence was felt throughout the city.

The Red Chinese were the barbarians growling outside the gates of the great metropolis.

That's how it was in Hong Kong in 1949. Four years after the Japanese surrender, the stone walls and pillars of the Tsing Lin Temple remained pockmarked with bits of razor-sharp metal shrapnel and jagged clumps of paving rock thrown up by the force of explosions. A handful of miles away, Mao's millions hovered menacingly. It was a time for shattered nerves and shattering nightmares.

Looking down on how mankind had ravaged and threatened their holy place, the Chinese gods were much more than angry; they were furious—especially with outsiders. For millennia the Chinese had kept to themselves, and were isolated and xenophobic, going so far as to build a Great Wall to keep foreigners away. The Chinese gods were ready to lash out at all foreigners and to terrorize any of their own who dreamt of other lands.

The Tsing Lin Temple was rectangular, with a two-tiered pagoda roof made of blue tiles and arched in the center like a crossbow. The corners of the twin roofs arched upwards toward heaven and were decorated with grotesque figures of animals. There was a serpent on one corner, and a lion on another. A leopard and a dragon perched angrily on the other corners.

The four main pillars were made of stone that had been polished to the smoothness of ivory and painted red. Each pillar was entwined, like half-living totem poles, with blue-and-green snakes with gleaming eyes that bulged out above six-inch ivory fangs. The wall was made of red, blue, green, and gold panels. Along the wall was a frieze meant to scare the faithful into a state of awed fearfulness. The mural sculpture depicted a row of gods and warriors, some half-beast, some with fearsome black faces that sprouted boar-like tusks. Some wore helmets and breastplates that

2

seemed to have been made from the scales of a gigantic fish. Others carried weapons: short and long swords, pikes, daggers, and bows.

Some were familiar Chinese gods. Man, the god of literature, was dressed in green and held a writing implement. Mo, the god of war, wore red and carried a sword. Pao Kung, the Chinese god of justice, had a jet-black face. Shing Wong, god of the city of Hong Kong, looked stern. Some of the other figures grimaced in pain, while others vented bare-toothed fury. One or two smiled sweetly, perhaps to suggest, as does Chinese mythology, that nothing in life is wholly evil or entirely good. Around the figures and sometimes gashing them were pockmarks left over from wartime shrapnel.

It was in the moments before sunset when the nine-year-old Lee Jun Fan—not yet known as Bruce Lee—stepped from the damp and cavernous inside of the temple out into the long shadows that cut across the war-scarred old gods of the temple facade. He wore crisp, white linen school clothes, slacks and shirt, and carried a canvas book bag at the end of a strap.

The street that ran alongside the temple was curiously empty. The only other soul was an old beggar, crippled by disease, years, and malnutrition, who sat propped against a pole, his toothless mouth gaping wide open as he slept. Lee's black hair was neatly parted but his face was pale with worry. The hideous gargoyles, demons, warriors, and guardians of the temple glared down on him, their weapons and bared fangs all too real for a boy of nine. But he had to pass by that wall to get home, where his father would miss him were he not to arrive soon. So Lee hurried along the wall, his teeth chattering as he tried to pull his head down into his shoulders like a turtle.

An eerie wind came up from nowhere, blowing softly like

3

the horn of a freighter following the channel that cut across Repulse Bay and out into the South China Sea. The demons of the temple seemed to suck in that wind and blow it back through flaring nostrils. Lee was nearly paralyzed with fear by the time he got to the end of the wall and the last statue, a seven-foot Ming warrior from the 16th century.

The wind stopped suddenly, but was replaced by another sound. The stone statue seemed to crack, and the boy swore he saw the muscled arm of the statue move, shedding bits of stone scales as if they were crumbling autumn leaves. Lee froze and gaped in abject terror. *Yes, it moved! The arm of the warrior moved! He's reaching for his sword!* The leather-armored giant was unsheathing his razor-sharp sword! Cracks were forming in the stone as centuries-old muscles broke free of their bounds.

With a whoop of fear, Lee began running down the street. But the old beggar was suddenly awake, and grinning horribly, four-inch fangs now gleaming from his old mouth. Then he disappeared and the street itself turned to blackness, a curtain of sheer black that must have come from the edge of the world. The boy stopped, whirled, and ran back for the safety of the temple.

Running as fast as he could, he leaped up the several steps and raced across the terrace, only to have the gigantic brass-and-ivory-trimmed oak doors slam in his face. Lee gasped in fear and pounded on the doors until his little hands were raw. There was the sound of ripping and tearing, and stones falling. Behind him, the Ming warrior had gone. His place in the wall was empty, a black hole to match the blackness that seemed to have gripped the entire street.

The back door! I can get in through the back door! The boy dashed off the terrace and ran down the narrow and cramped alley that led to the north side of the temple. There was a small door there that the priests used. Surely it would

4

be open. If not open, it might be weak enough to force. But halfway down the alley, as darkness closed in behind, there appeared a pulsing light that grew in intensity until it became a searing white wall that blocked the way.

Lee froze and dropped his book bag. There was no way out. The wall of light was blinding, but behind was blackness from the edge of the earth. Then from out of the light came fog, a sickly sweet-smelling fog that carried the aroma of funeral flowers. A figure began to emerge from the light—the Ming Warrior. Now he looked even taller than seven feet, and he was no statue. He was the real thing, smelling of death and old leather, his breath reeking, his razor-sharp sword poised overhead.

Lee slumped to the ground, unable to move, his face contorted in silent screams. The sword rose high overhead, nearly to the starless sky, then came searing down through the perfumed air.

The force of the impact woke Lee Hoi Chuen from his nightmare. His eyes snapped open to feel the sting of sweat that poured down his brow like the flood rains that raced down Victoria Peak and turned the steep, ladder streets of Hong Kong's old Western District into waterfalls.

The room was illuminated by the garish glow from the store signs, including a few primitive neon ones, that filled the narrow streets outside. Lee Hoi Chuen's bedroom was sparsely furnished, the walls decorated only with family photos and a small frame that held an octagonal *pat kwa* mirror and the likeness of Tsao Kwan, the household god to whom many Chinese families turned to protect them from the evil spirits that were thought to be everywhere. The mirror was to ward off the spirits; Lee Hoi Chuen picked it up and carried it into the kitchen, where a shrine to Tsao Kwan held a small porcelain figure of the god. Lee Hoi placed a shiny new Hong Kong dollar at the feet of the god, then carried the *pat kwa* mirror into his son's bedroom.

Lee Jun Fan slept peacefully, his jet-black hair contrasting with the freshly washed and pressed white pillow. Lee Hoi stroked his son's hair gently, then reached over and placed the mirror on the windowsill along with several others like it. There Tsao Kwan could watch over the boy and protect him. No evil spirit—no Ming Warrior from the 16th century—would get past that barricade of charms. Lee Hoi was sure of it. That feeling was bolstered when the boy woke, saw his father, and gave him a sweet smile, then fell back asleep.

❧ 2 ❧

YOU COULD GET ANYTHING YOU WANTED IN HONG KONG IF YOU knew where to go. The neighborhoods had their specialties. Queen's Road and Queen Victoria Street were the places to buy foods of all kinds. Li Yuen Street held bargain clothes. Cloth Alley sold fabric, while Wing Sing Street sold eggs—all sorts of them, from quails' eggs to one-thousand-year-old eggs. Bonham Strand was filled with traditional shops, most of them spilling out onto the sidewalk, selling, among other things, live snakes for use as food or medicine. Funerals and coffins were sold along Hollywood Road. Everywhere traffic roared at breakneck speed—despite the nearly impassable streets. For their part, pedestrians stepped into traffic without looking, seemingly without regard for their lives. The Chinese fear of spirits had melded interestingly with modern, motorized society: Many pedestrians felt that the cars whizzing behind them would surely kill any evil spirits who happened to be following them around.

With the young Bruce in tow, Lee Hoi Chuen walked purposefully through the narrow lanes, stopping often to exchange greetings with shopkeepers. For if the citizens of Hong Kong were fearful of spirits, they were even more ardent in their pursuit of money. Sixteen-hour days were common in the family-run shops that crowded every street,

7

their narrow, tall signs and banners stretching often from pavement to rooftop. Lee Hoi seemed to know everyone, even the miserable old man on Macau Alley who was making a living by selling American candy to children. His rack of Mars Bars, Baby Ruths, Hershey's Chocolates, Three Musketeers, and Wrigley's gum perched on the cobblestones between a maker of "ancient" Chinese vases and a purveyor of shark's fin soup.

Young Bruce eyed the candy hungrily. He said, in Cantonese, "Buy me some candy, Dad. I want some candy."

His father answered in English: "When you learn to ask in English, I will buy you candy."

"But English is so hard."

"You simply must speak English. Everyone must know it. It will be very important to you one day. You will see."

The boy pouted, but knew enough to behave. His father was boss, there was no denying it. You simply did not talk back. And the old man had been acting odd lately. The young Bruce could think of no reason for it, and it would have been improper of him to ask. He was afraid of something—what, Bruce could not tell. He made offerings to Tsao Kwan *twice* daily, and carefully polished the magical mirrors left on the windowsill.

Lee Hoi led his son down a brick alley not far from Tang City Hall. The straight line of solid brick was broken by only one door. Lee Hoi kissed his son on the forehead and urged him inside. The boy looked inside the door nervously, then looked back at his dad and smiled bravely. Lee Hoi had been saving his pennies for this moment, and Bruce knew that what he was about to embark upon was a great honor. He knew most of all that it would make his father very, very happy—and perhaps, in a way, ease the fear that had been gripping the man of late. Bruce said good-bye to his father and stepped bravely inside alone.

Yip Man had been born in the town of Fatshan, but had left in advance of the Communist takeover and settled in Hong Kong. It was there that he'd founded his *kwoon,* a training place or club, and become the leading teacher of the *wing chun* ("beautiful springtime") style of kung fu.

His *kwoon* was in an abandoned temple with roofless courtyards flanking it front and back. The familiar, blue-tiled pagoda roof—much smaller, of course, than the ones atop the Tsing Lin Temple—held a shrine to Pao Kung, the god of justice, and a six-foot-tall golden dragon that guarded an arched nook in which sat the master. A *wing chun* dummy stood by itself atop a practice mat.

Yip Man poured *cha,* tea, into two delicate cups, and held one up for Bruce. "Come, take it, and sit," said the old man, ever so gently urging the wide-eyed boy onto a silken cushion next to his own. There was something about this old man that set him apart from everyone else Bruce had met. He had an aura, an inner strength, and a sense of destiny that, with scarcely a word being said, filled the young Bruce Lee with admiration bordering on awe.

Yip Man rose, bowed to Bruce, and silently took the tiger stance. He began to work out on the dummy, and the instant he did his old body was replaced by a young and lithe one that moved with the grace and inner strength of a true master. Imagine being so old yet so young, Bruce thought. Think of having no more fears, not of man, beast, or spirit. Imagine having such *chi,* such inner energy. Another thought fixed in the boy's head. *I've found my calling,* it said.

And so it went for thirteen years. From 1949 through 1962 Bruce's routine centered around Yip Man, the master of *wing chun,* and the training sessions in his *kwoon.* As he

9

grew in years from nine to twenty-two, Bruce grew in *chi* and skill. *Wing chun* was suited to him. Bruce was slightly built, and *wing chun* had been developed by a Chinese village woman under the tutelage of a Shaolin nun. It had economy, using the minimum force to do the maximum work. And it was a fluid, beautiful style perfectly fitted to the boy's outgoing personality.

By the age of twenty-two, Bruce was a *wing chun* adept and had begun to form his own ideas of style. He knew that kung fu was whatever an adept made it. Each movement was like a brick that could be put together with other bricks to make a road that led anywhere. His physical skills were perfectly honed. His mental abilities were likewise polished. Bruce was as good on the chessboard, and had the generally calm and peaceful mental attitude essential for him to be a kung fu master.

It was 1962 and he was ready to prove himself. He had already proved himself in one arena. His father, long a star of light opera who was important in Hong Kong's growing film industry, had helped Bruce get roles in locally made films. As a boy his face was seen now and again on the movie posters that were sold in small shops that specialized in movie memorabilia. He was not a name then, only a face. Now the young man was ready to take the bricks of kung fu and start building a road that he himself would travel. It would take an event of nearly seismic proportions, however, to get him started down it.

🕱 3 🕱

1962

THE CIRCLE OF HEAVEN DANCE HALL WAS IN ONE OF THOSE LONG streets just off the waterfront where the dance halls, girlie bars, and pornographic shops seemed to go on for miles. It was the Chinese New Year Celebration, and the city seemed to be coming apart at the seams.

The World War II devastation was long forgotten in 1962. In the place of quaint, handmade store signs of wood and paper were towering neon constructions. If Hong Kong itself could be likened to New York City crammed into Central Park, the nightlife district was Las Vegas stuffed into a sardine can. The signs were electric and gaudy, and seemed to leap across the street in the same way that the canopy formed by maple trees leaps across country lanes in small American towns. The double-decker buses crawled beneath the signs, bristling with a clamoring mixture of local thrill-seekers, tourists out for a look at the seamy side of town, and sailors, legions of sailors.

Hong Kong had grown to be many things over the years, but it was first and foremost a port—the greatest port connecting the great East Asian mainland with the Pacific and the Americas. Sailors of all nations came there, wallets

11

thick with money to spend, hungry from long months at sea without the company of women. A pack of British sailors, fresh from the Naval Dockyard in Wanchai, got off a bus and looked around for a minute before their eyes focused on several pretty young Chinese girls going into the Circle of Heaven. One of the sailors was waving a bottle of Gordon's Gin, and swaggering with an attitude that was superior to begin with, and more than a little drunk on that fine Saturday night in Hong Kong, they all pushed inside.

It took American dance crazes a few years to reach halfway around the globe, and so the five-piece band struggled with a cha-cha that had been popular in the States before Elvis was swallowed up by the U.S. Army and sent to Germany to drive trucks. So did a dozen Chinese couples, while perhaps a hundred more Chinese watched, swayed with the music, and talked. The hall was decorated in the management's impression of what an American high school sock hop must be like. Crepe-paper ribbons in pink, blue, yellow, red, green, and orange were draped along the wall, hanging off lighting fixtures and coat racks. Accordion-like Chinese lanterns hung from the ceiling, as did an old fishnet stolen from the docks, which had plastic lobsters and starfish tangled in it. A mirrored ball twirled madly from the center of the ceiling, the spotlights trained on it creating a swarm of bright dots that raced around the room.

Occasionally a wandering spotlight illuminated a poster-sized sign, hand-lettered in Chinese and English, that proclaimed that this was the night of the 1962 New Year Elimination Cha-Cha Contest. Top prize was a dinner for two at the Viceroy of India. Judges in red sports jackets circulated among the dancing couples, checking name tags and making notes on clipboards. As they worked, the judges paid particular attention to the clear front-runners: a slender, college-age Chinese man wearing a salmon-pink blazer dancing with his girlfriend, a willowy and beautiful Chinese girl with jet-black hair styled in the manner of Jackie Kennedy and a mint-green crinoline dress worn with black patent leather pumps.

There was something of a commotion at the door when the British sailors pushed their way in. The deck crew of Her Majesty's Destroyer *Antibes* had been in port only a few hours after a grueling passage from the Persian Gulf. They were drunk and horny and, like generations of Her Majesty's subjects before them, inclined to treat Hong Kong natives like servants or worse. The deck crew of any ship must be a rugged bunch, used to doing heavy hauling under all kinds of conditions. On one tour they might be frozen by winter winds in the North Atlantic and tossed about by forty-foot seas. The next voyage they might be sweltering beneath a tropical sun that heats the deck plates to 150 degrees. The man who keeps this tough bunch in line is the boatswain, the nautical equivalent of a sergeant.

The boatswain of the *Antibes* was Billy Cox, who before he entered the service had been a soccer bully from Newcastle. In those days, he and his mates had delighted in getting beered up and thrashing the daylights out of the fans of opposing teams. When they weren't doing that, they went Pak-bashing—beating up Pakistanis who had the misfortune to wander into the wrong part of Newcastle. In short, practically everything in Cox's life had prepared him to be a boatswain on a destroyer and a drunken party-crasher at a Hong Kong New Year's dance.

Having elbowed aside the ticket-takers at the door, Cox went straight for the punch bowl, which sat on a crepe-paper-decorated cafeteria table not far from the bandstand. He grabbed the ladle away from the white-haired Chinese woman who had been serving the concoction of Kool-Aid and papaya juice to the young Orientals at the dance. He held it up while one of his crew uncapped the gin and poured it into the ladle before adding the remainder of the bottle to the bowl.

Cox swigged the gin from the ladle while the rest of his men commandeered cups and dipped them into the bowl. All of them looked around the room, drooling at the sight of so many lovely, available-looking Chinese girls. So many women in Hong Kong were available; these must be too. That was the thought going through Cox's addled brain as he bulled his way through the crowd on the dance floor to reach the girl in the green crinoline.

Cox cut in on the young man in the salmon-pink jacket, shoving him aside by virtue of sheer bulk. The boatswain then grabbed the girl by the waist, a beefy hand reaching halfway around her reed-like midsection. She was startled, her big, chipmunk-like eyes darting about in surprise and confusion. But she danced with the man, who took her hand and twirled her with amazing grace for someone so big.

Although half the Briton's size, the Chinese man tried to reclaim his girl. "She's mine," he said in Cantonese. Cox spoke not a word of that language, but understood the meaning of the words. With a huge left arm, he swatted the man away. The young fellow tripped, tumbling backwards, and fell to the floor.

The several couples dancing nearby broke apart, providing a circle in which the drama could unfold. The girl was terrified. Angry now, her Chinese beau scrambled to his feet and charged the boatswain.

Cox responded by letting go of the girl and unleashing a tremendous right hook that caught the young man in the face and sent him sprawling. He was unconscious before he hit the floor, where he skidded into the feet of onlookers at the edge of the circle. The girl screamed, and several others

14

joined her. The band stopped playing as the dancers quickly pulled back out of harm's way.

The dance floor was left to Cox and the girl in the green crinoline. She was stiff with fear as he grabbed her again and pressed her tiny body to his. He moved her in a slow dance around the floor as she began to sob and push fruitlessly against him. The rest of the crew laughed and looked around for more women to assault. There was no music other than a guttural humming that Cox made to entertain himself.

A shadow came down the hall then, a long shadow made by the neon glow from the street as it passed around a solitary, stoic figure that moved, with leopard-like grace, into the dance hall. Sensing his *chi,* the crowd parted to let Bruce pass. At five-foot-seven and 135 pounds, the handsome twenty-two-year-old Lee commanded attention and respect far beyond his physical size or years. Like a leopard—or a dragon—he moved people aside by the sheer force of his internal strength. In addition, he was far from unknown among the young people of the city. As a child actor he'd appeared in enough movies, often playing a street tough, to make his face familiar.

He walked across the mostly empty dance floor, unafraid, perfectly focused, wearing black slacks and a dark burgundy polo shirt. The dance hall stumbled into silence, and Cox looked up from where he had been kissing the girl on the nape of her neck, holding her in a vise-like grip. When he looked up, he saw Bruce standing nearby, staring intently at him.

"What do *you* want?" Cox said with a laugh.

"I want to dance with her," Bruce replied calmly.

"This one's mine. Get one of your own—Shorty."

He resumed dancing and humming, all the while pressing the helpless girl against his groin.

15

"She *is* one of my own," Bruce said. "You could get one of *your* own, except I haven't seen any gorillas loose in Hong Kong lately."

The boatswain let go of the girl, who scurried off to join her friends and sink to her knees to hold the head of her fallen boyfriend.

"You're a big pig, I hope he kills you," she shouted in Cantonese.

Cox looked at her and then at Bruce, who smiled at her words. Cox was big but hardly a pig. More like a rhino about to charge. But that was all right with Bruce. As a *wing chun* master he was trained to handle much bigger opponents, largely by turning their own forces against them. But already, in Hong Kong in 1962, Bruce was formulating his own version of *wing chun*. He had no name for it yet, only an idea torn from the mean streets of the world's busiest and, in some ways, most crime-ridden city. Few martial arts masters have the experience of being assaulted by another martial arts master while walking to the corner deli. Few kung fu practitioners become muggers and other types of sidewalk criminals. The most likely opponent you will run into is a big idiot, probably high on booze or pills and low on brains. It's not likely you will have a chance midnight encounter with a karate or tae kwon do master who will want to get into his set position, bow respectfully, and fight. The key, Bruce knew before he ever left Hong Kong, was adaptability. See what your opponent can do and then, quickly, do unto him.

Cox growled then and tossed a massive right fist. His searing paw came within millimeters of Bruce's chin, but missed as Bruce's head slid just out of harm's way. Frustrated, Cox lunged for the much smaller man, hoping to get his arms about him and choke the life out of him.

Bruce sidestepped, and Cox stumbled a few paces across

the floor, having partly lost his balance. A few people laughed.

Cox snarled, "Stand still and fight, you yellow bastard."

"Whatever you say," Bruce replied.

The boatswain came forward again, this time in an American boxing stance. He feinted with his left fist and threw another mammoth right. It hadn't worked before, but he figured eventually he would land it.

This time Bruce stepped to the side but blocked the punch with his left hand while grabbing the fist with his right. Pulling Cox forward using his own momentum, Bruce hit him with a right-hand claw strike that covered half the boatswain's face.

Lee spared the man's eye but left the lower lid torn at one corner. And a clawing thumb left torn skin and ruptured capillaries below the jawline. The boatswain jerked his head back, fighting the tears and blood that were creeping into his eye.

Furious now, Cox lunged again. This time Bruce answered with a combination of straight-arm punches to the kidneys. Stung, his ears hearing increasing laughter from the young Chinese men and women he had tried so hard to humiliate, Cox feinted with his right and tossed a left cross.

Bruce caught the punch, jujitsu-style, and twisted the arm, bending the sailor's wrist back. He smashed it down on his rising knee. The sickening crack echoed off the crepe-paper-strewn walls of the Circle of Heaven Dance Hall.

As Cox staggered, grasping his broken paw, Bruce gave him a high kick right into the bandstand. He landed amidst a clatter of drums and cymbals, and only got to his feet when two members of his crew helped him.

"You okay, Billy?" one asked.

"I'm fine. The son-of-a-bitch broke my wrist, though. I'll kill him."

17

"You got another wrist," the man said, handing the boatswain a ten-inch cake knife.

"I'll turn him into sliced pork," Cox said, then advanced on Lee with murderous fury in his one good eye.

Bruce whipped off his belt—except it only looked like a belt. It was the pull chain from an old-fashioned, overhead-tank toilet. In Bruce's hands it became a worthy substitute for nunchaku fighting sticks.

As Cox lunged, Bruce wrapped the chain around the knife hand and twisted the arm up against Cox's own neck. Suddenly the nearly beaten man felt the pressure of his own arm against his own throat as Bruce strangled him from behind. When he was weakened Bruce shoved him forward, and he staggered across the floor. Then Bruce leaped into the air and hit Cox in the shoulder blades with a flying kick that propelled him into the cake table.

The table snapped in half as the big man went down in a shower of crepe paper and pastry. The crowd roared its approval as Bruce turned and faced Cox's fellow crewmen.

"Next," he said.

"Not me, mate," one of them said, holding up open palms in the universal gesture of surrender.

"Nor me," another added, and the rest seemed to agree.

"Why don't you be good boys and carry out the trash?" Bruce said, indicating Cox.

The crowd roared again. This was the first taste of crowd approval for Bruce, and he found he liked it. It was wonderful to have Yip Man, his *sifu,* his instructor, approve of his fighting. But there was something raw and powerful in having a crowd of people, *his* people, applauding. It also felt good to have done a good deed, and Bruce was reminded that kung fu had originated in the Shaolin Cha'n Buddhist Temple in the Songshan Mountains, in the northern Chinese province of Hunan. Bruce was no Shaolin monk, not by a long shot, but having aided a helpless person in distress felt good. Between the applause and the feeling of having done some good, he sensed something, something akin to the feeling he had had upon first setting eyes on Yip Man. Fate was presenting itself.

At that moment, however, the girl in the crinoline dress ran up bearing nothing heavier than gratitude. *"Lee Sue Long,"* she said in Chinese. The words mean "little dragon."

He smiled at her and gently touched her white corsage. "Thanks."

His smile grew broader, then disappeared as the sound of police sirens could be heard converging from several directions. He left her and ran toward the back door.

🏮 4 🏮

DAWN WAS RISING IN HONG KONG, THE FIRST RAYS OF SUNLIGHT
illuminating the top of Victoria Peak and glinting off the
cables of the tram that took tourists to and from the apex.

It was true that the city never entirely slept, but in the
moments before dawn it yawned a little. No tourists were on
the streets. Most of the prostitutes had turned in for the
night. The heroin sellers were out in force most of the day
and night in the years since the British authorities banned
opium smoking and addicts switched to heroin because
there was no telltale smoke to give them away. But by dawn
they too were bedded down for a few hours.

For the most part, the only ones up and around were street
sweepers, garbagemen, deliverymen, and merchants preparing their stores for the next sixteen-hour day. Perhaps there
were a few evil spirits about, discontented phantoms of
age-old ancestors who had been improperly revered by their
descendants. And certainly the police were out in force. On
avenues and alleys of the old quarter, sirens blared as a
small army of lawmen searched for Bruce Lee.

Looking warily around, he ran up a ladder street that rose
at a nearly sixty-degree incline from the flat boulevards of
the harbor area. On the streets and on the rooftops of the old
buildings where the common people lived, men and women

did their morning tai chi chuan exercises and sipped steaming cups of tea.

Bruce zipped around the corner of his apartment building and, unwilling to be seen going in the front door, scaled a wall and scampered up the bamboo scaffolding that served as both laundry rack and fire escape.

He glanced around long enough to verify that no one had seen him, then slipped up the window to his bedroom. He removed the several *pat kwa* mirrors that his father had placed on the sill and gently lowered them to the floor. Then he squirmed inside, shut the window, and replaced the mirrors. *I'm safe now,* he thought with a sigh.

Then a rough hand grabbed him by the shoulder and turned him around. It was his father, Lee Hoi Chuen.

He pushed Bruce against the wall. "The cops were here. They're looking for you."

"I know. Hey, don't surprise me like that."

"That young man you assaulted is in the hospital with a punctured lung. He might die."

"I didn't assault him. He was making trouble. He started it."

"That's not what the police say. His friends say that you started it."

"And you believed them? I'm supposed to have picked a fight with a man twice my size?"

"It does not matter what I believe."

"That British sailor was making trouble—he beat up a local boy and nearly raped his date. I tried to stop it and he threw the first punch."

"Yip Man taught you too well," Lee Hoi said, shaking his head ruefully. "Come into the kitchen and have some tea. There is much we must discuss."

He led the way. Bruce followed, protesting: "This mess will blow over. That man was another drunken sailor who

21

tried to have his way with a Chinese woman and paid for it.''

Now in the kitchen, Bruce's father said, ''The man you beat up—his father is the cousin of the assistant police inspector of Kowloon. Did you know that?''

Bruce stared at his father hard, without his usual optimism. Nonetheless, he said, ''It'll blow over. I can hide out with my friends.''

''You don't have any friends now,'' Lee Hoi said.

''That's not true.''

''You can't trust them not to betray you. The police are powerful and your friends mostly poor boys like yourself. There is no place that they can hide you.''

''Yip Man will hide me. He has family.''

''Yip Man's *kwoon* is the first place the police looked. And his family? They are all on the mainland. Do you think the Communists will sympathize with you?''

''For beating up a British sailor, probably they will. But I get your point. I can't go there. That would be worse than being hung by the British.'' Bruce softened his tone and added, ''I hope that man doesn't die. He was only a drunken fool. No one deserves to die for that.''

Lee Hoi poured two steaming cups of king tea from a teapot that had a dragon's head and neck as a spout. The implication that the gods were involved in Bruce's fate was everywhere, from the shape of the teapot to the extra offerings that had been made overnight to Tsao Kwan. Honey had been rubbed on the lips of the deity, and nearly a dozen dollar coins sat at his feet. A thin trail of scented smoke rose from an incense burner set at the base of Tsao Kwan's pedestal.

''Sit down,'' Bruce's father said.

Bruce did as he was told, and took a sip of tea. It was hot but full and good, and stirred his spirits as it went down.

"The cops will be back," Bruce said. "I should get out of here."

"I have thought about this for a long time," said Lee Hoi Chuen. "You must leave Hong Kong."

"Leave Hong Kong? For how long?"

"Forever."

"This is a joke, right? You're joking." Bruce was astonished. For while he realized that there was a much bigger world that he might someday want to see, the notion of leaving was as far off as the lands he might visit.

"Listen to me, Sai Fong. You'll die in Hong Kong."

"That fate awaits us all."

"True, but you are fated to die before your time if you don't take care. I have seen it."

"You're too superstitious."

"It is not just I who have seen the future. I have been to the *feng shui* man."

"The old man in Kowloon with two-inch fingernails?"

"Don't be so scornful. He saw the future in my palm. You will die young if you don't get out of Hong Kong. The demon will come for you."

"I can beat any demon," Bruce said confidently.

"No man can do that. Not me, not Yip Man, not you. The best you can do is put him off."

Bruce shook his head and said, "I love you, Papa, but this is silly."

His father was insistent, however. Magic remains powerful in the lives of many Chinese. The *feng shui* man, the fortune teller, is as much a part of the family as the corner shopkeeper. Many Chinese will not make an important decision without consulting their *feng shui* man. At his direction houses alongside rivers face upstream to avoid having the family fortune carried off. Or hillside graves are

23

dug at a particular angle. Or household furniture is rearranged to ward off evil spirits and please the good ones.

Lee Hoi told his son, "You're a man now . . . almost. You have a right to know everything. You had an older brother, you see."

"What?"

"He died in childbirth. The demons took him from us."

"I never knew."

"It is unwise to speak too much of these things. A firstborn man-child is very valuable. When you were born, I named you Sai Fong—a girl's name. We dressed you in dresses so the demon wouldn't know I had another son. We were afraid he could come and take you too. I made you speak English to fool him more. Perhaps it was wrong of me to let you play in those movies. Now the demon knows who you are and he's coming for you."

In spite of his natural confidence, Bruce was unnerved. Perhaps there was some truth to what his father said of spirits and demons. Certainly, many of his friends believed in them. "You must leave at once," his father said.

"Where, Papa? Where can I go?"

"Come into my study."

The walls of Lee Hoi Chuen's study were covered by framed photographs documenting his long and successful career in regional opera and local films. A sturdy oak desk with a polished top dominated the room, and one wall was taken up by the old man's *kang*: a low horizontal brick fireplace with a mat atop it for sleeping. In this case, the mat was for smoking opium. A rack of pipes sat discreetly nearby.

Lee Hoi pulled open a desk drawer and rummaged around for a moment. Then he pulled out an ancient leather binder and carefully undid the silk cord that bound it. From the folder he took a silk wrapping. He laid it on the table and

24

unfolded it carefully, as an archaeologist might unwrap an ancient papyrus. Inside was a document, written in English and just beginning to show the yellow of age.

Curious, Bruce moved closer. "What's that?" he asked.

"You love American movies. You love American cars. You'll go to America."

He showed his son an American birth certificate.

"America!" Bruce exclaimed.

"I was in America on tour with the Canton Opera in 1940. I was in San Francisco, doing *The Drunken Princess*. It was November twenty-seventh."

"My birthday!"

"Yes. That morning I got you and three good reviews! I was very proud. This is your birth certificate."

"You never told me I was born in America."

"It was a difficult time, an uncertain time. The Japanese had taken over China and it was impossible to know what to do. Your brother died and we had no idea where to live. To make the future more secure for you, I took out an insurance policy. I made sure that you were documented as an American citizen and I gave you an American name."

"What?" his son exclaimed.

"Bruce Lee," Lee Hoi said, with a slight chuckle. "It sounded very American."

"It sure does." Bruce laughed. The two men giggled, almost like schoolgirls.

Lee Hoi gave Bruce the birth certificate. "Give this to the immigration man. Show them that you are one of them and they have to let you in."

America loomed. America brightened up Bruce's eyes. But it was so far away.

"You need money to go to America," Bruce said.

His father went to the wall and from it plucked an old, framed black-and-white photograph. It showed father and

25

son on the set of *The Orphan,* the last film Bruce had performed in as a young actor.

"I remember that," Bruce said fondly.

"You were good in this film. You were a good young actor."

"I was okay."

"Juvenile delinquents you always did well. In America they are fascinated with troubled youth. Did you see *West Side Story?*"

"Papa, that was about Puerto Ricans and whites in New York. I'm Chinese."

"That was before. You're an American now. Remember that." He opened the back of the frame to reveal several stacks of bills. Each stack was neatly tied with a silk ribbon. Bruce's eyes widened at the sight of the stacks of Hong Kong dollars.

"You earned this doing those movies," Lee Hoi said. "This money is yours. I saved it for you, for a day like this. I knew it would come. The *feng shui* man told me long ago."

Bruce was overwhelmed. "I don't know what to say."

"Say you'll do better. Tell me you'll make a big noise in America. So big I can hear it over here."

He hugged his father, and said, "I'll be back and show you personally."

"No, you must never come back."

"I must, if only to finish my chess game with Yip Man. He was beating me when we stopped."

"Remember the demon. He cannot get you in America."

"Sure, Papa," Bruce said.

They were about to hug again when they heard the sound of footsteps coming down the outside hall. After that came the pounding of a heavy, angry fist on the door.

Someone shouted in Cantonese: *"It's the police! Open up, please!"*

Lee Hoi rushed Bruce out of his study and back to the young man's bedroom. He urged his son to the safety of the fire escape. The pounding at the door grew more intense, but Bruce took a moment to scoop up some keepsakes.

"Remember one thing," Lee Hoi said. "You must remember this one thing about America. Everything depends on it."

"Open up now!" the voice demanded.

"Yes, Dad?" Bruce asked.

"In America . . . remember to drive on the right."

He cuffed his son's chin. It was one last joke. Then the old man shoved him toward the window. Bruce put one leg outside, then paused to grab his father in a tight embrace.

"Go now," he said, and then his son was gone, scrambling down the bamboo scaffolding.

Lee Hoi watched him go, then turned to face the police. He mussed up his hair and pulled his shirt halfway out of his pants. The old actor was at work. Doing an Academy Award-winning imitation of a drunk just roused from sleep, he lurched toward the door.

"Coming . . . coming," he muttered angrily in Chinese.

✺ 5 ✺

THE S.S. *MENENDEZ* WAS A 140-TON STEAMER THAT, ON THAT steamy night in 1962, debarked from Hong Kong carrying a cargo of Chinese merchandise to Seattle by way of Hawaii. As she coursed through the Lamma Channel, which led from Hong Kong out into the South China Sea, the newly renamed Bruce Lee worked hard to shed the last vestiges of Lee Jun Fan. That was a name he would use again only rarely, only when it suited him.

It was hard being in steerage, the cheapest passage overseas. Millions of persons had emigrated to America in just that way, of course, but in Bruce's case what awaited wasn't the Statue of Liberty and New York, but an unknown future in San Francisco's Chinatown. Many Chinese before him had taken that route, and many of them had died building the railroads through the West during the 19th century. Bruce felt an odd kinship with all those Chinamen who'd gone before him as he returned from the galley bearing a leg of fried chicken.

He sat on his pallet, a thin wooden frame covered with cotton, in a dark and smelly compartment built to accommodate twenty passengers and now holding fifty-five. He took a hungry bite, then offered some to his neighbor. He said in Cantonese, "I got it from the cook. Do you want some?"

The man shook his head, so Bruce finished off the chicken leg while looking around at his fellow travelers. A few were young but most were older—men in their forties and up. A few lay on their backs watching water condense on the cold pipes that ran along the ceiling. Most slept. There would be little to do during the three-week passage. The ship was doing the work: plastic flowers and dolls to Honolulu, ceramic tiles and sewing machine parts to Seattle. Along the way a hold would fill up with canned pineapple. It was not inconceivable that some heroin had found its way into one or two of the thousands of innocuous wooden crates. No one knew. Now everyone searched for a way to pass the time. In a corner of the steerage compartment, four men were playing mah-jongg.

Bruce switched languages and said, "Do you speak English? I'm practicing my English for when I get to America."

The neighbor grunted. He was a skinny man with bones that protruded through a thin layer of skin. He looked fifty years old, but could easily have been older. There was some lung problem in his past, Bruce thought, noting the raspy voice and deep, moist cough.

"I've always wanted to go to America," Bruce went on. "You know: John Wayne, French fries. The sky's the limit, that's what they say."

" 'Not a Chinaman's chance.' They say that too. You ever heard that?"

"Sure. But I don't know what it means."

"We built the railroads, right? They lower Chinamen over the cliffs in baskets to set the dynamite. Get pulled up too slow—bang! Ropes break—bye-bye! Americans say, 'Not a Chinaman's chance,' and laugh."

"What's that got to do with me? That was a hundred years ago. Things are different now."

The neighbor, and in fact all those within earshot, burst out laughing. Bruce glared, ready to fight, then shrugged it off. Old men were always so pessimistic.

"I'm different. You'll see."

The neighbor said, "I know your face, young man. Where have I seen you?"

"No place," Bruce said quickly. Police informants could be everywhere—even on ships bound for America.

"What's your name?"

"Bruce Lee."

"I know your face. You are the actor, the one who plays juvenile delinquents in the movies."

"You've mistaken me for someone else. My name is Bruce Lee."

"Who is going to America to be like John Wayne, right?"

"I'm planning to go to college, that's all. What happens after that I have no idea."

The man said, "Well, Bruce Lee, you will wind up washing shirts or dishes like the rest of us. You will see."

"I won't argue with you," Bruce said, and leaned back to watch a fat water beetle as it crawled through the droplets of rusty water that were condensing on a pipe a few feet above his head.

Flames shot up around the sides of woks, chicken and pork simmered in deep fat fryers, and the sounds of chopping filled the air in Gussie Yang's Restaurant. Waitresses dressed in red cheongsams slit up the thigh screamed orders in Chinese while busboys carried huge trays brimming over with aromatic dishes.

Yang's was on Sacramento Street in Chinatown, which,

like the Chinatown in New York, was located, oddly, next to the financial district. Every weekday at lunchtime, the many restaurants that peppered every block filled to capacity with stockbrokers, bond traders, and bankers. In the tiny haven of Oriental life in San Francisco, the manipulators of American wealth came to eat every day.

Bruce caught occasional glimpses of them from the vantage point of the kitchen. Most of the time, however, he stood with his arms plunged elbow-deep in scalding-hot water, washing dishes. All around him were the smells of shredded pork in garlic sauce, General Tseng's chicken, and sliced beef with oyster sauce. While they worked, Bruce and the rest of the kitchen staff paid on-again, off-again attention to a small black-and-white television set high on a wall that also held shelves of spice and other ingredients. On the small screen today, the American actors Paul Muni and Louise Rainer were made up as Chinese peasants for the film of the classic novel by Pearl Buck, *The Good Earth*.

Bruce had only been in San Francisco and working at Yang's for a short while, but already he had made both a friend and an enemy. The friend was April Chun, a waitress. The enemy was Ts'ai Lun, the head chef.

April was a pretty girl a year younger than Bruce, with fine features and long black hair that she parted in the middle and wore long and straight, in the manner of American folk singer Joan Baez. Baez had appeared the year before at the Newport Folk Festival wearing her hair that way, and in an instant created a fashion that quickly replaced the beehive hairdos of the 1950s. Bruce liked April, and the feeling was mutual.

Ts'ai Lun was another matter entirely. He was a huge man with a gut the size of a small steamer trunk and thick, brawny arms that made him look positively homicidal when wielding a meat cleaver. Lun's belly was perpetually on the

31

edge of bursting out of one of his oil-stained T-shirts. The one he wore that particular day bore a replica of Candlestick Park and the team logo of the San Francisco Giants, relocated several years before to the Bay Area from New York City.

It was late in the day, and Paul Muni was scurrying about his rice paddy. Bruce looked at the American actor trying to be a Chinese peasant, and felt a mixture of amusement and disgust. Just then April squeezed by him, looking sexy in her red cheongsam. As she did so, she purposefully bumped her hip against his.

"Hi, Bruce," she said. "How's the movie?"

"Terrible. I know it's a classic, but that guy looks about as Chinese as Tonto looks like an Indian."

"Who's Tonto?"

"You know . . . the Lone Ranger's sidekick? Don't you watch television?"

"Who has time?" She picked up a platter containing rose prawns, Lake Tung-Ting shrimp, heavenly duck, and sliced beef with bamboo shoots and black mushrooms. As she squeezed back past Bruce, she bumped her behind against his and gave him a wink.

Ts'ai Lun saw what she did. He scowled at Bruce and then went for the girl himself, reaching for her round, red-clothed bottom with a ham-sized palm. She squirmed out of reach, making several other kitchen workers laugh. For that they got dirty looks both from Lun and his three under-chefs, all of whom were his stooges.

Ts'ai Lun flicked an elbow and sent a bottle of rice vinegar hurtling off the counter and onto the hard concrete floor, where it shattered into dozens of pieces.

"Clean that up, Lee," he snapped.

Tension filled the kitchen as surely as did smoke and spice. Ts'ai Lun had been on Bruce's case ever since he'd

32

taken the job and moved into a small room on the second floor. Bruce had avoided conflict so far, but there were limits.

But before anything could happen, Gussie Yang walked into the kitchen. She was an elegant woman of sixty or so who had a magisterial bearing that left no doubt who was in charge. She looked at the mess on the floor.

"Clean it up, Bruce, please," she said evenly.

"Sure thing, Miss Yang," he replied, and went to get a mop and bucket.

Much later that night, when customers were long gone and only a cleanup crew remained working in the dining area, Bruce had the kitchen to himself. He was done with washing dishes and mopping floors, but not with the television. He was enjoying his first exposure to American television, and so what if he had to work late to get the TV set to himself.

On the agenda that night was a non-title fight by the young Muhammad Ali, then fighting under his given name of Cassius Clay. Clay had won the gold medal in the 1960 Olympics, and was making noise about taking on the "unbeatable" heavyweight champion Sonny Liston, a hulking bruiser who had manhandled every opponent foolish enough to climb in the ring with him. Liston didn't scare Clay, though, who now put on a demonstration of his style as Bruce watched with naked admiration.

"The man could be a Shaolin temple boxer," Bruce marveled to himself as he imitated Clay's moves, shadowboxing around the kitchen. Unlike many martial arts adepts, Bruce was willing to pick up useful moves from styles other than his own. Even a black American boxer like Cassius Clay had something to offer. Bruce also liked Clay's attitude—thumbing his nose at his opponent and the world.

In his upstairs room, Bruce stripped down to his jockey

shorts, tossing his clothes into an already overstuffed closet. He did a handstand in the corner, followed by a quick set of vertical push-ups. The day's heat had given way to a typically cool San Francisco evening, with fog blowing in off the bay accompanied by the deep lowing of a foghorn. The solitary window looked out on a Chinatown street that was a pale imitation of the ones he knew in Hong Kong. It was wider and cleaner, and the signs were mass produced and brightly lit with neon, with none of the endearing folk quality of his hometown's colorful, handmade placards.

It occurred to Bruce that, while he had made it to America and found a place to live and a job, he hadn't really come that far. He was in *Chinatown* and not mainstream America. He was not, certainly, in Beverly Hills. So he would *learn* to be American. He would study . . . read all he could. Strewn around his room were piles of books, both borrowed from libraries and bought at bargain rates from the used bookshops that lined the streets near the nearby college.

His push-ups done, he collapsed on his olive-drab army cot and grabbed a used paperback from atop the nearest pile. It was Ernest Hemingway's *For Whom the Bell Tolls*. Bruce opened it to the last page he'd read, and carefully dog-eared, the night before. He read aloud to improve his English:

" 'And I have made a mistake,' Robert Jordan thought to himself. 'I have told the Spaniards we can do something better than they . . .' "

There came a quiet knock on the door. Bruce put the book away, slid off the cot, and opened it. It was April. "I came for my lesson," she said.

He pulled her against his chest and wrapped his arms around her. Then he lifted her off her feet, cradling her in his arms. As he carried her to the cot, their lips still locked, he kicked the door shut with a well-practiced foot.

He awoke an hour before dawn and covered her with a

34

clean white sheet. Then he dressed quietly and slipped out into the empty, pre-dawn city. He caught the 38 and 28 municipal buses to the Presidio and Fort Point, where a lofty knoll overlooked the majesty of the Golden Gate Bridge. As the sun rose over the vast American continent, Bruce stripped off his shirt and did his kung fu exercises in front of the bridge and God himself.

6

THE LAST BOOTH BY THE ENTRANCE TO THE KITCHEN SERVED AS Gussie Yang's daytime office, equipped as it was with a mechanical adding machine with a crank handle, a black dial phone with a long, knotted cord, an abacus painted bright yellow with red beads, and a stack of bills which she glared at while yelling at a supplier over the phone.

"You call that bok choy? I tell you what to do with that garbage! You understand me? It will be a cold day in hell before I ever buy from you again. You what? Damn right you take it off the bill."

Having made her point, she hung up and looked at Bruce, whom she had summoned a moment ago and who stood there awaiting instructions.

"What do you want?" she asked.

"You wanted to see me, Miss Yang."

"You know where the college is?"

"Yes. Sure I do."

"I want you to take menus over there and put them up on every bulletin board. Give some to every frat house too. College kids got lots of money. Hungry all the time."

"Sure thing," Bruce said, excited at the prospect of getting out of the kitchen.

"You've done a good job washing dishes and cleaning up

the kitchen. Now I would like you to take menus around. Take one of the delivery bicycles. Maybe later you can get a bike of your own and make deliveries. Would you like that?"

"I can ride a motorcycle," he replied.

"First things first. Get lots of college kids calling me for food and we will see what happens."

"I'll do a good job. I promise it."

He picked up a shopping bag filled to the brim with menus. Gussie said, "And Lee, don't listen to anything you hear over there. You might learn something." She said it with a smile, which he returned.

"I want to go to college," he said.

"You're a bright boy. First, deliver menus."

"Okay," he said, and hurried out the door.

Bruce slipped on a red-and-white silk jacket emblazoned with the name of the restaurant, and got a rusty old Schwinn that was chained to a rack in front. He hung the shopping bag over the handles and started down the street toward the college.

He chained the bike to a street lamp outside the wrought-iron main gate of the campus. He hefted the shopping bag and walked down the street known as Fraternity Row.

The frat houses were wooden-shingle Victorian town houses, nearly all of them on a sharply inclined street. The houses were four stories tall, with steep gables and small front porches, many of which were lined with newfangled, three-speed English racing bicycles. Tennis and squash racquets were carelessly strewn onto white-cushioned Adirondack chairs. Clean-cut college men and, occasionally, women came and went in a continual stream. They had cashmere sweaters tied around their waists or draped over their shoulders, and many carried books. Many students were blond, blue-eyed, and good-looking.

Using his natural charm and good looks as well as the confidence he'd gained as a child actor in Hong Kong, Bruce talked his way into one house after another, finding the inevitable bulletin boards and tacking up menus. He also slipped menus under individual doors and left a stack in each house's kitchen. American college men, he was sure, were often too lazy to cook, and perhaps would pick up the phone and order something from Gussie's. If they bought enough, she would help him get enrolled at the college. He had enough money left over from *The Orphan* and his other movies to take at least a few courses. Once he got his foot in the door he knew there would be no stopping him.

When he was done with Fraternity Row, Bruce went straight for the Sports Center. The gleaming new steel-and-glass building was set at the western end of the Quad, that mostly square array of old, traditional campus buildings wherein most classes were held.

The Sports Center was a gold mine of bulletin boards. There was one for each sport, and there must have been thirty or forty sports what with the varsity teams and the intramural clubs. Bruce tacked up a menu on each, pausing just long enough to remove and destroy menus from competing Chinese restaurants. As he walked down the long hall that linked the various workout rooms with the locker rooms and the pool, Bruce listened to the sounds of basketball, squash, and wrestling. He heard the footfalls of men running on the indoor track that looked down on the pool—ten laps to the mile—from an encircling second-story balcony. From yet another room, the sounds of free weights and other body-building equipment could be heard.

Bruce ducked inside a door marked "University Pool" and found himself on the edge of the Olympic-sized facility. It was two in the afternoon, a time when the pool was reserved for the diving team. Normally it would be crowded with swimmers doing laps, but now it appeared to be totally empty, the water shimmering mirror-smooth and reflecting sun streaming through the skylight high above.

Bruce was about to leave when he saw her, a gorgeous vision high over his head, approaching the tip of the ten-meter high board. She had short blond hair and a slim body with shapely, toned legs. She held her stomach flat beneath a black tank suit, her rib cage high. Bruce thought she looked like a tai chi adept as she focused her energy on the exercise to come.

Fascinated and more than a little attracted, Bruce watched as she launched herself into the still gym air and executed a perfect half-gainer with three twists. She knifed the water like a descending angel. When she surfaced, they made eye contact. She was beautiful, and the first thing she saw after her dive was this intensely handsome Chinese wearing a silk jacket advertising a restaurant. Their eyes locked for a second, and he swore he saw the beginning of a smile. Then she swam to the far end of the pool, climbed from the water, and with a quick glance over her shoulder disappeared into the women's locker room.

Half an hour later, Bruce was in the Humanities Building tacking his last menu to a bulletin board that announced the activities of the college literary magazine. From a half-opened door beside it there came snippets of a lecture. Bruce leaned against the wall and listened to the voice of a professor who was locked in an interchange with a student.

"What is vital here are the elements of style," the professor said. "Words. How they're put together. That's what we want to get at. Hemingway's style—define it."

"Heroic code," said the student.

"Stop reading Lionel Trilling. Hemingway's style. Try again."

"His sense of irony," the student said.

Bruce smiled.

"Tone is not a style," the professor said more sharply.

Despite Gussie's warning—or maybe because of it—Bruce had been listening very carefully. But so far he hadn't heard anything he didn't know from his own reading, alone at night on his army surplus cot.

"Does anybody know what Hemingway's style is?" the professor asked the class.

"Simplicity," Bruce said to himself.

"It's simplicity," the professor told his class. "The approach to language without frills, rooted in journalism, spareness, and truth."

Bruce leaned back against the literary magazine's bulletin board and smiled. College wouldn't be so hard after all, he realized. It was just reading and common sense. And it certainly was better than life as a dishwasher.

His arms once again were plunged into hot water. It was the height of the noontime rush at Yang's, and the kitchen was in its usual chaos. Pots boiled and woks sizzled. The air was thick with smoke and spice and the shouted orders of waitresses. The black-and-white TV blared *Charlie Chan in Paris*. Actor Warner Oland walked down a foggy street looking inscrutable, his western eyes taped back to his ears to make him look Chinese.

On a ten-minute break, April stood alongside Bruce toying with his increasingly long black hair while he worked. He nodded his head in the direction of the TV.

"Do you see that crap? They take an American and make him look like a Chinaman. I guess it's supposed to be funny to watch this little 'Chinese' guy walk around Paris dressed like an English aristocrat and calling his kids by numbers. You know. 'Come here, Number One Son.' What crap."

"I never paid attention to it before, but you're right. Maybe they can't get good Chinese actors."

"What, we can't act? *I* acted in a couple of movies, back in Hong Kong."

"You did? Really?"

"Yeah. Nothing big, though. I mostly played teenagers. That was what they wanted."

"Maybe you'll go to Hollywood some day," April said.

"Man, I got to go *somewhere,* if only to the college. This job is for the birds."

"It's a living."

"For you, maybe. At least you don't have to get your hands wet all the time. You don't spend all day in the kitchen."

"I thought Miss Yang was going to make you a delivery boy."

"Oh, *that's* a step up."

"It's out of the kitchen," she argued.

"I guess you're right," he agreed begrudgingly. There simply weren't that many jobs available in 1962 for a young Chinese man who didn't have a college degree. Maybe it wasn't so bad if he had to deliver food for a while. At least he'd see daylight on occasion.

It was then that Ts'ai Lun's deep voice boomed: "Stop bullshitting, Lee, and wash dishes. Get going on this." With that he tossed a red-hot wok across the room. It landed in the water with a scalding splash, splattering steaming hot water all over Bruce and April.

His fists balled up in fury, Bruce leaped across the room and delivered a kick to the chef's chest. That shoved him back against the stove, where his apron caught on fire. He screamed in pain. Then one of his assistants dumped a bucket of ice water on him.

The kitchen staff scattered as the furious chef picked up

a gigantic meat cleaver and charged the young man, bellowing like a rhinoceros in heat. Bruce used his left forearm to block the blow and, in true *wing chun* style, simultaneously attacked. He hit the chef two sharp blows to the rib cage with his right fist. That knocked the wind out of the man, and he staggered backwards.

But not for long. Ts'ai Lun knew some martial arts. Feinting with the cleaver, he moved in on Bruce and hit him with a back elbow to the side of the head. That sent Lee reeling out the rear kitchen door. April screamed as the chef charged again, the cleaver held high.

The three under-chefs ran out into the daylight to help their boss. All were armed with kitchen weapons. It was four to one in the cramped space of the alley, which still gave Bruce more fighting room than he'd had in the kitchen.

The back of the restaurant was under reconstruction. The old bricks were being torn off and replaced with new material. To do the job, the construction crew had erected two-story scaffolding on both sides of the alley. Both structures were made of steel pipes and were connected by thick steel spanners, I-beams barely six inches wide.

Bruce ducked and weaved as the chef sliced at him with the cleaver. The big man was fast, but Lee was faster, alternately ducking under and sliding around the blows. And whenever the chef got too close, payment swiftly followed. Two times Bruce slipped inside his waving arms to deliver a back fist, which the chef blocked with his cleaver hand, and a reverse elbow that couldn't be blocked. The second one caught the big man on the left side of his head and left him woozy.

At that point one of his henchmen stepped in, carrying a carving knife. He came at Bruce from the right side, announcing his charge with a loud yell. The man could cook and he could scream, but he had no idea how to attack a man with a knife. He went straight in stabbing with elbow locked. Bruce blocked the blow with a forearm, then spun and delivered a vicious kick to the jaw that shattered teeth and bone and left the man bleeding on the ground, propped in pain against a pile of old bricks.

The chef had regained his composure, and he and the two remaining helpers moved toward Bruce, weapons at the ready. They pushed him backwards toward the blind end of the alley, from which it looked like there could be no escape. Bruce saw that, and backed them up with several high cross-kicks that threatened their throats.

That gave him time to spin and race toward the wall, taking two steps up it and using that as leverage to flip over to the scaffolding. He quickly swung up to a standing position on the catwalk.

The two younger assistants ran to the ladders that let construction workers get to either end of the scaffolding. They held their knives in their teeth like 17th-century pirates while climbing the ladders. Once on the catwalk they had Lee boxed in, trapped again.

Undaunted, Bruce ran out on the south spanner. He looked like a tightrope walker as he balanced at center span, ten feet off the ground. The under-chefs weren't sure if they were more afraid of height than they were of Bruce. One thing they *were* clear about was what Ts'ai Lun would do to them if they didn't catch the young man. They ventured out onto the spanner and, knives at the ready, moved in for the kill.

Bruce simply jumped to the north spanner—a simple jump of six feet performed ten feet in the air with no net. He stood there, facing them, bouncing on the balls of his feet, egging them on in the same way he had watched Cassius Clay do.

He dared them to join him and, with prodding from their

43

boss, they did so. Inelegantly they jumped to the other spanner, one of them nearly falling off and the other taking several moments to catch his balance. Bruce was between them, hands on hips, looking proud and confident. When at last they were steady on their feet, they charged toward Bruce, swinging their knives like Cuisinart blades.

He dropped down vertically, catching the spanner in his hands as a gymnast does with the high bar. He kicked his legs to gain momentum and then swept up and over, and as he went over the top Bruce hit both henchmen with kicks that came out of nowhere and sent them crashing to the pavement, unconscious. They would fight no more that day.

Bruce swung around the spanner twice more, then spun off and landed on the pavement in a perfect dismount. He felt like he had just won a gold medal in the Olympics. Unfortunately, Ts'ai Lun charged again; and this time his slashing cleaver made contact. Although Bruce pulled back from the blow, the razor-sharp instrument sliced the skin of his upper arm, cutting the shirtsleeve and causing a red streak of blood to erupt.

Everything stopped. Perhaps thinking he had ended the fight, the chef backed up. Perhaps he was just stunned by Bruce's calm reaction to being cut. In any event, Bruce had focused his *chi,* and once again had about him the aura of a tiger, a leopard, in short a very dangerous man. The intensity made Ts'ai Lun back off more, and then even more as Bruce ran his fingertips over his wound, collected the blood, brought his red-stained fingertips to his lips, and licked them clean.

His eyes glowed with an unearthly light, and then he threw himself into a furious attack, tying up the big man's knife hand while pummeling him with a rain of fists and elbows. *Wing chun* stressed close in fighting, and Bruce had become a master of it. He struck with balled fists, with the

44

back of his fists, and with his elbows, at the same time immobilizing his opponent's legs with strategically placed low kicks and blocks.

Finally, with an overwhelming burst of strength, Ts'ai Lun bulled Bruce against the wall, pinning him there with his considerable stomach while winding up for one last, deadly knife stroke. Lee squirmed to one side as the deadly blade seared past, hitting the wall and sending up a monumental spray of white-orange sparks.

Bruce broke free and kicked the knife hand, finally breaking the man's grip on the cleaver and sending the deadly instrument hurling, end over end, right into Bruce's outstretched fingers. His eyes blazed anew. So did the chef's, but with fear more than anger. Ts'ai Lun backed up against the rear door of the kitchen, and was about to duck inside when Bruce hurled the cleaver. It sliced through the air and embedded itself in the wood of the door frame—an inch from the chef's head.

His broken jaw forgotten amidst the rush of adrenaline that heated his body, Ts'ai Lun's chief under-chef rejoined the fray. He came at Bruce hard, twisting and throwing a turning kick with his right foot.

Bruce sensed it coming and dropped down beneath it, spun 180 degrees, and with his right leg swept his attacker's standing leg. The man went down on his back. Bruce then cocked his knee for a turning kick, which he planted firmly in the man's solar plexus. The wind was not only knocked out of him, it was knocked halfway up Nob Hill. The under-chef lay on his back, gasping for breath like a beached whale.

When Bruce got to his feet, he found himself encircled from behind by Ts'ai Lun's powerful arms. He was caught in a bear hug from which he struggled to escape. One of the tenets of *wing chun* was to avoid being caught, especially by

45

a much larger man, but if that was unavoidable, to quickly turn his force against him. It was hard at first, for the chef ran Bruce across the alley and rammed him against the newly installed brick wall.

Bruce lifted his legs, ran up the wall, and flipped over his opponent backwards. The two of them went down in a heap. Bruce managed to get in two elbows to the gut before the chef got him in a suffocating scissor lock. As Ts'ai Lun squeezed with all his might, Bruce's neck muscles bulged like steel cables. At last he freed his trapped right hand and, jabbing quickly, got in a tiger claw strike to the chef's groin. That got the man's attention: Ts'ai Lun howled like a beast and, of course, relaxed his grip.

Bruce back-flipped to his feet, landing in a praying mantis stance.

"Funny," he said. "The story was you don't have any balls."

Infuriated, the chef lunged forward with a vicious right jab. But Bruce deflected it with a forearm while launching a clawing attack at the man's floating ribs. Ts'ai Lun howled in pain and lurched backward. Just then Bruce hurled himself into the air and hit the man squarely in the chest with a double kick. That sent him bouncing off the same brick wall he'd had Bruce pinned against a moment before. This time Ts'ai Lun fell flat on his face, then rolled onto his back, beaten.

As his eyes cleared he looked up at the afternoon sky and saw Bruce sailing through the air, his foot poised to fall on the chef's windpipe, crushing it. Ts'ai Lun shrieked, and then there was a sickening crunch.

Gussie Yang ran out of the kitchen in time to see Bruce take his foot off the Ballantine Ale can he flattened like a flower. Ts'ai Lun was still alive. Down the street, though, there was the approaching sound of sirens.

Bruce shook his head. "A wanted man in both hemispheres," he said.

He was mistaken. The sirens were those of an ambulance going to a car wreck on the Embarcadero.

7

GUSSIE CLAPPED HER HANDS OVER HER HEAD AND SAID, "GET BACK inside, all of you."

Kitchen workers hauled off the chef and his cronies, all of whom had been reduced to slabs of bruised and bleeding meat. Bruce straightened his clothes, and pressed his palm against the still-bleeding knife wound on his upper arm.

"Are you okay?" April asked, running outside to care for him.

"I'm fine. You should see the other guys, though."

"I did. You nearly killed them. How did you learn all that?"

"I had a good teacher. Some I got from watching Cassius Clay."

"Who?"

"The boxer. The rest I got from all over."

"Oh, Bruce . . . you're *bleeding*."

"It's nothing, really."

"Let me help you," she said. She pulled a linen handkerchief from her pocket and used it to dab at the wound, pressing the fabric against the cut until the bleeding stopped.

"See, I told you. It was only a flesh wound," he said.

"God, you're so crazy."

"You're right," Gussie said. "He is."

Bruce smiled. The older woman looked at April and, with a glance, sent her back to work waiting tables.

"I'm sorry about the mess, Miss Yang. I had no choice."

She replied, "Lee, you're good at fighting. You're good with the ladies. You make a fine American. Come into my office and we'll talk."

She meant her upstairs office, which was similar to the downstairs office, only quieter during the day. It was a back booth in the second-floor dining room, and like the office downstairs was equipped with an adding machine and an abacus, and also had an ornate wooden cash box.

She took a seat and told him to do likewise.

"What do you want?" he asked.

"To do you a favor."

"What is it?"

"I'm letting you go."

"What?"

"You're fired."

She opened the cash box, and from it took out a wad of Hong Kong dollars. She tossed them at him.

"Why are you firing me? I didn't start the fight."

"No, and I agree that Ts'ai Lun is a bad man. But he is a good cook, and they're hard to find these days."

"This isn't fair, Miss Yang."

"It's for your own good. If you stay here he will only buy a gun and shoot you. Your kung fu won't protect you from that."

"Not all the time," Bruce agreed reluctantly, looking down at the pile of money in front of him.

"That is your father's money," she said. "There is no need to count it. It's all there. I kept every dollar safe for you, as I said I would. You take it and be gone now."

She added some American dollars to the pile.

"Two weeks' pay. Two weeks' severance."

Finally she peeled off some more money from a large stack of American dollars. That money too she handed to Bruce.

"What's this money for?" he asked.

"It's an all-purpose loan. Now you got a lot of money, Lee. What are you gonna do with it?"

"Maybe I should hire a bodyguard and live a less aggressive life," he said with a shrug.

"That is a good thought, but one I doubt you will keep in your young mind. I tell you what to do. Take April out on the town. Buy her nice clothes. Check into a big hotel, the Mark Hopkins. Have lots of sex. Have food brought to you in bed. Drink champagne and whiskey. Buy her expensive jewelry, very expensive. Buy yourself a car, but not a second-hand car. A nice new one. You know what?"

"What?"

"Now money all gone. Soon April be gone like money. You come back to me. If Ts'ai Lun doesn't shoot you with a big gun, I put you back to work in kitchen. You can wash dishes to pay loan. Live upstairs like you do now. By the time you pay back loan you no longer young, you no longer handsome, you nothing but a dishwasher."

Bruce squirmed and looked depressed.

"That is one choice," Gussie went on. "There are others."

"Like what?"

"They say education is good. I see you reading books. I notice how much time you spend at the college. Were you looking at books at the college or looking at girls?"

"Both, actually."

"See, you becoming really good American boy." She smiled.

"I've made up my mind. I'll enroll in the college. I will

study English and philosophy. I already know Hemingway's style.''

''Whose?''

''Hemingway. Ernest Hemingway, the writer.''

''Oh, the man who killed himself last year. I read all about it in *The Saturday Evening Post*. As always, you keep good company.''

''No, no. It's not that about him I admire. Never *mind*. I'm going to college. You don't have to worry about me wasting the money, and I thank you for the loan. I promise to repay it some day—with interest.''

''Send me a check,'' she said sharply.

''In other words, don't come back,'' he replied.

''Me personally, I hope you spend the money on April,'' Gussie said. ''I can always use a good dishwasher.''

She laughed, a high-pitched cackle that, on a dark night, could have been mistaken for a sound from one of the demons from Lee Hoi Chuen's nightmares.

▩ 8 ▩

1963

BRUCE THOUGHT THAT ALL AMERICAN COLLEGES, LIKE ALL CHINESE
temples, were somehow alike. For although it was cramped
by its location within the boundaries of one of America's
great cities, the college he had chosen to be his key to
entering the mainstream of American life seemed like all the
campuses he'd ever read about.

The open spaces were green and lush, with carefully
tended grass broken up into symmetrical patches by criss-
crossing red brick paths. On the larger swatches of grass,
students lounged. Some sat in groups and talked. Two girls
sunbathed, wearing generously cut, not-very-revealing bi-
kinis. Two guys tossed a football back and forth (it would be
a few years before the discovery, by New England college
kids, that the aluminum plate made by the Frisbee Pie
Company of Connecticut made a fine projectile, which
would spawn a national craze). On a broad brick path
directly in front of the Administration Building, several card
tables were set up. Behind them sat students who distributed
literature about and collected signatures on petitions backing several causes that were popular in 1963. Among them
were students protesting the presence of American military

advisers in South Vietnam, and others upset about China's refusal to join America, Britain, and the Soviet Union in signing the nuclear test ban treaty. A third group recruited for the Peace Corps, founded two years earlier by President John F. Kennedy.

Bruce was a student on an American campus at last. Even after a year at the college he still ate up the sights and sounds of it. He sprinted across campus, dressed Ivy League-style: khaki pants, a blue, button-down Oxford shirt, and penny loafers worn without socks. In one hand he carried a gym bag marked with the logo of the San Francisco Giants baseball team. Tucked under the other arm was a bunch of textbooks: on philosophy, history, and biology. He also had copies of Ernest Hemingway's *The Sun Also Rises* and Hegel's *Science of Logic*.

Lee pushed open the door to the gym and walked up to the security guard, who stood watch over an aluminum turnstile that restricted entrance. Prominently hung on the wall was a sign that read: "Admission restricted to students with ID only."

The guard was a thin but surly-looking white man of about thirty years of age. His uniform was dark blue with white trim, including epaulets. At his waist was a billy club that he drummed the fingertips of his right hand on. Bruce had seen that often enough among the military policemen in Hong Kong. The club was displayed prominently and the man drummed his fingers on it as if to say, "Mess with me and I'll beat your brains in." It was a common method of intimidating the impressionable. Bruce wasn't impressed; moreover, the affectation made him smile.

"You a student?" the guard asked, his voice a skeptical growl as he glared suspiciously at the young Chinese-American.

"You bet," Bruce replied.

"Let's see you prove it."

"Is there a problem?"

"Not unless you can't show me ID."

Bruce put his books down on the narrow, vinyl-topped table that served as the guard's desk. "These books aren't good enough?" he asked.

"Books can be stolen."

"Are you accusing me of being a thief?"

"Let's see the ID."

Bruce shrugged and plucked a fine leather wallet—made in Hong Kong—from his pocket. He flipped out the identification card that carried his picture as well as documentation of his status as a college student.

The guard seemed almost disappointed. He looked like he might relish using that club. But he handed back the wallet and, perhaps sensing he had been too hard on the young man just because he was Chinese, said, "I'm sorry, but I gotta be careful. We been having a lot of problems with people breaking into lockers."

"I'll keep a lookout for them," Bruce said cheerfully, scooping up his books and pushing through the turnstile.

"You just let me know if you see anything funny," the guard said, patting his billy club.

Smiling to himself, Bruce found the men's locker room and dumped his stuff into the bottom of a full-length locker. He stripped off his street clothes and hung them carefully on the hooks provided for that purpose. Then he pulled on a T-shirt, a pair of black kung fu pants, and socks and sneakers. Bruce twirled the dial on the combination lock and went off in the direction of the weight room.

The weight machines used in 1963 were heavy and clunky, made of raw steel that rusted overnight if it was not constantly lubricated by the sweat of straining muscles. In those days there were no gleaming stainless-steel wonder-

54

workers set in "fitness centers" carpeted in tones of beige and salmon. Gyms were all biceps and business. There were few women in gyms, and no one went there to make friends.

Bruce held the sweat-darkened bar with two fingers of each hand, doing chest curls the hard way. His biceps and pectorals gleamed with perspiration, bulging out with each tug at the two-hundred-pound weight. Before him the machine's cables whizzed like a serpent, and the lead clanged as it scraped the vertical steel supports. The sound merged with others like it from the dozen or so college men who shared the room and contributed to its sounds and smells. Their grunts were punctuated by the thud of dropped weights and the occasional gasp of satisfaction as the hard-fought end of a tough set of lifts was reached.

Looking around with casual interest, Bruce was struck by the number of blonds. It was like being in one of those small Western towns where a passing dark-haired stranger might well be treated like a visitor from Mars. This was San Francisco, however, where a goodly portion of the population was Oriental. Yet at times Bruce felt like the only one of them who was going to college. At least, he was the only one to violate the white sanctuary of the weight room. And he was curling two hundred pounds with two fingers of each hand.

There was a noise in the hall, a mingling of deep voices and the sound of bragging. Into the weight room came about ten members of the college football team. All were over six feet, and two were nearly six-four, pumped up with self-importance magnified by aggressively colored team jerseys and sweat pants. Joe Henderson was their leader. One of the team captains, he was bigger than the rest with a square crew cut and a face and arms so bruised from athletic combat as to give the impression he liked to crash into things. On his left shoulder was the tattooed emblem of the

Army Reserve Officer Training Corps. In 1963, when memory of victory in World War II was fresh and Vietnam simply a vaguely known and faraway place where American Army advisers would surely whip the yellow-skinned natives into shape, an ROTC tattoo on a football player was almost mandatory.

Henderson walked straight up to Bruce and looked down at the muscled but hardly tall young man. "Time's up," Henderson growled.

Bruce kept pumping. "I can't hear you," he said.

"I said, time's up."

"You'll have to talk down lower. The air is thin up there where your mouth is." He pumped on still.

His face flushed with rising anger, Henderson snarled, "You're finished."

"No, I'm not."

"Yeah, you are. We work out here every day at three. See the clock? It's three."

The large, round wall clock hung over the door, as it did in classrooms across campus. Bruce glanced at it, but the information meant little. He had no idea if there was some rule that let the football players take over the weight room every day at that time.

"Where's it say that in the rule book?" Bruce asked.

"Have you been reading the book?" Henderson asked. "*Can* you read the book? It ain't printed in Chinese. You gotta read it in English."

The rest of the players laughed, and those others in the weight room who weren't involved put down their weights to watch. The gauntlet had been thrown down, and it remained to be seen if the young man from Hong Kong would pick it up.

Bruce stopped pumping iron, letting the bar roll off his fingertips, which were curled like angry claws. The lead

56

crashed to the floor with a resounding thump that sent a vibration like an earthquake rumbling across it.

"What's that mean?" Bruce asked, looking up at the much bigger man.

"What I mean is, your kind doesn't understand English."

"My kind?"

"Yeah, chinks . . . gooks . . . your kind."

Bruce's fingers, curled into claws from using the bar, tightened into iron balls.

Henderson went on: "You guys killed my brother at the Yalu River. I don't want to see you in my gym."

He reached out with a beefy finger and poked it at Bruce.

"Don't touch me," Bruce snapped.

At five-seven, Bruce didn't have the stature to frighten the bigger Henderson. But something in the voice backed the giant off. His hand froze in midair; then his fingers also clenched into fists.

"Or what?" he growled.

"Or I'll touch you back." The words were mocking, and no one in the crowd had seen anyone go up against Henderson before. The members of the football team sucked in their collective breath.

"C'mon, touch me, dink."

Bruce smiled, laughed faintly, then turned and walked to the door. A smirk curled across Henderson's lips. He thought that Lee was backing down, leaving. The same thought occurred to the rest of the team; several smiles broke out. Then Bruce hesitated in the door, turned, and called back to Henderson: "Coming?"

"Where?" Henderson asked incredulously.

"To the wrestling room. I need to finish my workout, and I might as well finish on you."

One of Henderson's buddies "ooh'd" mockingly. Another laughed and said, "Uh, oh, Henderson."

"You gotta be kidding," the big man said, starting after his adversary.

Bruce walked down the hall, a green-tiled showcase for the framed portraits of decades of college athletes. There were fencers in white bearing masks and sabers, basketball players lined up at center court, tennis players lining the net, and football players looking bulked up and angry while a succession of coaches stood with arms folded.

Bruce was a modern Pied Piper followed by a rapidly growing crowd of very big children. For as the members of the football team followed their burly leader to what they were sure would be his latest bloody victory, some ducked into workout rooms and reappeared with new spectators. They were coming to watch the slaughter, all of them, and so they followed Bruce up to the door of the wrestling room.

With an exaggerated gallantry that only made Henderson angrier, Bruce held open the door. Once inside, Henderson moved to the center of the room and assumed a boxing stance, his right fist close to the chest while his left probed the atmosphere in Bruce's direction.

The wrestling room had high ceilings, the walls cut by narrow vertical windows that let in shafts of late afternoon light. The shafts cut swaths across the dusky blue wrestling mat, which reminded Bruce of the light that illuminated the Tsing Lin Temple back in Hong Kong, half a world away.

As the room filled up with onlookers who formed a ring around the combatants, Henderson moved in for the kill, his eyes blazing fire and his left fist probing toward Bruce.

Smiling, Lee said, "Wait a minute," and backed off.

"What?" Henderson exclaimed, surprised as Bruce bent to remove his sneakers and socks.

The big man rolled his eyes. "Are you gonna stink me to death?" he asked.

He moved again toward Bruce, who again smiled and held up his hand. "Wait, wait."

"Stop stalling."

Bruce peeled off his T-shirt and tossed it atop the pile of sneakers and socks. He stood, bare-chested, at last ready to fight.

"What is this, a strip tease?" Henderson asked.

"Ready now," Bruce said, and then, affecting a Hollywood version of a Chinese accent, said, "So sorry." It came out sounding "So solly," and made some in the crowd laugh. Henderson wasn't laughing, though, for the accent only reminded him of his brother's death at the Yalu River, a key battleground where American and Chinese troops had fought during the Korean War.

Infuriated, he hurled a massive fist at Bruce's head. The punch was a bomb, a death blow, but it never found its mark. Bruce slid beneath it, his head bending ever so smoothly out of harm's way.

The momentum of the punch carried Henderson past Bruce, who came up behind him, pausing only to flick the giant's ear teasingly as he passed.

"Over here," Bruce said, "behind you."

Henderson wheeled and turned with a series of punches. Bruce backed up, using reflexes that would make a housefly seem slow in comparison. Henderson caught nothing but air, and the crowd around the two fighters began to sense that something quite unexpected was happening.

"Very good shadowboxing," Bruce said.

Crazy now, Henderson launched himself in a flying tackle. Bruce uncoiled his spring-like legs and leaped five feet into the air. Henderson flew beneath him and crashed in a heap in the center of the mat as several spectators gasped, then laughed.

Bruce landed with his feet straddling Henderson's head.

59

Lee could have hurt the man; killed him, even. But that was not Bruce's intention. He merely wanted to take the guy down a few pegs and, maybe, impress the gorgeous blond woman who out of the corner of his eye he saw push through the crowd.

"Chinks can jump really high, huh?" Bruce said, tousling the fallen man's hair with the ball of his foot.

Henderson rolled and grabbed for Bruce's legs, but they had vanished into thin air. He climbed to his feet, only to see Bruce standing a few paces off.

"I'll kill you, you bastard," Henderson fumed.

"I'm no bastard. The name's Bruce Lee."

Bruce offered his hand, but Henderson lunged at it. He would tear the arm off—if he could only grab hold of it. But that would not happen that day. As Henderson grabbed, Bruce swept with his right leg and took him down, sending the big man crashing onto his back with a resounding thud that provoked a gasp from the onlookers.

Unable to take their friend's humiliation any longer, teammates Paul Nunnemacher and Chris Townsend charged in, fists balled and raised. Bruce moved into Nunnemacher with a double punch, then whirled and smashed Townsend with a double kick. Townsend flew backwards, taking the stunned and staggering Nunnemacher with him. The two friends landed in a heap atop Henderson.

Bruce strolled over and looked down at Henderson. All the fight was gone from the man. What was left was pure amazement.

"I'm sorry about your brother," Bruce said. "That was the Chinese Communists who killed him. I'm an American."

Henderson said nothing, but closed his eyes for a moment before struggling slowly to his knees.

The crowd parted as Bruce headed for the door. As he

walked down the hall he heard a voice, a melodious one. "Hey, Bruce."

"Yeah?" he asked, turning to face the blond diving queen, who'd just stepped out into the hall. She held his shirt, sneakers, and socks in her hand and offered them to him like a trophy.

"You gotta learn to pick up after yourself," she said with a smile as broad as the Pacific Ocean.

"I've never been very good at that. I mainly leave things lying around." There was a twinkle in his eye as he said it.

"Yeah, I *see*. That was pretty impressive."

"Not really. That was fooling around—playtime. I could have really hurt them if I wanted."

"Could you have *killed* them?"

He looked embarrassed. "That's not the idea," he said, turning once again to walk down the hall toward the locker rooms. She followed him, unable to give up her fascination with him and the display he had just put on.

"It isn't? I thought karate was to kill."

"Samurais worked very hard not to unsheathe their swords, for if they ever did they had to take a life or die themselves. So they tried to scare people so much that they never had to use their swords."

"I see. Are you a samurai?"

"No, and what you saw wasn't karate—it was kung fu."

"I never heard of it. What is it?"

"A Chinese martial art, like karate but different. I learned in Hong Kong, where I grew up. I can teach you if you like."

"Really?"

"Sure. Why not?"

"I'm a girl, if you hadn't noticed."

"I noticed," he said, stopping outside the men's locker room and facing her yet again. "I *noticed*."

61

She blushed slightly.

"You would make a good student of kung fu. You have poise and inner strength. You can focus your energy very well."

She looked at him quizzically, and he said, "I've seen you on the diving board several times."

"Oh. But diving is different."

"Not so different. Both our skills require the ability to concentrate and focus energy. You must strike the water perfectly. I must strike an adversary with the same perfection and economy of form."

"Well, yes, I guess so." She laughed. "Since you put it that way. But won't being a girl make it hard for me to fight much bigger men?"

"I'm only an inch or so taller than you. And my style of kung fu was invented by a woman. I will tell you that story in time. Well, what do you say? Will you let me teach you kung fu?"

"Unh, sure. Okay," she said, breaking into a happy laugh. "My name is Linda Emery."

"Bruce Lee. I was born in San Francisco and am very much an American."

"That's great," she said.

"Give me your number and I'll call as soon as I can arrange for a workout room to teach you in."

She wrote a phone number on a matchbook, and as she handed it to him, she smiled and said: "You really *are* an American. You work fast. I never give out my phone number that easily."

"What was easy?" Bruce asked. "I had to beat up three guys to get it." And with that he disappeared into the locker room, leaving the girl to shake her head in the hall, wondering what in the world she was getting herself into.

9

BRUCE HAD JUST GOTTEN HIS LOCKER OPEN WHEN HE HEARD footsteps racing up behind him. He swirled into the dragon stance, which had the virtue of looking very frightening to someone not in the know.

"Hey, ease up, man, we come in peace," said one of two students. He was taller than Bruce and had the broad features of an American Indian. His black hair was longish for 1963 and pulled back behind a white beaded headband. With him was a taller college boy, a blond with Nordic features.

Bruce smiled and straightened up.

"Bruce Lee," he said, offering his hand.

"Benny Sayles," said the Amerindian. "This is Tad Overstreet. We just want to ask you a question. That jujitsu stuff . . ."

"It's called kung fu."

"Kung who? I never heard of it."

"Kung fu. The name means something like 'hard work and applied skills.' "

"It's Japanese?" Overstreet asked.

"Chinese."

"Can anybody do it?" Sayles asked.

"Many people can, with time and dedication."

"Well, we got the time and we're dedicated. Can you teach us?"

Bruce turned away from them and looked into the darkness of his locker. "To teach is to become a master, with a *kwoon* . . ."

"A what?"

"A training ground. A club."

"We can find something. One of the workout rooms in the gym."

"You don't understand. To teach one must be a master, and I'm nobody. Just a practitioner. I . . ." He wasn't explaining himself well because he was thinking of Yip Man, the graceful old grandmaster, with his *kwoon* and his chessboard.

"Never mind, Benny," Overstreet said, leading his friend away. Under his breath he said, "I told you it was that secret chink stuff."

Bruce turned around and say, "Hey."

"What?" Sayles asked, walking back.

"You guys have money?"

They smiled. "You mean, for lessons?"

"No," Bruce said, "I meant for liniment. Meet me tomorrow at two—out on the quad."

The quad was filled with sunbathers soaking up the last bit of the warm autumn weather. A few wannabe football players lobbed a pigskin around, and under a radiantly yellow maple tree the English professor Bruce had overheard on his first trip to the campus was holding forth on the subject of F. Scott Fitzgerald. In front of the Administration Building, a few activists were collecting signatures in support of the Free Speech Movement at the University of California at Berkeley, across the bay.

Bruce's class had begun with just Sayles and Overstreet,

but soon had grown to include a handful of others. The Bruce Lee legend was beginning to spread across campus, and more and more students gathered around his weekly outdoor kung fu lessons just to get an idea of what it was all about. These onlookers included, from time to time, Nunnemacher and Townsend. Their bruises had healed just in time for them to get new ones on the football field, and eventually the memory of the Bruce-inflicted pain had subsided. What did not subside, however, was their fascination with the martial arts. In America in 1963, not one person in a hundred had heard of the martial arts, which mostly meant judo or jujitsu. It would take the young man from Hong Kong to popularize kung fu and start the craze that, decades later, would see a martial arts training facility in nearly every small town in America. The craze began in a small way with Bruce's college class.

With Sayles and Overstreet sweating from a good workout, Bruce said: "Be like water. Water is the softest stuff in the world but it can fit in any container. Water seems weak but it can penetrate and destroy rock. Be like the nature of water."

"To get inside your opponent?" Sayles asked.

"More than that. To get inside and *around* your opponent. To be slippery, so he has nothing to grab onto, and to be everywhere, so you can attack when you are ready."

"You mentioned the white crane style," Overstreet said.

"Yes. That is one of the popular kung fu styles."

"I don't understand how being like a crane, an awkward bird, can help you fight."

"Actually, the crane is tall and elegant, not awkward at all. The style developed far back in history when a monk watched a crane defending her nest from an ape that wanted to steal the eggs. When the ape attacked, the crane used her

65

wings and feet to move back out of range, and her beak to strike when that was advantageous.''

Said Sayles, ''You mean we should use evasive tactics, waiting for the enemy to show weakness before making an attack.''

''That's one thing I mean.''

''In the Army they call it 'strategic retreat.' Running away.''

The unexpected voice came from Joe Henderson, who with Chris Townsend and Paul Nunnemacher had finally worked up the courage to walk up and join in.

Bruce smiled and said, ''You guys still mad at me?''

''No, no,'' Henderson said quickly. ''I learned my lesson and am man enough to admit it. Now I was wondering if you could teach me and my friends. Sayles and Overstreet here look pretty good when they work out.''

Bruce said, ''I would be glad to teach you. But you and your friends are big men. Oriental martial arts evolved because most Orientals aren't. You may not need it.''

''Hey, look,'' Townsend said. ''Last Saturday I nearly got my neck broke because I couldn't move fast enough to get past this big tackler from UCLA. Anything you can do to make me be . . . well, like water . . . you see what I mean?''

''Sure thing. I will teach you the drunken monkey.''

''The what?''

''Another style of kung fu. It will make you agile. As agile . . .''

''As a drunken monkey,'' Henderson said, and they laughed.

''That's it for today,'' Bruce said to his class. ''We'll meet on Friday. It's supposed to rain, so let's make it in the wrestling room at three. Be prepared to spar.''

The class broke up with some small talk and some

exchange of cash. Bruce had begun to charge nominal fees for his classes, and was beginning to wonder if teaching kung fu might be a calling for him. Certainly it would be better than washing dishes.

A hand tapped him on the shoulder. Linda Emery said, "Is this class only for guys? It looks like you only teach guys."

"I teach anyone who wants to learn," Bruce replied. "Usually guys are the ones interested in fighting."

"I've dated some of these animals. I did plenty of fighting. Listen, I'd like to take lessons. I thought about what you told me before and have decided to study under you."

"I was wondering what took you so long to call."

"And *I* was wondering why you never called *me*."

Part of the reason was April, but Bruce thought it wise not to say that. In any event, April was no longer in his life. As Gussie might have predicted, when he'd gotten all that money and spent very little of it on her, she'd lost interest.

"A teacher teaches. He does not go out and call students."

"This is America, Bruce. If you want to get a girl's attention *you* have to call *her*."

"I'll keep that in mind," he said. "Class is Friday at three in the wrestling room."

"That's a date."

"No, that's an appointment. There's a difference."

"See ya, Bruce," she said, walking off with just enough wiggle in her hips to keep his gaze on her. *That,* he thought, is a real American woman.

The kung fu class, Bruce Lee-style, got into session at three P.M. in the wrestling room, as planned. The group was enthusiastic, and soon asked to meet more often. So the schedule went up to twice weekly and continued for a month, until all of the group had at least a basic idea of kung fu.

There were ten students, half of them football players who had witnessed the brief fight between Bruce and Henderson. Linda was there too, and was quickly proving to be one of Bruce's better students. She showed much of the natural athletic talent Bruce had seen on the diving board. If ever there was a natural to learn kung fu, it was Linda.

Sayles and Nunnemacher were sparring now, trying for the first time to use what Bruce had taught them. Sayles was using the crouched sparring position, the better to fight the taller Nunnemacher who used the upright free sparring stance, which was more like Western boxing. Nunnemacher was the aggressor, but Sayles, who had been in the class longer, blocked every punch or kick that the bigger man threw. Frustrated, Nunnemacher tackled Sayles.

That was something Sayles had not yet learned to handle, and the two of them crashed to the mat. The sparring soon became real. A brawl was starting.

"Break it up," Bruce said. "Break it up."

"I couldn't get inside him," Nunnemacher complained as he got to his feet.

"So you went for brute force. You are bigger than him, so you took the easy way out. That is exactly what kung fu is supposed to guard against. You were like the bull in a bullfight. Sayles could easily wear you out, force you to expend your energy missing him, then go for the kill."

"I didn't know how to block his tackle," Sayles admitted.

"That will come."

"Sometimes it just seems easier to go for the straight kill," Nunnemacher said.

"If you give in to emotion, you lose yourself. You must

68

be at one with your emotion, because the body always follows the mind. This is not about winning. This is about perfection.''

''Then why do they have all those keen colored belts?'' Sayles asked.

''That's karate, not kung fu. In kung fu a belt is good mainly to hold up your pants. If you two guys are finished sparring, let's see who next can show me what they learned today. How about Linda and . . .''

He surveyed the class.

She was the only woman present, and she was surrounded by beefcake. The only one close to her size was Bruce. He said, ''I guess it's Linda and me.''

She bowed to him at center mat and assumed a free natural fighting position, her body half turned to protect the vital organs, leaning forward to confront him. She tried a low roundhouse kick with her right foot. Bruce blocked it with his right knee, then entered with a *pak-sao* trap, a *wing chun* move. His block had destroyed the effectiveness of the kick, so he immobilized her right arm with his, then jabbed at her chin with his left hand. He pulled the punch a millimeter from her face.

She flinched.

''You were open,'' he said.

She nodded and resumed her stance.

''There are four ranges where combat takes place,'' Bruce said, explaining as he circled her. ''There is kicking, punching, trapping, and grappling. Most martial arts students stay in the kicking range, because the legs are most powerful.''

Perhaps to illustrate, she threw a roundhouse kick at him. He jumped over it.

''I saw it coming,'' he explained. ''The legs are powerful, but hoping to stay at kicking length doesn't help you when you are fighting a raging lunatic who charges straight in. That is why you must learn to turn an opponent's power against him.''

Linda feinted with a straight arm punch, which Bruce countered. But she caught his inward motion and flipped him over her hip. He crashed to the mat while the class broke out in whoops and hollers.

''Like that,'' he said, jumping to his feet. ''It isn't size or strength that counts. It's focus. You all have a *chi,* an inner spirit. Focus it and there is no force you cannot bend to your will. Just like you saw.''

''How can we use this on the football field?'' Henderson asked.

''Surely you have all seen a player who had a certain look in his eyes.''

''Intimidating,'' Henderson said.

''Yes, but more than intimidating. The weak are easily intimidated, but the weak seldom are seen on football fields. So to be intimidating, a player must have *chi,* must feel an inner strength and be able to focus it.''

Linda's success had made her cocky and she came at Bruce with a straight punch. Bruce blocked it, then used his other hand to gain a wrist hold. He used her own momentum to guide her forward past him, then slipped a hand on the back of her head and kicked her legs out from under her.

She went down on the mat and he fell on her, going in for the kill in more ways than one. She smiled demurely.

''I kinda like this position,'' she said.

The guys all laughed. Bruce put his lips to her ear. ''Good. Then say yes to a date.''

''You mean all of us?''

''No, just you and me.''

He jumped to his feet and helped her up.

''Why?'' she asked.

"What do you mean, why?"

"Why me?"

"Why not?" he asked. "We already fell for each other."

She liked the answer, and smiled her reply. A chorus of "ooh's" came from the guys in the class.

❡ 10 ❡

THE SYLVANIA BLACK-AND-WHITE TELEVISION WAS A TOP-OF-THE-line model. It shared a mahogany cabinet with an AM/FM radio and a stereo that played 78, 45, and 33 1/3-rpm records. There was a space for albums. Included were several of Linda's recent ones, The Beach Boys' *Surfin' USA* and *The Freewheelin' Bob Dylan,* and one of her mother's: the songs from *My Fair Lady.*

The TV "entertainment center" was placed near the front window of the living room in the Emerys' comfortable house. The white lace curtains swept down and behind the collection of family photos atop the TV cabinet. There were black-and-white shots of Linda as a baby, Linda as a young teenager making her first dive, and finally of Linda as a well-developed college athlete.

The TV was tuned to the nightly news, in this case *The Huntley/Brinkley Report* on NBC. It was a news-filled time on American television. There had been the Cuban Missile Crisis in 1962. There was the increasing number of American military advisers in Vietnam. And it was a new Presidential election season, with the ultra-conservative Barry Goldwater fighting for the Republican nomination to oppose the expected 1964 reelection campaign of President John F. Kennedy and Vice-President Lyndon B. Johnson.

72

In his familiar, clipped tones, newsman David Brinkley said: "Senator Barry Goldwater kicked off his race for the Republican nomination today in Phoenix. Goldwater lashed out at Communists and what he termed 'their fellow-travelers' in American political life . . ."

Vivien Emery, Linda's mom, busied herself paying bills while watching the news. A car horn honked outside and Linda rushed down the stairs, wearing jeans with rolled-up cuffs and a flannel shirt. She carried a bowling bag.

"David Brinkley, now there's a man," Vivien said, nodding at the screen.

"I like the other one better, Mom," Linda replied.

"Who, Chet Huntley? He has jowls, like Mr. Gibson next door. You don't want to marry a man who will wind up looking like a basset hound."

Linda said, "I'm not looking to get married, Mom. I'm going bowling."

Vivien scanned her daughter's outfit and said, "It looks more like you're going to a lumberjack convention."

"Close. I'm going bowling *at* a lumberjack convention."

"You'll never find a good man in the bowling alley."

"Mom," she said, a bit exasperated, "I'm just trying to improve my score. I can't bowl 120 forever."

"Listen to your mother. You use too much follow-through and are hooking to the left. Put less English on the ball. Then you'll bowl 200 easily."

"I'll give it a try. I have to go."

"Have fun. Don't be too late now."

"Bye, Mom," Linda said, and gave her mother a peck on the cheek and then was out the door on the run.

Linda's friend, Sherry Schnell, was parked outside in her father's 1961 Mercury convertible. It was white with red interior and had sword-like tail fins that swept past the trunk, making the car look like it could slice a panel truck in half by getting too close.

The convertible top was up that night, by design. As soon as the car pulled out of sight of the house, Linda flipped into the backseat and pulled off her jeans. Beneath them she wore beige panties, garters, and stockings. She unzipped the bowling bag and from it took a blue sheath dress.

She removed the flannel shirt and quickly slipped the dress over her head. The subterfuge was necessary, at least as far as Linda's mother was concerned. In America in 1963, interracial couples were rare—even in big cities.

"I hope he likes blue," she said. "You think this dress is too wrinkled, Sherry?"

"So what if it is? I'm sure he can always get it pressed for you. Don't all Chinese run laundries?"

"That isn't funny," Linda said, zipping up and rejoining her friend in the front seat.

"All this for a Chinese guy," Sherry said. "I can't believe you're going out with a Chinese guy."

Linda hiked the dress up long enough to straighten her stockings. The rubber-and-metal catches that kept them suspended from the garters had twisted and were uncomfortable.

"Let me tell you, if you met him, you'd understand."

"Explain it to me."

"First of all, he's *gorgeous.* Second, he used to be a movie star in Hong Kong. Okay, a child star."

"A movie star in Hong Kong? Isn't that sorta like being a snowball in Acapulco? You're not very big and you don't last long?"

"You're a riot, Schnell. You should be in the circus. And there's a third thing—he's a *wing chun* master, and . . ."

Linda saw the look on her friend's face, and added,

74

"Don't ask me. He has the most *incredible* body and an inner calm that you wouldn't believe."

"An 'inner calm.' What is that?"

"I know what you're thinking. That and a nickel will get you on the cable car."

"I don't care how gorgeous he is. I don't think I could kiss someone who wasn't white. I don't know if I could."

"I'll try to live with that thought, Schnell. I really will."

Linda checked her makeup. Everything was ready for Bruce.

"*You'd* kiss him?" Sherry asked, a slight look of disgust on her face.

"I'd kiss him—at least. Who knows, maybe more."

Sherry laughed. It was a nervous laugh. She said: "You're dangerous, Emery. You pretend to be a jock, but you're really just a . . . a beatnik!"

"Pass the bongos, Daddy-o," Linda replied, looking out the window at the passing city lights and thinking of Bruce.

La Truffe Restaurant had three stars and a view of the Golden Gate Bridge, which contradicted the old gourmet's law that really good restaurants never have a view. It was old and elegant, with a rich history, having survived the 1906 earthquake, Prohibition, the Depression, and several recessions with its reputation intact.

The road to it was narrow and steep and passed numerous exclusive shops, mostly small and expensive clothing stores of a sort new in American cities. They were called boutiques. A few trendy bars filled the block leading up to its cut-glass front door and crystal chandelier foyer.

The Mercury pulled into the semi-circular driveway, and right away the parking attendant ran up and pulled open the driver's side door.

"Here for dinner, miss?" the Chinese attendant asked.

Sherry looked at his uniform outfit, which included a red frock coat with tails and a black French kepi. "I'm not staying," Sherry said. "*She* is."

"Sorry, miss."

Then she turned to Linda and whispered, "Is that him?"

Linda scowled and said, "I hate you."

"Have a nice evening, Linda."

"Thanks for the ride."

Linda got out of the car, still struggling with a twisted garter. She fixed it and patted her dress smooth, then made her way through the fancy main door, held by yet another uniformed Chinese attendant. Couples of all ages were seated in the elegant main dining room, and more waited at the bar. All were well-dressed. The smell of French wine and sauces permeated the crisp evening air.

She spotted Bruce waiting at the bar. He wore a slick black suit with micro lapels and looked nervous. She thought he was adorable: His *chi* had abandoned him for the occasion of his first date with an American girl. Bruce Lee was as nervous as any teenage boy before his first date.

She hurried up to him. "Am I late?"

"No. Not at all. Hey, you look great! Blue really looks good on you."

"I'm glad you like it. You look pretty good yourself. I've never seen you with so many clothes on."

He laughed. "I was going to say the same thing about you."

"I don't go out to fancy places that often. This is a beautiful restaurant. I've read about it in the papers, but never thought I'd get to go here."

"Would you like a drink first?"

"If you do."

"I'd just as soon get our table. I made a reservation for eight, and it's eight now."

He ushered her over to the maitre d'hotel, a thin and arrogant-looking Frenchman who had the attitude of a bantam rooster.

"Sir?" the man asked.

"Lee. We have a reservation for eight."

The man's eyes flicked suspiciously from Bruce to Linda and then back to Bruce again, where they focused on his ultra-narrow lapel and tie, longish hair, and yellow skin.

"I'm afraid we don't have a thing right now," he said, looking down his nose at a massive, leather-bound reservations book.

"But I made a reservation," Bruce protested.

"It isn't written down, so you'll have to wait. If you would like to have a drink at the bar, I'll see what I can do."

"Thank you," Bruce said politely, and walked Linda back to the bar. He ordered a Coke for her but nothing for himself. He stood leaning on the bar, keeping a wary eye on the maitre d', especially since the man had just seated a white couple. They had come right in the door and to a table with no waiting.

Linda said, "So, tell me more about yourself than kung fu. What are you majoring in?"

"Philosophy."

She laughed. "A philosophy major? What can you do with *that* after you graduate?"

"Teach other philosophy majors, I guess. We Chinese are philosophical about everything. We're deep thinkers. What can I do with a philosophy degree? Maybe think deep thoughts about being unemployed."

"You're a great teacher," Linda said. "Did you ever think of teaching kung fu?"

"What do you think I've been doing?"

"No, I mean really going for it—the American way— make a business, a chain like McDonald's."

"You want me to sell hamburgers?"

"Be real. I think you can sell martial arts the way McDonald's sells hamburgers. A lot of people will be interested in it."

"In kung fu? You've got to be kidding. Where did you get that idea? Americans are interested in boxing, maybe, or baseball and football."

"Did you ever see that James Bond movie?"

"*Dr. No*? Sure. So what?"

"James Bond used kung fu."

"Don't make me laugh. That was sort of polite judo. That's not fighting."

"Maybe not, but the next day ten thousand kids were trying to imitate him."

"Besides, he tossed around a lot of Chinese actors in that movie. That kind of bothered me."

"So you can be the Chinese actor who tosses around a lot of Americans."

"I just want to be a good American, and I like teaching."

"Sure, it's fun to throw helpless girls around."

"You're not very helpless. Seriously, I like the way teaching changes people. You can't change people with your fists. I learned that."

He watched as the maitre d' seated another white couple. Under the rim of the bar, where Linda couldn't see, Bruce's knuckles balled up.

"You sure changed Joe Henderson," she argued.

"But not by fighting. My beating him up just served to get his attention. It was my showing him how he could improve his life that changed him. Now the next step for him will be this: You learned how to fight better, now learn how to *not* fight."

"Have you learned that lesson?" Linda asked.

"I think so. Sometimes I forget." He watched a third

white couple being ushered to a table ahead of Linda and him. "When people see something strange, something they don't understand, they get afraid. You teach them the beauty of that strange thing and they're no longer afraid because it's a part of *them*. Their knowledge frees them from fear."

"Sometimes strange things can be so beautiful," Linda said, gazing deeply into Bruce's eyes and feeling, for an instant, his inner strength.

At that moment, though, Bruce's thoughts were focused on his inability to get a table at La Truffe. "Excuse me," he said, and went over to the maitre d'.

The man looked a bit uncomfortable when he saw Bruce, but his attitude didn't soften. If anything, it became harder.

"I'm sorry, sir, there's still nothing open."

"I've been here half an hour and I keep seeing people being seated ahead of us," Bruce said.

"Don't exaggerate," the man said. "It's been barely twenty minutes."

The man looked down at his book, making it perfectly clear to Bruce that he was *never* going to be seated, not as long as he remained a Chinese man with a white woman. Bruce's jaw set hard with humiliation. He'd like to teach the man a lesson with his fists, but realized that would just earn him another encounter with the police to match the first one in Hong Kong and the near miss at Yang's.

He went back to the bar, where he ordered a large tomato juice.

"You know what I been thinking?" he said to Linda.

"What were you thinking?" She was still gazing directly at his soul and was up for anything at that point.

"I was thinking I'd like to take you someplace else . . . someplace good. This place, I don't think the food is so good after all."

"I'll go wherever you like."

"One tomato juice, sir," said the bartender, delivering it in a large brandy snifter.

Bruce tossed a few dollars on the bar and escorted Linda off her seat and back toward the maitre d'. He carried the tomato juice as if it were a halberd, a long-handled sword one type of which was used in kung fu.

He said to the maitre d', "I'm sorry . . . we just ran out of time."

"What a pity," said the maitre d' just as Bruce checked his watch and, in so doing, rotated his wrist far enough to dump the entire glass of tomato juice over the priceless reservations book. Without that book, the rest of the evening would be a long apology to important customers.

The tomato juice covered all the open pages of the book, obliterating names and reservations, before dribbling down into a drawer that had been packed thick with valuable credit card charge slips.

"Gee, I'm sorry," Bruce said.

He pulled the maitre d's white handkerchief out of his pocket and began to sop up the red mess.

"Let me clean that up for you," Bruce said.

"I'll do it! I'll do it!" the man exclaimed, suddenly fearful for his job.

"Okay," Bruce said, tucking the sopping-wet handkerchief back into the man's jacket pocket. Bruce then smiled and led Linda to the door and outside. Once in the clean air, she asked, "What was that all about?"

He smiled inscrutably. "Confucius say: When pupil is ready, teacher appears."

☗ 11 ☗

THE NEON SIGN FOR YANG'S CHINESE RESTAURANT GLOWED YELLOW just outside the windows of the second-floor dining room. It filled the room with an electric glow to augment the romantic light of the small candles set on each table.

Bruce and Linda had gotten a good table at last. It was right by the window with a view of the neon sign and, beyond that, a busy Chinatown street in the full blush of evening. Their waitress was April, who at first gave the couple a withering glance that was hard to interpret. It could have meant, *Not an American girl*. It could also have meant, *Maybe I was wrong about him*. In either case, she served them a plate of beef with oyster sauce, which they shared.

Bruce told her an abbreviated version of his relationship with the restaurant (he left out the fight). April was an efficient and even friendly waitress after her initial reaction. And if Ts'ai Lun knew who he was cooking for, he refrained from spicing the food with arsenic. Bruce showed Linda how to drink Chinese tea (very delicately, and no sugar) and when the meal was done, took her to a movie.

Breakfast at Tiffany's was a romantic hit that featured, among other things, Mickey Rooney's wild caricature of Holly Golightly's Asian landlord. His eyes taped back, he

81

was bucktoothed and out of control emotionally, staring bug-eyed through Coke-bottle glasses.

He knocked on her apartment door, yelling, "Miss Go-rightly! You in there, Miss Go-rightly?"

Linda thought it was hysterical, and munched popcorn laughing with the rest of the audience. Then she looked over at Bruce, who wasn't laughing. To him it was like a black man watching a minstrel show where a white actor dressed up in blackface did a crude caricature of a black man.

Linda looked again at the screen to see Rooney squinting, licking his lips, appearing somewhat like the World War II American propaganda posters that portrayed Orientals as bug-eyed, bucktoothed fanatics. Then she looked back at Bruce, the real thing, handsome and almond-eyed, as he sat with arms folded, humiliated for the second time that evening.

She put the popcorn on the floor and took his arm. "Let's get out of here," she said.

Soon they were back on campus, taking a little-used way in and finding the one spot in which the two of them could be alone with the wind and the night. There would be no officious maitres d'hotel, no minstrel shows poking fun at Chinese. On campus they could have fun, and be free. So they gamboled across the empty green spaces in the fog. He chased her up to the colonnade, a secluded and dignified cloister of narrow brick walks and Greco-Roman columns covered with ivy.

He trapped her against a column, pressed her soft blond hair against ivy, and took her in his arms and kissed her. Linda responded, trembling, and wrapped her arms around his neck while his hands traveled up and down her fine, ripe body. When they started up under her dress, raising it, she pushed him away.

"I . . . I can't go this fast," she said. "I talk a good game. You think I'm experienced, but I'm not."

He could force her, certainly. He had that strength. But he could never make a woman do something she didn't desire.

"Do you want what I want?" he asked.

"Yes. Soon."

"Good. The body always follows the mind."

He kissed her, but tenderly this time.

"I'm cold," she said, shivering.

"It's getting cold out," he agreed, slipping an arm around her shoulders. He would wait. They turned, and slowly walked back, to safely deposit Linda at home.

1964

It was a cold January day in 1964 when Linda walked home from college, her gym bag in her hand. The wind was whipping up off the bay, and high stratus clouds whipped across the sky propelled by cold northern winds. The sound of the wind whistling in the street signs blended with the hum of the car engines and the occasional ringing of a cable car bell. Soon there came an odder sound, however, a tinny one, somewhat like a lawn mower engine strapped to an empty drum.

It was Bruce, barreling down the street on a decrepit 125cc Honda motorcycle. The cycle, more like a motor scooter than a true motorcycle, was painted red and yellow and sported decals from Yosemite and Death Valley. As for Bruce, he sported tight black jeans, a black motorcycle jacket, and fashionable Ray-Ban shades.

He skidded to a stop, and Linda's wintertime discontent

faded at the sight of him. "You look like Marlon Brando in *The Wild One*," she said.

"Oh, yeah? Is that good?"

"He's the best."

"Come on. You just have never seen a Chinaman on a bike before."

"I thought you guys pulled rickshas," she joked.

"I left mine home today. Hop on."

Without hesitation, she jumped on the back and threw her arms around his waist. The motorcycle darted off in a cloud of tinny engine noise, handlebar streamers chattering in the wind.

As she clung to him, Bruce drove down decreasingly pretty streets into an older part of town, a working-class neighborhood filled with small grocery stores, luncheonettes, and other establishments for the common man and woman. The area was safe but seedy, with low rents and some storefronts that had been vacant for months if not years. But cable cars and buses served the area, which meant that an attractive business started there could reach out to the entire city.

He pulled up in front of an abandoned storefront with brick walls inside and out and a layer of dust deep enough to leave footprints in.

When he parked the cycle and they got off, Linda gave him a quizzical look. He said nothing, but led her across the sidewalk and pushed open the unlocked front door. The hinges creaked like those in a haunted castle.

"Well, what do you think?" he asked.

Breathless, Linda looked around. It was indeed a wreck. The brick walls needed repair; some were chipped, others missing entirely. Paint had peeled off the ceiling in long strips that had eventually crashed to the floor, splintering into a thousand pieces, joining reams of garbage left by the previous tenant. Fluorescent light fixtures dangled like drunks hanging onto a bar. In the center of the room was something new, however. It was man-sized and covered with a sheet. Another new object, a Chinese screen, hid the far end of the room from view.

"What do you think?" he asked again.

"I think you should have gotten the license number."

"What license number?"

"The one on the back of the truck that ran over this place."

"I'm serious. I want to know what you think of it."

"I don't know what to think."

"What do you mean? This was your idea."

"My idea? When did I suggest that you move into a slum? I mean, the room above Yang's was tiny, but it was at least clean."

Bruce said, "This is no slum. This is the first branch of the Bruce Lee Kung Fu Institute."

Linda began to catch his enthusiasm. At first, she'd really had no idea what he meant to do with the place. Young people did live in abandoned storefronts here and there in San Francisco, mostly would-be beatniks—"hippies," the newspapers were beginning to call them—in the poverty-stricken Haight-Ashbury district. But Bruce did not seem like one of them.

"You talked me into it," he said. "You make me feel like I can do anything."

"You can," she said, moving closer to him, feeling once again his strength. It was especially strong that day.

He bent toward her, and for an instant she expected a kiss. Then he reached to the floor and picked up a pebble. He dropped it in her hand.

"When I came over on the boat, I knew this was an idea place," Bruce said. "Ideas make this country great. Here, a good idea makes a man anything he wants to be. You drop a pebble in a pond, you get ripples. Soon the ripples cross the whole pond."

He opened her hand. "Drop it," he said.

She did as she was told. The pebble clattered to the filthy floor, where it bounced and skittered under a crumpled McDonald's wrapper.

"See . . . it's begun," Bruce said.

"Okay," she said with a laugh, moving toward the mystery object in the center of the room.

"What's this, the first student?"

"No, you're my first student. This is Pete."

He whipped the sheet off, revealing a thick cylinder, a barrel almost, standing on one wooden leg. There were three wooden arms projecting at different heights and angles.

"Hey, Pete, how are they hangin'?" she asked.

"He's the perfect opponent. Always there. Always ready. Doesn't eat much."

"Don't fight him. Marry him."

"I'll use Pete for students to practice their offensive moves on," Bruce said. "He looks silly, but there are over a hundred specific moves you can try out on the *wing chun* dummy."

She wandered across the empty space, pulling Bruce along by the hand. "Here's where you can have the reception area," she said. "Over here's where you'll give the classes."

She peeked behind the Chinese screen and saw a box spring and mattress set, still in their plastic wrapping.

"And here's where you can give me my first private lesson," she said.

"You can count on that," he said, sitting on the mattress.

She sat next to him, held his hand, and rested her head on his shoulder.

"So you think I can make a go of this?" he asked.

"I think *we* can."

"Me too. I got a great bargain here—ninety bucks a month in rent, including gas and electric."

"And roaches."

"They came on their own. But hey, I'll buy a can of spray."

"Better make it a barrel of spray. Do you have the money to fix it up and everything?"

"Who needs a lot of money? We need some plaster and paint, a little wire, hammers and nails . . ."

"And a small army of friends," she added.

"I got it already. Sayles and Overstreet have volunteered. Benny's dad is a carpenter, and anyone can paint."

"The guys are gonna work for nothing?"

"If they don't I'll kick their asses," he said with a laugh.

"That's a powerful incentive," she agreed.

"I have enough money to pay the rent for six months. If we can't make a go of it by then—I guess I'll have to go back to washing dishes."

"We'll make it," Linda said. "I know we will. After all, I just dropped the pebble in the water and the ripples have only begun to spread out."

☖ 12 ☖

Fixing up the old storefront only took a few weeks, given the fact that everyone pitched in.

Plaster was repaired and painted over. Broken bricks were replaced. The wiring, which when Bruce first moved in had shorted out every time a bus passed and shook the ground, was redone. The fluorescent fixtures were cleaned up and rehung. A reception area was walled off, which also had the effect of making the workout and living space more private.

A used wrestling mat was bought from the college at a bargain rate. Pete, the *wing chun* dummy, was set up near the door to the reception area, where he would both impress onlookers and catch the ambient light from the street at night, discouraging thieves. He was, in that respect, something of an urban scarecrow. A set of free weights was added, mostly so Bruce could stay in shape without having to trek all the way to the gym.

Perhaps most important, the mattress and box spring that sat behind the Chinese screen were taken out of their wrappers. Bruce and Linda threw a party for the volunteers who had helped them build the *kwoon,* and a few minutes after the last of them left, made love for the first time. Their athletic bodies moved together in peace and loving harmony, glistening with perspiration and glowing in the street light reflected off the newly painted walls.

Pete's shadow lorded over and protected them. Linda saw him as being like the totem poles that guarded the homes of American Indians living in the Pacific Northwest. But Bruce saw Pete differently. He was like the Chinese dragon, who was not a fearsome thing as were European dragons, but a hearty creature that represented the vitality of the land. He was a protective dragon, not quite fire-breathing but very much a protective spirit. A bit like Bruce himself, Linda felt.

So when, in the middle of that first night, Linda awoke naked and alone on the mattress, she looked for Pete's shadow and saw that he had a companion. Bruce stood by him, doing curls, his naked body lit like a statue by the street light.

Linda walked from behind the screen. "Come back to bed," she said. "Don't you ever sleep?"

"I'll sleep when I'm dead," he replied.

"Don't talk like that. We're never going to die."

She walked up behind him, reached around, and grabbed the barbell. They did curls together, their bodies fused in the ambient light.

"Enough," she said, and he dropped the barbell. It landed on the mat with a deep thud.

He turned and faced her.

"There's only one thing wrong with making love to a Chinese man," she said.

"What's that?" he asked, a little nervous.

"You're hungry an hour later."

She jumped on him, straddling him with her muscular diver's legs.

"And I mean *starved*," she said as he carried her back to bed.

As winter turned to spring in 1964, they made love and

Bruce taught classes. At first just his usual college group showed up, but soon his reputation began to grow. Local men and women of all races were attracted by the goings-on, and they told others. By the first blossoms of spring the Bruce Lee Kung Fu Institute had a full roster of students. He was becoming a success.

What was making him a success, however, was a tempting of the gods. Bruce Lee was teaching Chinese secrets to Americans. He felt uneasy about that, though he didn't talk about it much. Yip Man had never left the Orient, after all. He had migrated from the mainland to Hong Kong to get away from the Communists, but once there he'd stayed.

The old Chinese insularity was raising its head—and that head sometimes took on the appearance of a creature with fury in its blazing eyes. And so it was one night, while Bruce was alone in the *kwoon,* the demon came to call. Bruce did not expect it. He had not thought of such things since leaving Hong Kong. The old fears seemed to have been left behind, with his father's offerings to the gods and the protection of the *pat kwa* mirrors.

He sat at a makeshift desk of bricks and boards, typing a term paper on Hegel's *Phenomenology of Spirit*. The old Smith-Corona typewriter clacked like a horde of beetles, and the desk swayed with every push of the carriage return. A cup of tea sat next to the machine, the green liquid magically staying in the cup despite the motion around it. It was early on a moonless night when the streets outside were deserted. Only the rats and an occasional wisp of tissue paper blowing in the wind disturbed the cemetery-like calm.

Suddenly the tea, which had sat for an hour and had cooled to room temperature, began to steam. Bruce noticed the cold then, the chill that made a cup of lukewarm tea send streams of mist blowing into the air. A noise came up outside, a thunderstorm, earthquake, or worse. There was a howling, a typhoon, and the door to the *kwoon* blew open so hard the glass shattered.

"What the hell?" Bruce exclaimed, getting to his feet as the pages of his term paper were lofted by the tempest and strewn around the room.

The *kwoon* was torn by a supernatural maelstrom. The edges of the mat lifted up and flapped like the wings of a devil ray. Pete was blown over backwards, crashing against the wall and to the floor. Papers, books, lamps were hurled about like autumn leaves in a nor'easter. The fluorescent ceiling fixtures, rehung so carefully only a short time before, swung wildly before flickering and going out.

Bruce tried to force his way into the wind, which was coming in the front door from the empty street. He was strong and agile, but neither his strength nor his ability meant anything against that unearthly wind. It blew him steadily backward, his T-shirt and workout pants plastered to his legs like second skins, until he was flat against the rear brick wall.

He looked up. The swirling wind became an onrushing white light, a wall of blinding light that hid the darkness of hell. From out of that light came the demon, the Ming Warrior of his father's nightmares. The smell that filled the room was of death and old leather, of breath reeking. The demon's leather-sheathed left arm held the sword. He pointed with his right arm, pointed a long and stiletto-like finger at Bruce. The demon said nothing but his eyes glowed yellow with the message: *You're mine.*

Lee Hoi Chuen's nightmare had followed his son to the promised land.

Half dressed, Bruce and Linda ate Gussie Yang's takeout while watching *General Hospital* on a small black-and-white television. Linda had gotten to the point where she

91

used chopsticks like a native, and Bruce was proud of her for that small obeisance to Chinese culture. They were between classes and the *kwoon* was empty. More than empty, it had about it the aura of an ancient battlefield. Perhaps the Romans and Carthaginians had fought there two millennia ago; the ghosts of the bloodshed remained, watching silently from behind the brick walls.

Said the soap opera actress, "Scotty . . . Scotty is not your son."

"Not my son? Whose son is he?" the actor replied.

Both man and woman on the screen were tall, angular, and good-looking white Americans. Bruce felt somewhat uncomfortable watching them, as if the suggestion existed that they were an ideal he could never match. It hadn't helped that Linda had switched on the show.

The music swelled and the picture faded. On came a commercial.

Unaware of her lover's mood, Linda said, "I hate to tell you this, Bruce, but Scotty is *my* son."

She put aside her chopsticks and got up. Linda shoveled her diaphragm and makeup case into her bowling bag.

"I gotta go," she said. "I told Mom I'd help her with dinner."

Bruce leaned forward and switched off the TV. He flicked on the radio. The Beatles sang "Please Please Me."

Bruce looked at her bowling bag and said, "Your mom must think you're a professional bowler by now."

That remark made her feel guilty. She avoided his gaze, and after a second he turned away and wouldn't look at her either.

"I'm going to tell her," Linda said.

"When?"

"When I'm ready."

"Well, we all know how long that can take."

"I don't like to be pushed," she said, beginning to feel defensive.

"Are you ashamed of me?" he asked, the irritation plainly showing in his voice.

She had no idea, nor could he tell her, of the nightmare vision he had had the night before. Should he breathe a word of it, she would surely think him crazy. Another crazy Chinaman whose world was filled with superstition.

"No, I'm not ashamed. My mother is very old-fashioned, that's all."

"Does she hate Chinese?"

"Of course not. That's ridiculous. Maybe I am reluctant to tell her because I didn't tell her long ago. She'll know I was hiding something. Maybe I'm a little embarrassed."

"Your friend Sherry knows. What does she think?"

"It doesn't matter what Sherry thinks," Linda said. "What about *you*? Are *you* ashamed of *me*? Did you ever tell your father about me?"

"Of course I did."

"Did you tell him about your little *gwei-lo* girl?"

"Yes."

"What did he say?"

"It doesn't matter what he said. What matters is I told him."

She sighed and placed a hand on his shoulder. "Okay, so I'll tell her. It's just . . . she's so . . . she's not gonna understand, Bruce."

"I thought you said she doesn't hate Chinese."

"I don't think she does. I don't know what she thinks. I only know she's not gonna *understand*."

He said, "I understand . . . you understand. That's what matters."

"It should be all that matters," Linda agreed, her expression turning a bit sad now. "But she's my mom."

93

Bruce knew he was forcing the issue, but spoke anyway: "Then don't bother."

"Don't bother what?"

"You don't have to tell her. Look, Linda, I think we should break up."

"What are you talking about?" she said, shocked.

He stood and folded his arms. He was about to make a pronouncement. His bearing had an air of finality about it.

"I've made some decisions," he began. "I'm gonna quit school. You were right—there's nothing much that I can do with a degree in philosophy."

"Quit school?"

"Yeah. I've gotta get things going in my life. Business is starting to take off and I need to expand. I saw a larger space . . . in Oakland. I'm gonna open up a school over there."

Linda was beyond shocked. She was furious. She said, "Thanks for giving me a lot of notice. Nice of you to talk it over with me. Nice of you to let me know you were scouting new locations *in Oakland,* as far away from me as you can get without going to L.A."

"It's better this way," Bruce said. "You did your crazy Chinaman thing. You went slumming and had a fling with a foreigner. Now you can marry a nice white doctor and everyone will be happy."

She slapped his face hard. He felt the sting of her hand and her anger, and resisted the temptation to retaliate. The urge to strike back showed in his face, though.

"Go ahead! Hit me back!" she yelled.

"Come on, Linda," he said, shaking off the anger.

She went right up in his face. "Hit me! Only this time why don't you make it above the belt."

He was unable to stare her down, although he set his jaw and tried hard. Try as he might to avoid it, he blinked first.

Defiantly, she grabbed her bowling bag and stormed out the door. Bruce watched her go, and when she was well out of sight he whirled and gave Pete a high roundhouse kick that send him flying.

Crying, her cheeks red with anger and embarrassment, Linda ran to the corner bus stop where she could get the Number 10 home.

A redwood bench with wrought-iron supports was occupied by two black nurses, dressed all in white, who were on their way to work at Central Medical Center. They looked enough alike to have been mother and daughter. The older of the pair read the *San Francisco Examiner,* the younger a well-worn paperback copy of *Peyton Place.*

"Come on, come on," Linda said out loud, looking in vain for the bus.

She couldn't wait to put some miles between Bruce and her. Their love, which had seemed so perfect—if a little bit illicit—for so long, had crashed in an instant. There had been no warning, not the faintest signal that he was unhappy. True, he had been restless all day, and had mumbled something about a "bad night." She'd assumed he'd had a nightmare. So what, she thought. What harm could a nightmare do? The whole thing was so hard to understand.

There was no sign of the bus, and soon her pacing and crying got the attention of the black women. "You all right, girl?" the older nurse asked.

"What? Oh, yeah. Fine. I got a headache, that's all."

"It look more like a heartache to me."

"I . . . never mind. What time does the bus come?"

"Half an hour this time of day. You best sit down."

"Half an hour, my God!"

She continued to pace until there came the sound of a tinny motorcycle. She stole a look down the street and saw

Bruce driving up on his funky Honda. Linda quickly wiped her eyes and assumed an aloof attitude.

The two black women saw what was going on and looked at each other knowingly.

"Sure do look like heartache," the younger one agreed.

Bruce skidded the rear wheel out as he pulled to a halt right in front of the bus stop. "Come with me," he said.

"I can take the bus, thank you," Linda said coldly, trying not to look at him.

"The bus can't take you where I can."

"You've taken me enough, thanks."

"Come with me to Oakland."

"I've been to Oakland, thank you. It gave me a head-ache."

"You'll like it better when we're married," Bruce said.

"What did you say?" she asked, looking at him at last.

"You heard me—marry me."

"You . . . you mean it?" she asked, her voice trembling.

"Of course I mean it," he said, revving the engine to keep it from stalling.

"I . . . I . . ."

"It won't be a fancy marriage," he said. "But I can afford a carriage." He revved the engine again.

There was a suspended moment between them, when time itself appeared to stand still. Neither was sure of anything.

"For God's sake, girl," the older nurse said, "take two aspirin and go to Oakland with the man."

Her words seemed to break the deadlock. Linda leaped on the back, her tears turned to tears of joy as they peeled away.

❦ 13 ❦

It was June of 1964 when Linda and Bruce sat down to have coffee with her mother and discuss their future. A light spring rain was falling. Its drops could barely be heard behind a Chopin nocturne that Linda struggled to play on the baby grand piano in the den.

Vivien Emery brought in a tray of coffee and cookies and offered a cup to Bruce, who sat on the couch looking nervous. He was scared in a way that no opponent had ever scared him. The woman stood in the way of his happiness in the United States as he saw it. Linda was the girl of his dreams, after all, and so what if they had an occasional spat. He wanted her for all time.

Linda's piano playing normally was quite good, like her diving. But at the moment, the tensest in her life, nothing came easy. She kept flubbing easy notes.

"Eight years of lessons," Vivien said, shaking her head. "Sugar, Mr. Lee?"

"Please," he said, accepting a spoonful and stirring it slowly around the dainty fake china cup.

"Linda, are you pregnant?" she asked.

"No," Linda replied, swiveling around on the piano stool. "I've been very careful."

"I should certainly hope so. Okay, let's look at this thing from all angles. First, you're awfully young, Mr. Lee."

"I'm twenty-four," he protested.

"Well, you look younger. And Linda has to finish college."

"I'll finish up from Oakland. I can drive to the campus."

"You have a car, Mr. Lee?"

"I'll get one."

"A motorcycle is exciting, but . . ."

"I'll get a car," he promised again.

Vivien was visibly relieved, enough to take a seat on the couch near, but not too near, to her future son-in-law.

"Okay, okay. You'll finish college from Oakland. But there are other aspects to marriage I don't think you two have considered. How will you live?"

"I'm going to open another school . . . in Oakland. Maybe one in Palo Alto soon. It'll be a chain . . . like McDonald's."

"I don't want to rain on your parade, young man, but people need hamburgers. They don't need judo."

"Kung fu."

"Whatever."

"More people want to study it all the time. It's an excellent discipline for the mind, and a way to relax, in addition to being self-defense. People need to discipline their minds and relax too. That's how I've been putting myself through school."

"All right, I'll give you that too. Maybe you'll actually become successful with this kung fu. So now let's address the real issue: children."

Bruce and Linda exchanged looks. They had never discussed it.

"After all, Linda, marriage is really about children," Vivien said.

"Sure, we want children. Some day," Linda said.

"What will they be? They won't be white. They won't be Oriental. They'll be some kind of half-breeds and they won't be accepted by either side."

Bruce felt his anger rising. *Half-breeds?* he thought. She's calling our children *half-breeds?* Who *is* this woman to talk like that?

"They'll be Americans," he said calmly. "Linda's an American. I'm an American."

"You're an American *citizen.* You're not really American."

Bruce could control it no longer. He gripped the coffee cup so hard that the handle snapped off, cutting his hand. He rose slowly, looking at Linda as if to say, *Does this woman speak for you? Is that what your family is* like?

She averted her eyes. "Bruce," she said.

Vivien said, "You should get a Band-Aid on that cut, Mr. Lee."

Without saying a word, he walked out.

Vivien turned to her daughter and said, "I treated him like a gentleman. You saw me."

The front door opened, admitting the soft sound of rain. Then it slammed. Vivien examined the broken cup. "This is my favorite china," she said.

"Mom . . ."

"You can do much better. Believe me, you'll forget him in a month."

Linda felt as if she were lashed to horses that were going in opposite directions.

"Can you really imagine yourself having yellow babies? Can you?"

"Yes, I can," Linda said.

Outside in the rain the motorcycle kicked over. The tinny

sound was like a call for liberation. There was a lot of it in the air in 1964.

"I'm sorry, honey," Vivien said. "All this man will bring you is pain. I can't allow it."

"It's not up to you," Linda said, and dashed out the door after Bruce.

The light rain had turned into a downpour as she raced down the steps and out the front walk. Bruce had the motorcycle in gear and was starting down the street, perhaps forever, when she called, "Bruce! Bruce!"

Relieved, he threw the bike into a skid on the rain-drenched street. Linda leaped on board and threw her arms around him.

"Don't ever leave me," she pleaded. "Don't ever leave me again."

"What about your mother?"

"Forget her. You and I are all that count."

"You and me together forever."

"Yes," she said, and kissed him on the back of the neck. He rolled the accelerator to the max. They zoomed off so fast they streaked between the raindrops.

It was August 17, 1964, when Bruce and Linda were married. He had bought a car by then—a big 1963 Chrysler that had been knocked around fairly badly during its first year of life. And he'd bought a tuxedo, a sharp-looking one that he wore proudly as he hurried through the crowded dining room of Gussie Yang's restaurant.

April gawked at him, but she was holding a tray of fu yung and couldn't talk. A few of the other workers smiled and said hello, but Bruce had one thing on his mind. He had to repay a kindness.

He found Gussie in her downstairs office. She looked up at him, and his tux, in amazement.

100

"It's a funeral, right?" she said. "You finally killed someone."

He laughed. "You know me better than that."

"Do I? My kitchen staff still is black and blue."

He slapped an envelope in her hand. "Now you can pay them better, so they can afford to go to the doctor."

"What's this?" she asked.

"The loan . . . paid in full. And I want to thank you for steering me in the right direction."

He planted a kiss on her astonished cheek.

"Where are you going in that tuxedo?" she asked.

"To a wedding."

"Whose?"

"Mine," he said, and walked toward the door.

But April was after him in a flash. She said, "Wedding? I heard something about a wedding?"

They stopped just inside the door to talk. Bruce fed a dime into a gum ball machine and got a handful of Chicklets. He popped the red ones into his mouth.

"I'm getting married," he said.

"To her? To the blonde?"

"Yeah, I'm marrying my *gwei-lo* girl. Do you have a problem with that?"

April thought for a moment, then said, "No. Of course not."

"I'm glad."

"I just . . ."

"We had some good times together. It just wasn't meant to be."

She nodded, looking out the door at Linda, who was sitting in the passenger's side of the Chrysler, which was all decked out with ribbons, shoes, tin cans, and "Just Married" signs.

"No, I guess it wasn't. Look, Bruce . . . are you happy with her?"

"Very."

"And your school? Is it going well?"

"I'm opening a bigger one in Oakland."

"That's great," she said. "That's really great. Look, I'm going to miss you but I want to wish you all my best. Good luck to you and Linda."

"Thanks. That means a lot to me."

They kissed briefly, and then he pushed out the door and across the sidewalk. He got behind the wheel of the car, which was filled to the brim with luggage and boxes. Pete was lashed to the top, looking very much like the figurehead in the bow of a Viking warship.

"Who was that?" Linda asked, more curious than jealous.

"A chapter of my life that's over," Bruce said as he put the car in gear and pulled out from the curb.

The sign over the door read "The Jun Fan Gung Fu Institute." The new *kwoon* was large and spacious, and fitted out with the best equipment Bruce's money could buy. Pete was set up in his customary place of honor, and a new reception area was completely separate from the training room. Out back, and well out of sight for a change, were the Lees' honeymoon living quarters, with an actual kitchen and a real bathroom.

Carrying bags of groceries under each arm, Linda walked into the loft building, up the stairs, and through the reception and workout areas. She walked past Bruce, who was doing thumb push-ups to keep busy, and stashed the groceries in their new kitchen. Then she returned to join him. He had finished his push-ups and was sitting cross-legged on the mat, listening to a radio discussion of the

102

enactment of the Civil Rights Act of 1964, the strongest such legislation passed since the Civil War.

It was a cold autumn day. Linda stripped off her bulky sweater and tossed it into a corner. Then she marched to the radio and changed the station. What came on was the Beatles singing "Love Me Do."

"Anything yet?" she asked.

"Nothing," he said, and got up to give her a kiss. "The phone rang once. You know who it was? It was the phone company calling to ask if the phone worked all right."

She smiled grimly. "I don't know why we haven't gotten any students yet. I put five thousand flyers out—one under every windshield in this city."

"You would think that everyone already *knows* kung fu. I mean, I can understand why my old students wouldn't come here. It's a long way across that bridge from San Francisco, and they were mostly college kids who didn't have a whole lot of money after all. But Oakland is a big city with lots of people."

"But not many college kids, and who else would be interested? Maybe we should have thought of that."

"Kung fu isn't just for college kids. They happened to be the first crowd I attracted, that's all. If I had given that little demonstration I put on in the college wrestling room in a steel mill, we'd be getting steel workers signing up right now."

"I'll go out with more flyers tomorrow and look for a steel mill," she said.

Just then the front door opened, and a handsome young black man stuck his head in the door. He was a bit tentative at first, not knowing exactly whether *gung fu* was the same thing as kung fu and exactly what that was. Perhaps he was also wondering whether he was welcome, although Oakland was a city with a large black population.

He waved one of Linda's flyers. "You open?" he asked.

"Come in, come in," Bruce said, rising and walking across the floor to take his hand.

"I caught the flyer. Thought I'd check it out. Seen some of that kung fu in them chopsaki movies."

"Chopsaki movies? Oh, I know what you mean. My dad's friends make them—back in Hong Kong."

The visitor made some crazy moves along with a few sound effects. He looked like a blind farmer using a rusty knife on an old hog. Linda laughed.

"Cool shit, man. Name's Jerome. Jerome Sprout. And you must be that cat Bruce Lee."

"That's me."

"And you must be his wife, right?"

"Hi, Jerome."

"You two are some pair. You get invited to a lot of fancy parties in white neighborhoods?"

"Not lately," Bruce said.

"I can dig it. So Linda, you any relation to Brenda Lee?"

"No," she said, laughing again.

"That's good. Hey . . . I'd like to take some kung fu lessons."

"I'd like to give them," Bruce said. He was relieved to have a customer, a student to teach, but he was equally happy to have found someone he liked in Oakland.

"No shit. You know I'm not Chinese."

"I noticed."

"And it don't bother you? Some of the other teachers around here just turned me down flat. Some wouldn't even talk to me."

"They have little imaginations and big bank accounts," Bruce said.

"That may be, but from where I stand they just didn't want to teach a brother."

"A what?" Linda asked.

"A brother. A *soul* brother, y'dig?"

"Unh, yeah," Bruce said. "Otis Redding . . . Sam and Dave."

"You got it. That Beatles shit on the radio *scared* me a bit."

Bruce turned off the radio.

"Those other teachers got attitude, that's what they got," Jerome said.

"Well, you got a teacher," Bruce said. "And if you like what I teach and have any friends who would like to learn too . . ."

"Maybe you'll take something off my bill," Jerome said with a smile.

"Nothing is out of the question." He pounded Jerome on the shoulder. "Let's go to work," Bruce said.

ꙮ 14 ꙮ

Jᴇʀᴏᴍᴇ ᴅɪᴅ ʟɪᴋᴇ ᴛʜᴇ ʟᴇssᴏɴs, ᴀɴᴅ ʙᴇꜰᴏʀᴇ ʟᴏɴɢ ʜɪs ꜰʀɪᴇɴᴅs began to come. Then the sight of blacks going in and out of the *kwoon* attracted more black students. Linda put out flyers every day, and soon the class grew from one to five to ten. Other classes were added, even a group of seven to ten year olds. Among the adults, Bruce's students ran the gamut from Black Muslims to white attorneys to secretaries of all colors. A few college kids signed up, as did some retirees. The Jun Fan Gung Fu Institute was a success.

But success attracts the angry as well as the eager. It was in December of 1964 that a young Chinese boy, perhaps ten or eleven years of age, ran up the stairs and into the *kwoon*. Linda was alone, straightening up between classes.

"Hi," she said brightly upon seeing the boy. "Can I help you?"

Shyly, he handed her a piece of paper. It was a hand-lettered parchment on, rolled up and tied with a silk ribbon. The boy said nothing, but smiled sweetly, so she thanked him.

"*Un goy,*" she said.

He returned her smile and ran out the door and back down the stairs. She went to the window and watched him as he ran down the street in the direction of Oakland's small but powerful Chinatown.

Bruce came out of the shower, drying his hair with a towel. "If you're looking for the Good Humor Man, he isn't due for an hour."

"Some little kid was just here," she said, walking to her husband.

"One of my younger students?"

"No. A strange little Chinese boy. He handed me this."

She gave him the scroll, which he took even though the touch of it burned his hand. He *knew* what was in there; had been expecting something like it—though not as formal as a scroll—for some time. Bruce undid the ribbon, all the while being reminded of the ribbon that had tied the packet in which his father had kept safe his American birth certificate.

"What is it?" Linda asked.

"A warning. A summons for Lee Jun Fan."

"What do you mean, 'summons.'"

"The elders of Chinatown want to see me."

"The *elders of Chinatown*? What is this, the Spanish Inquisition? Who are they to *summon* you to their presence? What do they want? Does it say?"

The scroll was in Chinese pictograms and done in a hand that suggested a Mandarin origin.

"It doesn't say. But I think I know what it is. They're mad at me for teaching kung fu to the *gwei-lo.*"

"Oh, great. And I can just imagine what they think of *me.*"

"You're not mentioned, but I imagine you're on their minds."

"This is like with my mother, but worse."

"A *lot* worse. I have to go there."

"I'll go with you."

"No. I have to go alone."

"Where? Go where?"

"A social club in Chinatown. That's where they meet."

She said, "Bruce, this is crazy. This is America. They can't just *haul you in* like they were cops."

"No, they can't. But I have to put in an appearance. I have to go and explain myself."

"When?"

"Now."

"I'm going with you."

"No women are allowed. Sorry."

"Jesus, President Johnson signed the Civil Rights Act."

"It doesn't apply to women. Maybe Jerome could come with me." He thought about it for a second, then said, "No. Bad idea."

That the council of Chinese elders would have any power at all over Bruce is rooted in the fact that China, unlike the world's other major civilizations, never developed a religion of its own. Confucianism and Taoism were systems of social order—ways of behaving, not religions. Buddhism was an import from India and never had that much of an impact in China. What remained were the ancient Chinese practices of worshiping ancestors and gods drawn from nature. Out of ancestor worship came the Chinese devotion to family and the wisdom of elders. If Bruce's father could not escape the pull of the household gods, Bruce found it hard to ignore the old men who summoned him. Directly disobeying them would be akin to disobeying his father— something he found difficult to do, no matter how hard he tried to be an American.

The council met in a social club located a few blocks away from Bruce's *kwoon*. It occupied a three-story building that sat on a block otherwise given to Chinese restaurants, food stores, and clothing stores. The club met in a single large room that was unremarkable except for how dark it was inside. A few stray shafts of light came in through western-facing windows that no one had bothered to clean, cutting dusky swaths through air made thick by tobacco smoke.

Several dozen men, mostly aged sixty or above, stood or sat around, drinking *cha,* reading Chinese newspapers, or playing fan-tan or mah-jongg. A few sat around a table that had a finely lacquered top, watching with jaded interest the young upstart who walked in from the street and slapped the scroll on the table before them.

In Cantonese, Bruce said, "You asked me here. I'm here."

The first elder was a man of eighty, as thin as a stalk of bamboo, with white hair that was unevenly cut and unkempt. It stuck out at differing distances from his pale skull, which sat atop a neck wrinkled like that of a turkey. He used long, thin fingers to unroll the scroll and inspect it slowly, the intent of the delay being to make Bruce uncomfortable.

"Lee Jun Fan," he said at last, "you've been charged with violating the martial arts code. We have had complaints from Wu Zuolin, Wong Jack Man, and many others. You have been teaching the *gwei-lo.* This must stop."

"My wife is a *gwei-lo,*" Bruce said defiantly.

"That too is unfortunate."

Bruce's anger grew. How dare they attack Linda as well as his work! He said, "I'll teach whoever I want—Chinese, Japanese, white, black . . . I'll teach Martians if they want to learn."

His defiance angered several council members, and

earned him shocked looks from others in the room who were not directly involved in the inquisition. A second elder, younger than the first by a decade and fatter by a hundred pounds, raised a pudgy fist and shook it in the smoky air.

"You betray your training!" he shouted. "You betray your race!"

The first elder raised a bony arm to restrain his friend. He said to Bruce, in English this time, "Look, Bruce—you like to be called Bruce . . ."

"It's the name my father gave me."

"He also gave you the name Lee Jun Fan, and I beg you not to forget it. You are new here. We do things differently."

"I came to America because I didn't like the way things were done in Hong Kong," Bruce said. "Now you mean to tell me you would have it the same in the United States?"

The first elder pressed on with his argument, undaunted. "One of the things we don't do is teach our secrets to whites."

Still angry, the second elder said, "Whites! Black devils! Any of them! They're the enemy."

"They're not the enemy. Ignorance is the enemy. The *gwei-lo* just don't know us. Our race has been closed for so long, outsiders have never seen the beauty of our culture. They don't know how to emulate the beauty of a crane or the ferocity of a tiger. I say let's show it to them."

"Pearls before swine," the second elder spat out.

"That's a Western expression," Bruce said. "From the Christian Bible."

The first elder smiled faintly, even as his friend's rage grew.

"Your hearts are filled with anger," Bruce said. "But you cannot teach if you cannot learn. If you cannot learn, you have nothing to offer anybody."

Several of the elders whispered to one another. Bruce couldn't hear what they were saying, but the tone of it didn't look promising.

"You speak well," the first elder said. "But we do not agree with you. You are ordered to stop teaching the *gwei-lo*."

"Or what?" Bruce asked.

"Or we will settle this by combat. If you refuse the challenge, you will have no face . . . no status in this community."

"What if I win?"

"You will be left alone."

"To teach who I want?"

"Yes. But if you lose the combat, you will close your school and leave the city with your *gwei-lo* wife."

Bruce burned at the second slur against Linda.

"This isn't Manchu China," he said. "You can't tell me what to do."

"Prepare yourself, Lee Jun Fan," the first elder said.

Bruce left the club's smoke and shadows, and was glad to be back in the bright daylight. He walked home quickly, and when he got there found Linda busying herself in the kitchen, making dinner. A huge pot of vegetables simmered quietly next to a steaming pot of rice. The radio carried a discussion of the Gulf of Tonkin Resolution, passed by Congress, which had authorized President Johnson to escalate the war in Vietnam.

When Bruce walked in the door he was still angry, but seeing her in the kitchen changed him. He softened his mood, and while he wanted to talk about what happened, he

111

felt he should protect her from what he had to do. She could not understand how he had to fight to protect his work and his family from a bunch of old Chinese men. She was an American and accustomed to the rule of law. As little as the rule of custom and superstition meant to Bruce, it meant nothing to her.

He came up behind her, wrapped her in his arms, and kissed the back of her neck.

"What happened?" she asked, putting down her wooden stirring spoon and turning to face him.

"Pretty much what I expected. They ordered me to stop teaching non-Chinese."

"That's outrageous. What did you tell them?"

"I told them they were a bunch of silly old men and to leave us alone."

"Good. Then that will be the end of it?"

"I think so."

"They won't try to stop you?"

"They might *try*. I might not get any Chinese students for a while. I mean, the younger ones who don't have the old customs, they may still come. I may lose some older students."

"It doesn't matter," she said. "We're doing okay now. We have plenty of American students, and more are coming all the time. We don't need the Chinese students."

"Only the *gwei-lo,* huh?" he said, offering a grim smile.

"Yeah," she said. "Only them."

He kissed her again, on the lips this time, then walked away stretching his arms.

"I need a workout," he said.

"You can have it after dinner," she replied, going back to her cooking. "I'm starting my night classes this evening, and I may be late. You can have the place to yourself three times a week for the next month. Get as good a workout as you like.''

"Learn lots," he said.

"You too."

"Oh, I learn something *every* day," he said, wandering onto the mat and giving Pete a playful whack.

☗ 15 ☗

1965

BRUCE TRAINED FEVERISHLY AND ALONE FOR A MONTH, WORKING late into the night on his exercises. Linda learned nothing of the reason why he prepared himself, as the council of elders had advised him to do.

A challenge had been issued and communicated to him with another scroll. This one he'd intercepted before Linda could see it. He was due to fight for his right to run his business as he liked—even if it meant teaching ancient Chinese secrets to the *gwei-lo*.

The night before the match was a hard one. He trained as if his life depended on it, and perhaps it did. Now he toweled off, standing in the center of the mat and feeling not quite right, as though a great storm was coming just over the horizon. A full moon cast a pallid light in through the large front windows, and silence was the rule, as it often is before a storm. The street was empty, although the evening was young. A winter wind blew down the streets of Oakland, tossing leaves and scrap paper around with equal abandon and rattling the old and poorly sealed windows.

Pete was decorated with a strand of colorful love beads. It was the time for that sort of thing, what with the hippie movement of be-ins and happenings growing across the bay, back in San Francisco. Jerome Sprout had brought the beads in as a joke, but Bruce had liked them and draped them around Pete's neck. Now the beads seemed like the only glimpse of color in a world suddenly drained of it.

Then the wind came up higher, a high-pitched whining sound like the far-off screams of the dying. "Not again," Bruce whispered in fear as the lights flashed off, on again, and then off, to be replaced with the same ghostly light he saw the last time the demon came to call.

Pete's beads began to shake, then rattled against his wooden frame. Bruce dropped the towel and looked around for the Ming Warrior, but he was not to be seen. In his place came the low, terrifying rumbling from the bowels of the earth that signified an earthquake, or worse. The floor shook and Pete wobbled from side to side, the beads now swinging wildly.

The portrait of Yip Man, which hung proudly on the wall, crashed to the floor and its glass shattered. Bruce looked around in horror, then sucked in his breath as the floor collapsed beneath him and he dropped into the pits of hell.

He fell into a hollow, where he scrambled to his feet, thigh-deep ground fog sucking at his legs. A dead tree arose from a moss-covered knoll, its spindly branches clawing at the foul-smelling air like the fingers of the Chinese elder. On all sides of him, near enough to see but far enough away to never reach, were figures of the devil's disciples: A man used a *timbe* shield and *rochin* spear, making stabbing gestures at Bruce. Another used *ryukyu kobojutsu* sticks. A third brandished a *katana* sword, while a fourth reached toward Bruce with a gigantic hand gnarled into a praying mantis clawing position.

Bruce spun around as if to fight these apparitions, but they disappeared into the fog. He turned left and right, protecting himself with the tiger stance, but saw nothing. Then the ground shook again as the Ming Warrior rose from the earth behind him, the soul of a million dead ancestors rising from the graves. Bruce turned to fight, but there was no strength in his arms or legs. He was paralyzed, unable to move, unable even to scream, as the demon grabbed him by the shoulders and raised him over his head, high enough almost to touch the treetop.

The Warrior held him as if he were as light as a dead and dried twig, an offering to the gods. Then the monster smashed Bruce down on his rising knee. Bruce tried to scream, but nothing came out of his mouth but blood as his back snapped like wood.

Abruptly, the nightmare was over. The phantom was gone and the air once again smelled of sweat and *kwoon*. Pete was there and the picture of Yip Man back on the wall, the glass unsmashed. The street was silent no more. Traffic noises came in through the closed windows. Gone was the banshee wind and the ghostly light.

Bruce lay on the mat, his chest in pain. He clutched at it, felt his ribs, and arched his spine. Nothing was broken. His skin was drenched with perspiration and his jaw ached from clenching his teeth, but he was alive and in one piece.

He jumped to his feet, shaken and alone. The pain went away. He shook his head to clear it, and then he heard Linda coming up the stairs. *She must never know about this,* he thought desperately. *Whatever happens to me, I have to protect my family.* That, he knew, is the way of his people.

The following morning he sat alone staring at his teacup while she showered. Linda had made him a fine breakfast of eggs, bacon, and home fries, but it sat on the plate barely touched. The radio was on to a music station. The Byrds' ''Mr. Tambourine Man'' played in the background, com-

116

peting only with the rush of the shower and the drone of the refrigerator compressor.

She emerged from the bathroom with a towel wrapped around her head. The first thing she noticed was that he hadn't eaten. "Not hungry?" she asked.

"No." He shook his head.

"What's the matter, honey?"

"Nothing."

"Not feeling well?"

"I'm okay."

He wasn't very convincing and knew it. He thought he should say *something*. "I didn't sleep well," he said, telling no lie.

"Sorry," she said, kissing the top of his head.

"I had a nightmare."

"Poor baby. What was it about?"

"I can't remember," he sighed, putting aside his teacup and standing.

"Are you teaching today?" she asked.

"No. I have to take care of some business downtown."

"What business?"

"Tax stuff. It's getting to be that time of year. In order to be a good American, I have to pay taxes."

"You're a *very* good American," she said, going to him and holding his shoulders. "Do we owe a lot of money?"

"I owe everything . . ." he said.

She looked concerned. Lines appeared in her brow.

". . . to you."

She slapped him playfully.

"Get outta here. See you later?"

"I can't. I'm taking the most beautiful woman in Oakland out to dinner."

"Good," Linda said. "She'll be hungry at eight."

He gave her a last look, as if he might never see her again

117

and wanted to remember her perfectly. Then he left to keep his appointment.

The gymnasium was old, with dirty windows like those in the social club. Once a busy public school facility, it was now a privately owned gymnastic club that served the Chinese community. The council of Chinese elders had scared or bought everyone off for the morning, and as a result the place had about it much the same aura as Bruce's *kwoon* had had the night before, just prior to the nightmare.

Basketball backstops hung quietly from their supports, and gymnastic rings dangled from the rafters like nooses. A set of parallel bars stood near a chinning bar. Wooden bleachers, scarred with old graffiti carved by schoolboys' ballpoint pens, were folded up against one wall.

A wrestling mat stood at center court. The council of elders sat in a circle around it, not talking. If they were even *breathing* it wasn't apparent.

Bruce walked in with Jerome Sprout, who he brought along as a second and also to thumb his nose at the elders. If they objected to Linda being in his life, what would they think of his star black pupil? So many of Bruce's students were black these days, it seemed appropriate to bring Jerome. Also, he was a good man with a lot of information at his fingertips. He was plugged in to everything that happened in the city, it seemed.

"What is this place?" Bruce asked, looking around at the gym with undisguised distaste.

"This used to be the Frank B. Witcombe School. My dad went here in the 1930s. What it is now is a Chinese gymnasium attached to an office building that's mostly empty. I think the gym is related to that social club you told me about, but I'm not sure. My contacts in the Chinese community consist mainly of you."

"That's very comforting."

118

"Yeah, well so is the thought of you kissin' the butts of these old men."

"They challenged me. I can't put up with that."

"Yeah, but they ain't got no power."

"They have power enough to get someone to fight me."

"That would have happened anyway. A lot of the other teachers are intimidated by you. You're popular. And another thing, all the brothers goin' to study with you. A couple of Panthers even."

"Black Panthers," Bruce said.

"You ain't kiddin'. You're a big deal in this city, Bruce Lee."

"And they're trying to run me out of it. So you see why I have to fight."

"Since you put it like that."

"What do you hear about this guy I'm fighting? I never heard of him."

"Let me tell it to you like it is. Bookies are layin' twenty to one against you."

"Who is he?" Bruce asked again.

"The name's Johnny Sun. He's got a school over on Thompson. I checked him out. He's a killer, man."

"So am I, Jerome."

"Yeah, if you had to be, maybe. But I'm tellin' you, Johnny Sun is a real bad guy."

"What are you, his press agent?"

"He's got *real* blood on his hands. Some brothers tried to rob him last year. Two went to the hospital. The one with the gun went to a funeral."

"You're a real confidence-builder. Did anyone ever tell you that?"

"Constantly. I hear it all over town."

"Were these brothers friends of yours?"

"What, *me* hobnob with bad guys? You got to be kidding. I heard about 'em, that's all."

"Yeah," Bruce said, stopping to assess the circle of elders as they stared at him and his black second. "So this Johnny Sun has it in for brothers."

"In a big way."

"And you knew this and didn't tell me?"

"You ain't black."

"Yeah, but you are, and I brought you with me. Aren't you scared?"

"Shit, not with you around. Besides, you taught me a lot of stuff. I can handle myself. Not against *him,*" Jerome said, nodding in the direction of Johnny Sun, who had just entered the room. "He's a killer."

The man came out of the locker room looking like he could make ice ache for the Arctic. His body was muscled and his face showed a level of intensity, a *chi,* such as Bruce hadn't seen since coming to America. With him was a younger brother, Luke Sun. He was bigger than Johnny and handsome despite a deep scar down his left cheek. He lacked the killer edge of his older brother, but still looked formidable.

Jerome said, "The younger cat is his brother Luke. They eat their Wheaties in that family."

"What do your friends say about Johnny's style?" Bruce asked.

"What do you mean?"

"How does he fight?"

"Oh, yeah, style. Well, my contacts ain't kung fu gurus, but I get the impression that Johnny is a traditionalist."

"Explain."

"He sticks pretty much to the one style he knows."

"Which is?"

"Leopard."

"Good," Bruce said. "Leopard is by tradition a power style. Fairly static. I think I can handle him. Remember what

120

I taught you: *Wing chun* was developed to give smaller fighters the advantage against bigger and more powerful ones."

"Just don't forget to duck," Jerome said, eyeing the much bigger Johnny Sun with considerable apprehension.

"Let him come after me," Bruce said. "You know the rule: 'My movement flows from your movement. My technique flows from your technique.'"

Bruce stepped forward, and as he did Jerome caught him by the shoulder and said, "On second thought, forget this shit, man. Forget all us *gwei-los* and let's get the hell outta here right now. Either that or stall while I go round up some brothers with guns."

Bruce smiled at him like an indulgent father, and then entered the fighting area.

The Sun brothers hugged and then Johnny joined Bruce. Standing side by side, Bruce looked like the "before" part of a body-building commercial. Although well-built and muscled, Bruce couldn't match the awesome musculature and size of Johnny Sun. And his brother was even bigger. *He* stood off to one side, glaring first at Bruce and then at Jerome.

Johnny and Bruce bowed to the council, then to each other. Then they turned and squared off. The ordeal by combat had begun.

Bruce wanted to keep the bigger man at a distance until he learned more about him, so he boxed with his left foot, using tae kwon do moves to keep Johnny off him. That didn't work for long, and Johnny charged in—bigger men usually do, preferring to grapple than spar—throwing a series of jabs and knee kicks. Bruce blocked all of them and parried with a flurry of punches to the chest. Johnny's assault did little damage.

"Float like a butterfly, sting like a bee," Jerome said.

The two men broke and re-set their positions. Johnny set

121

up in a forward-leaning leopard stance, while Bruce hung back and low, leaving himself free to either duck or jump. Bruce went on the offensive then, striking at Johnny Sun's head and neck. The killer spun away, and as he did sent consecutive kicks at Bruce's head.

The first missed when Bruce ducked under it. But the second caught him hard in the shoulders. Bruce absorbed the blow, back-flipping to his feet. He was ready again.

"Go get him, Boss," Jerome said.

Bruce attacked again. He got inside the big man's defenses, turning a block into the opportunity to launch a *jik chun choy* straight blast, overwhelming Johnny with a frenzy of fists and elbows. Bruce drove him all the way across the mat. The bigger man covered up as he was hammered from every angle, losing his balance.

"You got him! You got him!" Jerome said.

The Chinese didn't believe in high kicks except as a training exercise for the crane form of *wing chun*. To them, going onto one foot unbalanced the fighter. Most of the high kicks seen in martial arts movies are from tae kwon do, the Korean form. But Bruce was willing to borrow good moves from many other martial arts, and unleashed a high kick to Johnny's face. First one, then another. A third followed. First blood was drawn. Stung severely, Johnny fell down.

"Right on," Jerome said as Luke Sun winced on the sidelines.

Bruce charged then, flying into the air and descending with a drop kick. But Johnny Sun intercepted the leading foot and, with a gargantuan burst of strength, hurled Bruce back into the air. He landed on the edge of the fighting area, and several of the elders scrambled to get out of the way.

This time it was Jerome who winced.

Johnny was on his feet and attacking with all his might. He caught Bruce while he was still scrambling to his feet and hit him with two high kicks aimed at the head. Bruce blocked both of them, but at great cost. He was staying in close, suffering greatly, while waiting to find an opening.

When it came, he slipped inside Johnny's legs, catching his huge calf on a knee and tossing it up like a lever. Then he hammered the Goliath's kidneys with a pair of knuckle punches. When Johnny staggered and partly doubled over, Bruce hammered the side of his jaw with two back fists and an elbow. Sun went down again.

But he was far from finished. A street fighter, he mounted a defensive even with his back to the mat. Bruce aimed a low *wing chun* kick at the man's throat, but missed when he twisted away. Anchored on the floor, Sun jammed a powerful right leg straight into Bruce's sternum. It was a crushing shot, one that knocked him back and sent him to the mat.

''Shit, man, get up!'' Jerome yelled.

Johnny Sun came in for the kill, but Bruce pulled himself up and into the dragon defensive stance. He was hurt. His only chance was to gather his strength and wait for the proper moment.

The big man came on like the killer he was. Bruce took blow after blow, deflecting some and absorbing others, hoping that through conditioning and patience he could wear the man down. He backed around the perimeter of the mat. Glistening with sweat, blood still running down him from his mouth and nose, the killer glint in his eyes, Johnny Sun just kept on coming, throwing kick after kick. He had switched from the *wing chun* leopard moves and was tossing bombs from tae kwon do. They weakened Bruce without destroying him, and he kept moving back and away, waiting.

But his energy was leaving him, beaten out of his body by the brutal assault. A quick combination of kick and punch

123

staggered Bruce and he fell to his knees, his head bowed, apparently beaten.

"Get up!" Jerome yelled.

Egged on by Luke Sun, the council of elders began to cheer for its man. They were yelling at him in Chinese to finish Bruce off and end forever his teaching of ancient secrets to foreigners. They wanted him to deliver the killing blow.

Sensing the moment, Johnny leaped into the air, his right leg out and targeting Bruce's neck for breaking. Jerome shut his eyes. He couldn't watch.

It was then that Bruce rose into a low tiger position and, with perfect coordination, used one claw hand to grab and rip Johnny's floating rib cage and diaphragm and the other to tear at his groin. Gravity impaled Johnny on Bruce's tiger claw hands, which ripped and tore at his soft parts.

Johnny bellowed in pain and crashed to the mat. Bruce was on him in a flash, knee holding down his chest, right arm cocked with a blow aimed at the bridge of the nose. One punch and Bruce could drive the nose bone into Johnny Sun's brain, ending his fighting days . . . and all other days . . . forever.

As Bruce hovered above the beaten man, muscles quivering with stop-go energy, he said, "Do you give up?"

There was no response, so Bruce said it again. "Do you give up?"

He cocked his arm higher. Johnny Sun stared at the fist of death through blood-streaked eyes. He knew that Bruce could kill him on the spot if he didn't give in. He glanced toward his brother.

Luke Sun's fists balled in rage and he began to step forward, but was met with a hand on the chest from Jerome Sprout. Bruce's friend and star pupil had no hope of beating

Luke Sun at anything but poker, but Jerome bluffed very well.

"Hold it right there, pal," he snarled.

The trick worked. Luke knew that stepping in at that point would look very bad before the council of elders. He took a step backwards, but not before fixing Jerome with a look that said, *I'll deal with you later.*

With no help coming from the sidelines, Johnny Sun gave up. He nodded yes to Bruce, who leaped to his feet and turned to the elders.

"That settles it," he said triumphantly. "I'll teach anyone I want. The choice is mine. Mine. Maybe I've taught you something today."

He bowed to the council and walked off. As he did so, Johnny scrambled to his feet and, summoning up a killer burst of adrenaline, charged from behind.

"Bruce! Watch out!" Jerome shouted.

Bruce twisted his head around in time to catch a terrifying nightmare vision. Johnny Sun had been transformed into the phantom, the Ming Warrior demon of his deepest fears. He flew across the mat and, before Bruce could respond, kicked him in the small of the back. There was a sickening crunch and Bruce crumpled, screaming in pain. It was just like the night before—except this time the pain and the injury were real.

🔷 16 🔷

SISTER OF ANGELS HOSPITAL WAS RUN BY THE DOMINICAN ORDER
of Roman Catholic nuns, and members of that order scurried
up and down the corridor leading past the intensive-care
waiting room. The order had been founded by St. Dominic
in 1215. The brothers were sometimes called Black Friars
because of their white habits and black mantles, and the
brothers and sisters of the order wore rosaries in their belts
and were renowned for their preaching. On that bitterly cold
January night in 1965, however, they remained appropri-
ately silent in the room holding Bruce Lee. What do you say
to someone whose world has just collapsed?

Linda rushed to the hospital as soon as she heard about
the ambulance that had taken her husband to Sister of
Angels. She brushed past the downstairs guard and rode in
frightened silence in an empty metal elevator that seemed as
cold and as vacant as her life had become. Jerome paced up
and down in the waiting room, holding a rolled-up copy of
Look Magazine. He held the magazine as if it were
nunchaku sticks, smacking it into his palm as if to drive
away the evil spirits.

"Jerome! What happened?" she asked, allowing herself
to be drawn into his arms for comfort. Perhaps it was

Jerome, though, who was in need of comfort; he felt partly responsible.

"He lost. I'm sorry. I wanted to step in, but those guys were way out of my league."

"He lost *what*?"

"A fight."

"He didn't say anything about a fight."

"He didn't want you to know."

"Bruce said there was a problem with the taxes and he had to go downtown."

Jerome shrugged. "What can I say? The man wanted to keep you out of it."

"I'm his *wife,* for God's sake. I'm entitled to know. Who was this fight with?"

"The Sun brothers, Johnny in particular."

"Who are they?"

"Bad guys. Killers. Next time I *will* bring a gun."

"Jerome . . . I don't understand."

"Remember the Council of Elders that told him not to teach *gwei-los* like us?"

"Yeah. They sent a kid with a scroll. Bruce told them to take a hike."

"Well, not exactly. Like I said, he kept a lot from you. The fight was scheduled for today. If Bruce beat their champion, he would be left alone to teach who he wanted. If he lost, you and him would have to leave town. Well, he won."

"But . . ."

"But Johnny Sun suckered him after the fight was over. Gave up and then hit Bruce from behind."

Linda closed her eyes and felt anger rising. She fought it. Her anger would do her no good now. She had a husband to look after.

"How is he?" she asked.

127

"I ain't no doctor, but it don't look good. It's his back."

"Oh, my God," she exclaimed.

"Yeah, you see . . ."

Jerome's improvised medical opinion was interrupted by the appearance of the real doctor. The orthopedic surgeon was a mature man with white hair that was disappearing from the top of his head and a sheaf of X rays and medical records under his arm. He introduced himself and brought Linda down the hall a few paces to the partly opened door of a private room.

He said, "Your husband suffered damage to an area between the sixth and seventh vertebrae. There is evidence of crushed cartilage that is putting pressure on the spinal cord."

"He's not going to die, is he?" she asked.

"Of course not. Not for a long time. But the injury he suffered is severe."

"Can you fix it?"

"I could operate, but that is a sensitive area and surgery could make it worse. I think that physical therapy will be more productive."

"How long will it be before he's better?"

"If we're lucky, two years."

"Two years! It'll take him two years to get back to normal?"

The doctor lightly touched Linda's arm. "It'll be two years before he can *walk*. He might never get back to normal."

When she recovered her composure, Linda was shown into her husband's room. Bruce was lashed to a therapeutic bed—designed to help heal spinal injuries but resembling nothing so much as a medieval torture instrument, the legendary rack. But while the rack was used to dislocate a

128

victim's joints, the therapeutic bed kept the patient immobilized while his body healed. It only *looked* evil.

Outside the window, the skies of the bay area were dark with the pallid gloom of winter. Bruce was lashed tight, lying on his back, his head strapped to prevent him from moving it. He could look up at the ceiling, but nowhere else.

Linda pushed the door open and stepped inside.

The doctor tried to stop her. "There are some papers for you to sign, Mrs. Lee," he said.

She didn't hear him. She heard nothing but her husband's need as he lay partly paralyzed.

"Mrs. Lee?"

"Let her go, man," Jerome said behind the doctor. "There'll be lots of time to sign shit later."

Linda looked around at Jerome and the doctor, but said nothing to them. Instead, she pulled herself up tall and walked to Bruce's side. He looked straight up, perhaps ashamed to look at her. She brushed a strand of hair out of his eyes and still he avoided looking at her.

"This bed is kind of sexy," Linda said. "Maybe we can take it home with us when you're better."

He looked at her.

"I can think of some interesting uses for it," she continued.

There was anger in his eyes. The last thing he wanted was humor. She realized her mistake.

"Sorry. Bad joke. I know you're mad, but don't be. It'll only make things worse."

"Worse?" he said at last. "It would take a hell of a lot to make things worse."

"You could be dead."

"Johnny Sun would have been merciful had he killed me."

"Maybe he should have," she said. "What were you

129

doing fighting anyway? Jesus, Bruce, formal combat as a way of solving business disputes went out sometime during the French Revolution."

"It was more than a business dispute."

"And you should have told me what was going on."

"What would you have done?"

"I could have talked you out of that stupid fight, for one thing. That failing, Jerome could have brought a gun. I don't know, honey—you should have told me. I'm your wife."

"Wives have to be protected from some things."

"You are *so* old-fashioned. This is 1965. Hey, look, let's not fight over something we can't change. You got hurt and will take a while to recover, so let's order in for a while."

"Order in?" he asked.

"Dinner, remember? You were taking me out to eat."

Bruce tried to shake his head, but he was restrained, and he realized how difficult it was to communicate without simple movements. His temper rose even higher.

"The fight took too long," he said. "I left myself open. That's why this happened."

She shook *her* head. "Jerome filled me in. You lost because Johnny Sun cheated."

Bruce thought about that. Did Johnny Sun cheat—or did he have supernatural help? The vision of the demon lingered powerfully in Bruce's memory now that he had nothing to do but lie in bed and think. The thought was yet another thing that Linda would have to be protected from.

"I lost because *wing chun* has its limitations," he said.

"Whatever the reason, you should have told me where you were going. As your wife, I had a right to know."

"You might want to think about that," Bruce said.

"Think about what?"

"The wife part."

130

"What are you saying? You lost a fight so you want a divorce?"

"It's *you* who might want a divorce. Take a good look, Linda."

"Okay, I'm looking. I see my husband who's feeling sorry for himself. So we'll eat take-out and we won't go dancing for a while."

"We won't be doing lots of things for a while," Bruce said. "Maybe never."

"So we're in a little trouble," she said with a shrug.

"This is more than a little trouble."

"So this is big trouble. You're always going on about the beauties of Chinese culture. Well, let me tell you about the beauties of *my* culture—we love big trouble."

"That's what you say today. Six months from now you'll be looking for the back door. You might as well get it over with now. If you want a divorce you can have it. I'm no good to you anymore. I'm no good at all."

Her own temper was rising. Linda said: "It'll never be over between you and me. Get it? Never!"

"Go back to your mother, Linda," Bruce said. "I'm finished."

She stroked his forehead, but he clenched the muscles beneath the skin of his face as a way of driving her off.

"Baby, you're just hurt now . . ."

"Tell her you made a mistake. Do it! I don't want you here!"

"Bruce, I . . ."

"I don't want you—do you hear me? *Get out!*"

He was confused with anger, paralyzed inside and out, but his words fell on her like lethal blows. She was upset with him for leaving her out of things, mad at him for going into combat for such a flimsy reason, and furious at being rejected like yesterday's garbage. Destroyed, weeping for them both, she burst out of the hospital room, nearly knocking over Jerome Sprout. Soon she was out into the cold and rainy winter night.

One feature of the therapeutic bed to which Bruce was strapped was that it could be moved into practically any position according to how the doctors wanted to relieve pressure on the spine. It was still raining the following afternoon when Bruce was suspended upside down, strapped as he was the night before, except this time he faced the cold linoleum of the floor.

The window was open slightly to let fresh air in, and when the venetian blinds rattled in a certain way Bruce knew that the door had been opened. He couldn't see what was going on, but heard light, vaguely familiar footsteps moving across the bare floor.

Two black marble notebooks—the kind a million American kids have used in thousands of schools—skidded across the floor and into his sight.

"What the . . . ?"

Linda dropped to her knees, then rolled over onto her back and slid beneath Bruce, looking up at him. Her hair, longer now than when they'd first met, spread out onto the linoleum.

"Hi," she said cheerily. "I thought I'd improve the view."

He tried to turn his head away, but was unable to do so. She saw him try, though, and responded.

"Look at the big kung fu man," she said. "The first sign of trouble, all he can do is quit."

"Shut up," Bruce said. "Shut up."

"Make me. Make me, quitter! Beat me up. Come on, that's what you do best."

132

Furious at being mocked, Bruce strained against the leather straps. He was unable to budge them.

"I'll . . . I'll . . ."

She continued: "You'll what? Bust out of there like Superman and kill me? I doubt it."

Bruce was so angry and frustrated there were tears in his eyes. This was the first time she had seen him cry, or nearly cry. In his anger and emotion there was life, and hope. Linda knew it.

"See these notebooks? They look like the kind we had in school, right?"

"I suppose so," he said reluctantly.

"Wrong. They're your future. Our future."

"I have no more future," he argued. "I'm a cripple."

"Sure you do," she said. "All I hear about from you is that the fight took too long. There are too many fixed positions in *wing chun*. Too much tradition. Too much classical mess. You know everything that's wrong with *wing chun*, and maybe you're an example of it yourself, because you were beaten. So fix it."

"Fix what?"

"Fix *wing chun*, of course. Stop whining and start fighting. Fight back with your mind."

"And do what?" he said in disgust.

"Write down your ideas about how *wing chun* can be improved. You're always talking about borrowing moves from other martial arts—high kicks from tae kwon do, straight punches from American boxing. You like Cassius Clay, for God's sake. You know. 'Float like a butterfly, sting like a bee.' Well, you look like a butterfly now."

"Thanks for pointing that out."

"Use your mind while your body repairs. Fill up those notebooks."

"I can't write," he said. "I can't move."

"Whine, whine, whine," she said. "You talk, quitter. I'll write."

She cracked open one of the notebooks and picked up a pen. She held the book overhead so that when she began writing it would be almost pressing against his chest.

"I have a lot to say, but it will take forever."

"Well, the doctor says it will take you two years to heal. Personally, I don't believe it will take half that time. Still, that gives us the better part of a year."

"I've never written a book," he protested.

"Neither have I. We'll learn together. Come on . . . I'm waiting."

"It'll take forever." Even as he said the words he knew they would do no good. She was right.

"Are you going anywhere?" she asked. "I'm not."

They had locked wills and she had bested him. He knew it. He relaxed and surrendered to the inevitability of her willpower and logic. She could see it in his eyes and smiled warmly, yet offered an impish glance.

"Oh yeah, one more thing," she said.

"What?"

"I'm pregnant."

🌀 17 🌀

FOR NINE MONTHS THE IDEAS FLOWED AS BRUCE HEALED. LINDA stayed with him in the hospital every day, and they used every free moment for writing. When he wasn't sleeping or in physical therapy he dictated his theory of martial arts for the twentieth century.

The two notebooks filled up quickly. Soon many more were filled with Bruce's thoughts set down in Linda's neat handwriting. His personal experience plus years of researching all the major martial arts merged with what he learned from other masters while teaching in San Francisco and Oakland to form the basis of *jeet kune do*—"the way of the intercepting fist."

As the months went by and Linda's belly grew, Bruce was released from the prison of his therapeutic bed and put into a wheelchair. To celebrate his brush with paralysis and, perhaps, death, Linda ceremoniously unveiled a cardboard tombstone. On it was printed, "In memory of a once-fluid man crammed and distorted by the classical mess." The joke made him laugh for the first time in months.

It was September of 1965 when Bruce, going it alone in his wheelchair, made his way out of his room and across the hospital to the maternity ward to visit his wife and newborn son. He'd bought new clothes for the occasion—a mod

European cut of the sort very much in style that year—and carried a bouquet of flowers and a brown paper bag.

Smiling all the time now that he had been given new purpose by the birth of his son, Bruce did a wheelchair spin for the maternity nurses and pushed open the door to Linda's room. Mother and child slept peacefully, the baby boy nestled under her left arm. The room was full of flowers, and sunlight streamed in through partly opened blinds. It was a crisply beautiful autumn day.

Bruce rolled over to the bedside and gently placed the bouquet on Linda's breast, not far from the baby's head. The boy was beautiful, his face a little bit of both mother and father. Linda's mother could not have been more wrong about the prospect of children. The boy was a miracle.

Bruce wheeled himself to the window. He opened the paper bag and from it took three octagonal *pat kwa* mirrors. Like his father before him, he placed the mirrors on the windowsill to protect his son.

"Hey, kiddo, he's too young to shave," Linda said, with a yawn.

Bruce rolled back to her side and, stroking the baby's cheek, said, "They aren't shaving mirrors. They're called *pat kwa*."

"*Pat kwa*," she repeated. "What are they for if not for shaving?"

"The mirrors are like gargoyles on churches. You put them around to ward off evil spirits."

"Baby, the only evil spirits around here are the people cooking the meals."

"Nonetheless, my people believe in *pat kwa*."

"It's an interesting tradition. How do the mirrors keep the evil spirits away? Is this like with vampires, who can't be seen in mirrors and are afraid of them?"

"The *feng shui* men think that the mirrors work."

136

"The who?" she asked.

"*Feng shui*," he explained a bit sheepishly. It's always hard for a young man to explain his father's beliefs, especially when they are strange by American standards. "They are the fortune tellers."

"I see," she said, though it was clear that she didn't. "Did you go to fortune tellers in Hong Kong?"

"No, but my father did. He had *pat kwa* mirrors all over the place. He really believed in them, and in the *feng shui*. So do a lot of people."

"Do you?"

He wanted to confess his belief, and his dark knowledge of the demon that pursued him. But he couldn't bring himself to frighten his wife. Linda looked so vulnerable.

"No," he said. "Of course not. I'm an American and don't believe in demons."

She smiled at him, then down at the baby, who had opened his eyes and begun to stir.

"I want to call him Brandon," Linda said.

"Brandon. That's good."

Bruce pushed back from the bed and set the wheels on his chair. Then he rose, pushing himself up, slowly and painfully. The agony showed on his face as he forced himself to get out of the wheelchair. Linda had tears of joy in her eyes as she watched him take two steps forward, to the bedside.

"I stand for my son, Brandon Lee," Bruce said.

Her eyes alight with miracles, Linda handed him the child. As he held his son in his arms, Bruce felt his strength returning. The long period of pain and convalescence was over, as was, indeed, that first, unsettled period of his life. He had written a book, a martial arts method for the twentieth century. And he was a healed man and a father, with new responsibilities.

With those responsibilities came the necessity of tying up a loose end, one of family. That happened a month later, in October of 1965, when the Lees were at home, in their living quarters behind the *kwoon*.

While Brandon lay, entranced with the mobile that swayed above his crib, Linda sat on the bed writing thank-you notes to the many friends and well-wishers who had congratulated them and sent gifts on the occasion of the twin good news: Bruce's release from the hospital and the child's birth. Bruce was in his wheelchair, which he used to get around but rose from, frequently, to do therapeutic exercises and light workouts. He was reading through his notes, polishing them and making revisions. Already word of *jeet kune do* was spreading throughout the martial arts community. Nobody outside the Lees' circle of friends and students knew what it was yet. It was, then as now, something of a mystery very much attached to the personality of its creator. Light traffic noise came in from partly opened windows. On the radio the Lovin' Spoonful sang "Do You Believe in Magic?" Now and again, Brandon made a googly noise.

The doorbell rang. Linda said, "I'll get it," and sprang from the bed.

"If it's a kid with a scroll tell him I'm not home," Bruce called out.

"No kidding," she replied, and walked around the Chinese screens that separated workout and living areas. She walked briskly across the mat and pulled the door open to find herself staring, for the first time in almost a year and a half, at her mother.

Linda was shocked. The only thing she could say was a tart, "What do you want?"

Vivien was unsure of herself. She had never been to the *kwoon* and only had the vaguest idea what was taught there.

She knew about Bruce's injury, but then it was she who had predicted that he would bring Linda no good.

"I . . . unh . . . came to see my grandchild." She held up a present, carefully wrapped in blue paper and tied with a ribbon made of a deeper blue. Linda looked at it but didn't touch it.

"The grandchild you said would be a half-breed?" Linda snapped.

"I'm . . . I'm sorry I said that."

"You hurt me, you really hurt me, and you hurt my husband. Now you want to come into our house?"

"Maybe we can work things out," Vivien said, her tone changing from uncertainty to mediation. She was making a peace offer.

"I got you out of my life. I'm not sure I want you back in it."

Linda's posture was stiff and unforgiving. She was about to slam the door in her mother's face when Bruce wheeled himself out from behind the screens and across the mat.

"Brandon, it's Grandma!" he called out cheerfully.

Both women turned and watched as Bruce wheeled toward them, maneuvering past Linda and yanking the door wide open.

"Come in, Grandma. There's someone you ought to meet."

Linda glared at him, as if to ask, *What the hell are you doing?* Bruce did a wheelie as he pushed off toward the bedroom.

"C'mon," he called behind him.

Linda sighed, "Oh, all right, come in," and took the present from her mother's hands.

Unsure of herself again, Vivien followed. Still smoldering, but at least resolved to the inevitability of having her mother in the house, Linda led the way.

"How are you feeling, Mr. Lee?" Vivien asked.

"I think you can call me Bruce now. That would make me feel better."

"Okay . . . Bruce . . . how are you?"

"Like half-man, half-car."

"Glad to hear it. That was awful, what happened to you. Did the police ever do anything to that terrible man?"

"They never found out about it. But don't worry. Like we Americans say, 'What goes around, comes around.' The man who hurt me will get his."

"I hope so."

Leading the procession into the bedroom, Bruce looked back at his mother-in-law and said, "You know, Linda, your mom has great legs. Really great."

In spite of herself, Vivien was girlishly flattered. Bruce rolled up to the crib and tickled Brandon on the belly. The baby giggled and grabbed his father's finger.

"Cute, isn't he? Look at the tummy on him. He looks like a little Buddha."

Vivien's face was transfigured when she beheld her grandson. The year and a half of anger and resistance melted away like snow in the noontime sun. Her eyes glistened with tears of regret and joy; regret at the lost opportunity and joy at the reunion of her family.

Not entirely convinced, Linda hung back by the screens.

"He's beautiful," Vivien said. "He looks . . . he looks like . . . well, he looks like both of you. May I?"

She beckoned to hold the baby. Bruce said, "Ask his mom."

Vivien turned to her daughter and said, "Honey . . . may I?"

"Sure," Linda said with a shrug.

Vivien picked up the infant and held him close, smelling the top of his head and kissing his cheek. Tears streamed down her cheeks and Linda saw then, at last, the mother she used to know. Able to hold out no longer, Linda moved forward and slipped an arm about her mother's waist. The two women stood close, admiring the baby.

Bruce beamed. He said, "Oh, Brandon, you're a strong one. Only you could have done this. Only you."

ꙮ 18 ꙮ

1966

Fall and winter passed and Bruce healed. As he did, he put the finishing touches on his theory of *jeet kune do*. Gradually he set aside the wheelchair and walked normally. Then his light workouts increased. First he bench-pressed with only the bar—no weights. Gradually weights were added, and by the spring of 1966 he was strong enough to do handstand push-ups. Soon he returned to teaching and, when Linda wasn't looking, to doing closed-door tryouts of *jeet kune do*. The sparring sessions were absolutely essential. For in June he was due to present his theory before a gathering of colleagues: the Long Beach International Karate Tournament, scheduled to be held in the Long Beach ballpark on the outskirts of Los Angeles.

Bruce's teaching had made him well enough known on the West Coast to get an invitation to speak about *jeet kune do* and demonstrate it at the tournament. On the day of his presentation, the crowd was packed with martial arts adepts. They were restless, and at times looked more like something out of the French Revolution than a convocation of twentieth century martial artists.

When Jerome brought Linda onto the field, Bruce had

been speaking from the ring for several minutes, and already was facing a hostile response. Boos were common and loud; Linda heard them growing in ferocity, and wondered what in the world they had gotten into. Spurring Bruce to write down his theory of *jeet kune do* had been a good idea, she was sure. It had given him something to do while recuperating.

"I never thought this would start a riot," she said to Jerome as they pushed their way through the jeering crowd that had surrounded the ring.

"*What* would?" he asked.

"*Jeet kune do*. I encouraged Bruce to put his thoughts on paper."

"Yeah, well, it goes like this: Your husband is a revolutionary, and those folks usually don't get popular until a few years after they're dead and buried."

"A revolutionary? Bruce? Come on, he's the most old-fashioned man I ever met."

"To you, maybe, but to this crowd he's a trouble-maker."

They slipped by one especially large and vocal karate adept who was shaking his fist at Bruce.

"How so?" Linda asked.

"Are you kidding? He's upsetting their little worlds. These guys all spent years and years and collected a lot of bruises while learning very specific styles. In tae kwon do you kick high and do lots of it; in kung fu you kick low if you kick at all. These guys *live* what they've been taught. No one wants to go that far to learn something only to be told it's all a crock."

"I see what you mean," Linda said, as her husband's amplified voice finally became clear.

"The art of *jeet kune do* is simply to simplify," Bruce said holding a microphone in one hand and a notebook in

143

the other. "It favors formlessness so that it can assume all forms. It has no style so it can fit in with all styles."

"Go home," a heckler cried out.

"Go back to Oakland," another agreed.

Jerome said, "These people are gettin' *ugly*. We could be lucky to get out of here with our *lives*."

"Bruce takes me to all the best places," Linda said.

"Me too. The last time he nearly got his back broke. This time they're fixin' to fry his ass."

Bruce read on: "Kung fu, karate, tae kwon do, all the classical styles are attempts to arrest the flux of conflict . . ."

"There will be conflict right here," Jerome said, leading Linda past a bald man carrying nunchaku sticks who shouted, "Drop dead, Lee."

"But in actual combat, the opponent doesn't wait for formalities. He doesn't wait to bow to the judges and assume a stance. He's not a robot, but a human being, a fluid and alive human being who wants to *act,* not take a position."

Jerome and Linda finally pushed their way through to the edge of the ring. It was a boxing ring that had been slightly modified to make it work better for karate and the other martial arts on display that day. The spectators had pushed past the ringside seats to crowd around the ring, looking like bloodthirsty onlookers at a burning at the stake.

A group of Bruce's students and sparring partners held down one corner. Jerome led Linda to them, and for a moment she felt safe enough from the crowd to look around. The modified ballpark had attracted perhaps a thousand martial arts adepts, enough to make the promoters happy but far too few to fill the park. The ring was set on what was ordinarily the pitcher's mound. The crowd gathered around it reinforced her impression that she was witness to an execution. She was reminded of engravings she had seen of the cheering onlookers at public executions during the French Revolution.

"How many of us are there?" she asked Jerome.

"I count six, including the boss."

"Too few," she replied.

"Yeah. Damn, when am I gonna learn to carry a gun."

"When am I?"

Bruce's voice struggled to be heard over the mob. "Like the sculptor who doesn't keep adding clay to his statue, but strips away the inessentials until the truth is revealed, we've tried to develop a way of fighting with no fixed positions, no set movements."

He was ripping away thousands of years of tradition. They had invited him to give a demonstration of his new martial art, which many adepts assumed, without real information, was a simple extension of the *wing chun* taught in Hong Kong by Yip Man, and Bruce was telling them that *no style* worked anymore. They should take the best moves from over two dozen martial arts, including American boxing as practiced by Cassius Clay. The shock was like that a group of hard-core baseball fans might experience should a top player suggest doing away with bats.

"The fancy mess of martial arts solidifies what was once fluid," he continued. "It is nothing but blind devotion to the systematic uselessness of routines that lead nowhere."

Someone in the crowd bellowed in anger and tossed a wooden folding chair at Bruce. He ducked and it crashed behind him. The tournament director, Ed Barker, took the mike and held up his hands for order.

"Now hold on," he said. "Hold on."

"Tell him to prove it," yelled a heckler.

"Mr. Lee is not here in competition," Barker said.

"If need be, I am," Bruce said to him.

Linda was there, suddenly, pulling at his pants leg, reaching in from ringside.

"No you're not! You're not fighting!" she yelled.

He leaned over, reaching down to brush his fingertips against her cheek. "Don't worry," he said.

Barker said, "Mr. Lee has a point. There is a lot of truth in what he says. Now let him finish."

"Let him prove it," another man yelled.

The crowd began to murmur in agreement. Soon the murmur became a chant of "Prove it! Prove it!"

"Mr. Lee is not here to fight," Barker said again.

"He sure isn't," Linda called out.

The chant of "Prove it, prove it" grew louder.

Jerome looked around nervously and said, "Here we go again."

Without warning, Bruce took back the mike. He raised his hand to calm the crowd and said, "Okay! Okay! I'll prove it. I'll *prove it*! But I need someone to prove it on."

"No! No!" Linda cried, trying to hoist herself into the ring.

"That ain't a good idea," Jerome said.

"Help me up," she commanded.

"He won't like it."

"He'll like it less if someone puts him back in the hospital," she argued.

"You got a point," Jerome agreed, and gave her an assist up into the ring. As she squirmed through the ropes, Bruce made his challenge.

"I will beat anyone in this crowd," he said, adding, "in thirty seconds." He pointed at the huge, round competition clock that sat on a ringside pedestal.

The crowd went crazy. The blood lust rose in them and their voices grew louder, sensing pain. Some people go to sporting events to see artistry and skill; other go to see blood spilled. The prospect of watching Bruce Lee take on any comer and beat him in thirty seconds was turning normally cool martial arts adepts into the sort of bloodthirsty monsters who go to stock car races to see flaming wrecks and hear the wail of ambulance sirens.

Linda grabbed her husband by the arm. "What are you, crazy? The doctors told you no fighting."

"They told me I'd never walk again too," he replied.

"When will you be happy—when they're right?"

The situation with the crowd had gone from bad to worse. In the midst of Bruce Lee's challenge, his American wife was trying to talk him out of it. There were laughs, and boos. Bruce reacted as most men would, by stiffening his spine and preparing for the battle.

There was jostling around at ringside. Two men were pushing through the rest. One of them raised a fist and yelled, "I'll fight you."

It was Johnny Sun, who approached the ring followed, as always, by his brother, Luke. Bruce looked at Johnny the way a man regards an old, ancient enemy. Was he just a man, just another martial arts adept, or was he really the Ming Warrior, the phantom who stepped out of nightmares to wreak havoc in Bruce's life? The two images—man and monster—merged in Bruce's head until he shook them off.

"I beat this man before . . . I'll beat him again," Johnny said, climbing into the ring as the crowd roared its approval.

Linda dug her nails into her husband's arms. "Bruce, I'm begging you. If you love me, don't do this."

"This isn't about you and me," he replied.

He gently unpeeled her fingers from his arm and unbuttoned his shirt. As he stripped it off, she said, "Fine, fine. But I'm not going to go through it again. You understand me? If you get hurt, you're on your own."

147

She wheeled and climbed back through the ropes, lowering herself down with some help from Jerome. Bruce called after her, saying, "Don't go too far, hon. I'll be done in thirty seconds."

Linda didn't buy the bravado. She turned to Jerome, anger and hurt in her eyes, and said, "He's gonna get himself killed. I know it."

"Maybe not today. Check out that look in his eyes. He seems like a killer to me."

"That's what you said about Johnny Sun, and now he's back."

Jerome looked at Johnny, then at Luke, who was staring back with murder in his eyes.

"I noticed," Jerome said to Linda.

"I'm leaving. I can't take it anymore." She turned and started toward the exit.

"Where you goin'?" he called out.

"Home."

"That ain't right. You got to stick by your man even when you don't approve of what he's doing."

She turned back. "You don't understand. *Men* don't get it. Why do you always have to fight?"

There were tears in her eyes and her fists were balled up by her sides.

Jerome said, "That's the way life is."

She looked like she was about to cry.

"Get your tail back here and let him see you standin' by him. Besides, I kinda agree with the man."

"About what?" she asked, wiping her eyes.

"I don't think this fight is gonna take that long."

Linda returned to ringside and looked up at Bruce, who was stretching at center ring. Their eyes met briefly, and he smiled at the sight of her. *Trust me,* his smile said.

Ed Barker had the microphone again, and was struggling

to control both the crowd and his own excitement. He announced, "This is a challenge match to prove Mister Lee's theory of *jeet kune do*. Thirty seconds. Ready?"

Johnny Sun was in the ring and stripped to the waist. His wounds had healed in the time since he last fought Bruce, and if anything he seemed even meaner. The victory over Bruce—even if accomplished through cheating—had taken place in front of the elders and at their request. Winning had made him the acknowledged champion of traditional ways: exactly the ways that Bruce was threatening with his talk of formlessness and *jeet kune do*. And the crowd greeted him as if he were *their* champion.

Bruce Lee and Johnny Sun bowed to one another and squared off once again. Barker blew his whistle and the large sweep-second hand began its move across the face of the clock.

Johnny leaned into the forward leopard stance while his left hand contorted into a leopard's paw fist. Bruce, momentarily in the classical *wing chun* mode of keeping arms close in to protect the body's centerline and its vital organs, let his opponent make the first move. His idea was to let the bigger man betray his strategy and, maybe, let his anger and pride lead him into mistakes.

The assault came before the hand on the clock had ticked off three seconds. Johnny launched a massive attack, throwing a flurry of fists and elbows at Bruce. He blocked them all, protecting his torso while countering with a few textbook *wing chun* moves. In all forms of *wing chun,* defensive and offensive moves are made at the same time. A punch always accompanies a block. Maybe Johnny could be fooled into thinking that Bruce's much-talked-about *jeet kune do* was merely the *wing chun* of Grandmaster Yip Man, but packaged under a new name.

Unable to break through Bruce's defenses and eager for a

quick kill, Johnny leaned back and aimed a kick high at Bruce's head that connected to the cheekbone, snapping Bruce's head back. He sucked wind to counter the pain.

Linda shut her eyes, then turned away. Her fists were clenched by her sides and she started to walk away from the horrible, screaming crowd that wanted nothing less than her husband's blood. Twelve seconds were gone off the clock and the crowd smelled vindication. But then Linda heard Jerome's voice shouting support of Bruce, and she opened her eyes and turned back toward the ring. It was a good thing too. Had she had her back turned another few seconds, she would have missed it.

For Bruce spun, turning with Johnny's still-arcing foot, and moved inside his large, powerful, and sweeping motions. Bruce was like water, the water he always told his students about, seeping inside the cracks of the brick wall that was Johnny Sun. Then Bruce reached down inside himself and drew from the centuries the energy flow of the universe. From his throat there ripped a primal scream, the *kiai* that millions would soon know as the Bruce Lee scream, and it cut at his opponent like a razor's edge blade.

Bruce was inside Johnny's defenses then, and launched a blistering flurry of three-to-one punches. Delivered at a range of less than three inches, they shattered Johnny's jaw, crushed Johnny's nose, split his lip, and broke his spirit. Low kicks tied up his legs while another flurry of punches racked Johnny's torso, crushing his ribs and pounding his spleen, kidneys, liver, and diaphragm.

The big man staggered, taking a step backwards to steady himself, as blood poured down his face from the smashed nose and dripped down his chest.

Nineteen seconds had come off the clock. Jerome screamed "Yes!" and hugged Linda. His shout was nearly the only one in the stadium; only Bruce's half-dozen students and friends cheered the inevitable outcome.

Bruce pulled moves from the *jeet kune do* grab bag: a nerve destruction technique from *kali,* aimed at the arm; two kicks to the knees from southern *wing chun*; an elbow from *bak hoo-pai*; and finally a spinning back kick to the jaw from karate. Bruce's foot unerringly found Johnny's jaw, or what was left of it, and he staggered back.

Johnny took two short, faltering steps, then fell straight backwards, landing on his back with a *thump* that seemed to shake the ring. Bruce pounced on him, arm cocked high, his knuckles poised like spikes. With another shriek from beyond the ages, Bruce drove his fist forward and down into Johnny's face. The body shook and went still.

Bruce jumped to his feet, bowed to his opponent, then turned and looked at the clock. It was stopped at twenty-six seconds.

''Yes!'' Jerome yelled again.

☒ 19 ☒

"BRUCE!" LINDA CRIED OUT, BUT HER HUSBAND WAS AS STUNNED as the crowd. Stunned not by how easy the victory was—in his heart, he had expected it. But by the reaction around him, which had gone from noisy blood lust to stunned silence in an instant.

Linda began to climb into the ring. Jerome helped her with a lift, and then noticed a new face standing on the periphery of the knot of Lee supporters. The man was middle-aged, well tanned, and well dressed in a white linen summer suit and expensive shades. He stood out like a sore thumb amidst the crowd of martial arts experts and fans, nearly all of whom were casually dressed if not in combat or workout gear.

"Are you with Bruce?" he asked Jerome.

"Yeah. Who're you?"

"Bill Krieger."

"Let me guess. You're an undercover cop, maybe a narc. You're too well dressed to be a private detective or a bill collector."

The man laughed.

"Well, let me tell you something," Jerome went on. "You won't find drugs in this crowd. Maybe some ginseng tea, but that's about it."

"I'm a TV producer," Krieger said.

It was Jerome's turn to laugh. Then he said, "Oh, yeah, *right*. Well, you got to be lost. Hollywood is that way." He pointed northeast. "What you do is go north on the coast highway and hang a right by the airport."

"I know how to get there," Krieger said, smiling broadly. "And I *am* a TV producer. What's your name?"

"Jerome Sprout."

They shook hands.

"If you're looking for a bright young brother to take over for Bill Cosby in *I Spy*, I'm your man," Jerome said. "I don't play no tennis, though."

"I'm not here to talk to you. Sorry. Can I get to talk to Bruce?"

"Bruce? The way you talked before I thought you knew him. Yeah, I guess so, but not now. He's got a lot on his hands at the moment. You got a deal for him or something?"

"It could be. Where can we talk?"

"Bodine's Steak House. You know the place?"

"No. Where is it?"

"Long Beach Boulevard, by the corner of Delancey."

"I'll find it. What time will you be there?"

"We said we were going after the tournament. Today's session ends in an hour. Make it two hours."

"I'll see you then," Krieger said, pressing a business card into Jerome's palm before melting back into the crowd.

Jerome stuck the card in his pocket. "Hollywood," he said, shaking his head. "That's a very far-out concept." Then he climbed into the ring, where Linda had already found her husband still transfixed by the magnitude of it all.

"Hey, Bruce," she said.

Bruce whirled around and saw her. He had just snapped out of it and begun to look around for her when she pressed his wadded-up shirt and shoes into his hands—the same way she had done outside the college wrestling room.

"You never did learn to pick up after yourself," she said.

"Yeah. I'm still leaving things lying around." The twinkle was back in his eye as he glanced down at what remained of Johnny Sun.

He grabbed her and pulled her to him. They hugged tightly in the center of the ring, ignoring Barker, who was prowling the ring using the public address system in an attempt to get his tournament back on track.

"I would like to thank Bruce Lee for that amazing demonstration of *jeet kune do*. Would the ambulance crew please respond to the ring?"

A siren started up at the south end of the field. Soon a 1959 Cadillac ambulance was rolling across the sun-dried grass of the outfield.

Barker continued: "Ladies and gentlemen, after a brief intermission we will return to our program. I think you will join me in acknowledging that we have witnessed something very important today—the birth of *jeet kune do* and, more important, the arrival at center stage in America of Bruce Lee, who now must be considered the leading practitioner of kung fu in the United States."

A smattering of applause broke out, and that soon turned into a solid round of respectful, sometimes awed approval. There was one significant exception, however: Luke Sun. The towering younger brother of the beaten Johnny Sun climbed into the ring and spent a silent moment staring down at his broken, bleeding older brother.

Paramedics clambered into the ring and began to work on Johnny. Luke turned his mounting fury on Bruce then, and screamed, "I'll kill you! I'll kill you!"

He charged Bruce, who pushed Linda out of the way and used a jujitsu move to flip Luke over the ropes and out of

154

the ring. He crashed down into a group of spectators, who broke his fall. Luke regained his feet, still furious, and screamed, "I'll kill you. You hear me? I'll kill you." He tried to climb back into the ring, but the spectators restrained him.

Bruce led Linda to the other side of the ring and helped her climb down into the group of his supporters. When at last they rejoined Jerome he was brimming over with enthusiasm.

"Way to go, Bruce," he said, embracing his friend in a large bear hug. "I've seen some lopsided victories in my time, but you beat all. *Twenty-six seconds.*"

The other martial arts adepts who had helped Bruce develop *jeet kune do* also gathered around and exchanged expressions of amazement. Even Bruce was a little awed by the completeness of his victory. From its first test, *jeet kune do* seemed to be everything he hoped it would be—a martial arts system for the twentieth century. In defeating—destroying, actually—Johnny Sun in twenty-six seconds with the whole martial arts world watching, Bruce had assured the success of his training centers. Already popular in the San Francisco Bay Area and Oakland, the Bruce Lee training method could now be taught in other cities. Money would no longer be a problem. Brandon could have a new crib and stroller; maybe the family could stop living behind the *kwoon* and buy a house. Such things are important to a young man newly in America with a young family.

As if reading Bruce's mind, Jerome said, "You got to know one other thing—Hollywood called."

"You're kidding," Linda said.

"No one in particular? The whole damned city?" Bruce asked.

"Some guy named Krieger. I heard of a guitarist by that

155

name who lives around L.A. somewhere, but no producer. He's gonna show up at Bodine's, I think."

"Oh, great," Bruce said. "He's probably an IRS guy."

"I already checked out that possibility," Jerome said, shaking his head. "He's too well dressed."

"What's he have in mind?"

"I got no idea. I tried to sell myself to him, but bombed out."

"Let me grab a shower and we'll go eat," Bruce replied.

When they turned to walk to the locker rooms, the crowd parted as if to allow some mythical figure to pass. Linda took her man firmly by the arm, as if to assure him of lifelong admiration and support.

"I guess you're not walking out on me after all," he said.

"Don't try to put me on the defensive," she said. "I only said what I did to keep you alive."

"I look pretty alive, don't I?"

"Yeah, but the doctors . . ."

"The hell with the doctors. What do they know? They told me it would take two years to heal. I did it much faster."

"They said no fighting."

"Well, there are some things a man has to do to stay a man."

"Don't give me that. It's old-fashioned nonsense. Besides, I *love* you and want you to be mine forever."

"I will be," he said, kissing her on the side of the head.

"And you're not a single man living above a Chinese restaurant anymore. You have a wife and child to support."

"I know. That reminds me: We have to call Grandma and see how Brandon is doing."

Linda nodded. "He's probably got her buying him all sorts of stuff."

Bruce said, "What I did today sets us up. You know that, don't you?"

"I hope so."

"There will be offers. The school will expand. There will be lots more students and they will come from all over. Jerome said something about Hollywood. Well, we'll see about that. I haven't done a film in a long time, if that's what he has in mind."

"Jerome said he was a TV producer, not film."

"Whatever. My acting is a little rusty. And who in America would go to see a film about martial arts anyway?"

"Maybe he wants to cast you in *Bonanza*."

"Oh, sure. A Chinese kung fu expert on the loose in the Old West. What an idea! Charlie Chan meets Wyatt Earp. You got some imagination on you, woman."

She winked and replied, "I can imagine what I'm going to do to you once we get back to the motel."

He smiled at his wife and together they walked off the field and down the corridor that led to the various locker rooms.

Bodine's Steak House was one of those suburban roadside inns that gave the impression that the owner was raised in an antique shop—or a junkyard. Old stuff was everywhere. Framed sheet music from the 1920s and 1930s decorated the dark wood-paneled walls, sharing the space with black-and-white photos from World War II. Vintage warplanes and ships were everywhere, and a gigantic "Uncle Sam Wants You" recruiting poster hung behind the bar.

Every inch of space on the ceiling was occupied. An old sled hung near other memorabilia that spoke of a rich childhood and, no doubt, a fondness for garage sales. There was a ship's anchor, a fisherman's net complete with plastic lobsters and clams, two oars, a Schwinn bicycle, a red Radio Flyer wagon, a fly-fishing rod, a crab net, four duck decoys, and down the middle of the ceiling, a six-man racing shell.

The walls of the main dining room were an antique armory. Old rifles spanning a two-hundred-year history of American firearms hung on varnished racks. Each table and booth had its own table lamp, and the shade covering each showed a different theme from American history. The place mats were stylized American flags.

"You think these cats like Chinese and brothers?" Jerome asked, looking around nervously while attacking a mammoth black Angus steak smothered in mushrooms and onions. The other diners, like the restaurant staff, were white and the men had closely cropped hair. In 1966, it was easy to tell a man's political affiliation by his age and hair length. As the Lees and their friends celebrated their triumph in Long Beach, thousands of long-haired teenagers rioted against police restrictions and the Vietnam War on Sunset Boulevard in Hollywood. The Vietnam War was already beginning to turn America into opposing camps, one young and with long hair and the other older and with short hair. Members of the older generation were looking with increasing suspicion at Asians—including Chinese—and blacks and long-haired whites. All of those groups were represented at the Lees' table.

"I think they like our money," Bruce said, attacking a T-bone while an ex-Marine waiter looked at him as if he were an enemy Viet Cong guerilla preparing to invade Burbank.

The restaurant was only half full on a Saturday afternoon, and so Bruce's party was easy for Bill Krieger to find. When he walked through the restaurant he drew as many surprised glances as did the Lees and their group. What was this Hollywood type from the cream-colored Rolls Royce doing

158

with the long-haired Chinese kid and his black and hippie friends?

Jerome spotted Krieger halfway across the room. "Here comes Hollywood," Jerome said, waving a forkful of steak at the man.

"That's the guy?" Bruce asked.

"I remember seeing him at the tournament," Linda said.

"He's here just like he said. Remember, whatever you get, I want the part in *I Spy*."

"Huh?"

"Mr. Lee?"

"That's me."

"My name's Bill Krieger. How are you doing, Jerome?"

"Good. We left that angry crowd and came to have a restful meal in this here gun shop."

"What can I do for you, Mr. Krieger?" Bruce asked.

"Call me Bill. May I sit?"

"Sure thing," Bruce said. Linda moved to one side to make an empty place across the table.

"You looked pretty great out there today," Krieger said.

"Bullshit," Jerome said. "He took too long. He was too slow."

Several others of Bruce's party laughed.

"It seemed pretty fast to me. Do you think you can do some of that stuff in front of a camera?"

"I already have," Bruce said. "Did you ever see *The Orphan*?"

"Unh, no. I don't think so."

"It was made in Hong Kong five or six years ago. I played a juvenile delinquent then."

"And he's still causin' trouble," Jerome quipped.

Krieger said: "I'll check it out. Bruce Lee in *The Orphan*."

"My name was Lee Jun Fan then," Bruce admitted,

startling a few of his friends and sparring partners who didn't know. "You might have trouble finding the film. It was never released out of Hong Kong."

"So you changed your name when you came to America?"

"No, I was given an American name when I was born—here, in San Francisco. When my dad brought me back to Hong Kong with him—my parents were touring when I was born—they called me Lee Jun Fan. It's complicated, but the bottom line is that I'm an American."

"Your folks were entertainers? You said they were touring."

"My dad played in light opera. He was with the Canton Opera playing in *The Drunken Princess* in San Francisco."

"So you've been around film and theater people your whole life," Krieger said.

"Yes, but for the past few years I've mainly been teaching martial arts and romancing this lovely lady." He introduced Linda, who was flattered by the attention.

"Are you really a TV producer?" she asked.

"Absolutely. My Rolls is parked outside."

He winked. Bruce was coming to like the man, admiring him for standing his ground against Linda's skepticism.

"So what can I do for you, Bill?" Bruce asked.

"I'm casting a new TV show. Have you ever heard of *The Green Hornet*?"

"No."

"I've heard of it," Linda said.

"It was a comic book back in the 30s or 40s, right?" Jerome said. "Some dude in a funny outfit fighting crime with the help of some little dude. They all wore green. Is it something like that?"

"That's close enough," Krieger said.

"And you'd like me to play the little dude," Bruce said.

"Not the Green Hornet himself?" Linda asked.

"Sorry, but the lead role goes to an established star. That's the way it goes."

"Who is he?" Bruce asked.

"Van Williams."

Bruce and the members of his party exchanged quizzical glances. No one had heard of the man. Krieger saw their expressions.

"Okay, so he'll *be* a star by the time I'm done with him. So will you."

"Awright!" Jerome exclaimed, while Linda reached across the table and squeezed her husband's hand.

"Van will be the Green Hornet and you'll play his sidekick, Kato."

Bruce's smile faded. "Kato? I assume you're not talking about the ancient Roman stoic who opposed Caesar."

Krieger's face brightened. Lee was intelligent as well as handsome, charismatic, and one hell of a fighter. "Your character will have his resolve, his strength of mind, and devotion to duty."

"My Kato is Chinese?"

"He's whatever you want him to be but, yes, he's Van's character's Chinese sidekick. You know how Robin is Batman's ward who when called upon turns into a caped crime-fighter? That's what Kato is like. He knows karate."

"*Jeet kune do,*" Bruce said.

"Yes, of course."

"I'll do your TV show, Bill, but let's have an understanding. I'm very proud of my Chinese heritage and won't play any role that makes fun of my people. I just won't."

"The word 'sidekick' scared you," Krieger said.

"A little, yeah. I can't help thinking of Charlie Chan and his 'Number One Son.'"

"The Green Hornet will be done very respectfully, I promise you. Besides, Kato is the chauffeur."

"I *am* happy that you decided to cast an Oriental actor as an Oriental character."

"The days of a Warner Oland taping his eyes back to play Charlie Chan are over," Krieger affirmed.

"Well, then," Bruce said, "Let's do it."

"It's a deal," Krieger said. "Now, if you don't mind my taking over your dinner table, let's talk about scripts and money. Do you have an agent?"

"No," Bruce laughed.

"A manager?"

"Linda, maybe. She watches after me."

"Though not closely enough," she chimed in.

"If I took your advice this afternoon, we wouldn't be starring in a TV show now," Bruce said.

"You have a point," she admitted.

"I think I can act as my own agent and manager. So, Bill, let's look at a script and talk money."

Krieger opened an expensive leather briefcase and from it took a wad of papers held together by a spring clip: the script for the pilot episode. He handed it to Bruce, who flipped through it, scanning the fifty or so pages with increasing glee. Finally, what had been at first an enigmatic smile became an all-out ear-to-ear grin.

"You want me to *break a table in half*? With my *foot*?"

"We'll make it out of balsa wood. It'll split if you breathe on it."

"This is not *jeet kune do*. This is not the real world," Bruce said, though he didn't stop smiling.

"Who said anything about the real world?" Krieger allowed, throwing his hands up. "Welcome to Hollywood."

162

❧ 20 ❧

K<small>ATO'S OUTFIT WAS A</small> <small>JET-BLACK CHAUFFEUR'S SUIT AND CAP</small>,
which made him look vaguely like a lieutenant colonel in
the French Army. A black mask often covered Bruce's face,
though not enough to hide the fact that he was Chinese. In
1966 only one Oriental actor was featured on a network
television show: George Takei, of Japanese descent, who
played Sulu on *Star Trek,* then a low-rated show. Casting
Bruce Lee, a Chinese American, as one of the co-stars of
The Green Hornet was highly unusual.

Bruce loved it, and threw all his energy into the role. On
this particular day he was standing on the set, a re-creation
of a posh executive office. A mahogany-looking desk was
covered with a blue blotter that was held in a rich leather
frame. Two silver-framed photographs showed the villain's
smiling blond daughters. A Mark Cross pen and pencil set
sat alongside an in-box that held a few carefully arranged
papers. One wall had a fireplace with a brick mantle. Above
that was an oil painting that depicted the villain in all his
sneering, powerful glory. Across the room were a black
leather couch and a cherrywood coffee table.

Nearby was the area where all the action would take
place: a round conference table with a solitary, straight-
backed chair. To the chair was tied the Green Hornet in the

163

person of actor Van Williams. His green cape hung from his shoulders and spilled onto the floor, but without hiding the ropes that artfully bound his hands behind him. His feet too were tied. Two of the villain's henchmen guarded him. Both were six-foot-two bruisers; one held a fat, black, and ugly pistol. They chatted idly with Williams while the movie's stunt coordinator briefed Bruce on the upcoming action.

"Okay, Bruce, you get the cue light, you come through the door. The coffee table is between you and Van. Kick it over; it'll break in half. It's made of balsa and has been scored."

"It makes more sense fighting-wise to jump over it," Bruce said.

"Maybe, but it looks better if it breaks. Trust me on this. People like to see furniture break during TV fight scenes. Do you have any idea how many chairs they go through on *Gunsmoke*? Every two minutes someone is breaking a balsa chair over someone else's head."

"I got it," Bruce said.

"If you watched Westerns, you got the impression that the most secure job in the Old West was furniture repair. So trash this chair, preferably with one of those yells that you do."

"Okay."

"Next thing is Roy here"—the stunt coordinator indicated the gun-toting villain—"will point the gun at you, but he's startled because you broke the chair. So you kick the gun out of his hand and then threaten the two bad guys with some kung fu thing. You know, the one where you stick your hands out and make them into claws or something."

"I'll handle it."

The stunt coordinator, working at half speed, showed Bruce how the tricks should be done. He came in the door, then pretended to smash the table, kick away the gun, and threaten the bad guys. Bruce smiled indulgently at his imitation kung fu.

"You're good at that," he said.

"Yeah, sure," the coordinator said. "Thanks for the compliment, but you're the expert."

"I won't let you down," Bruce said.

"So anyway, after they run off, the Green Hornet delivers one of his classic lines . . ."

"Like 'Kato . . . what kept you?' "

"Yeah, like that. So you go behind the chair and start to untie him. That's the cut. Okay?"

"No problem."

From a distance away came the authoritative voice of the first assistant director calling, "Positions, everyone." Bruce went to his assigned spot behind the closed door.

Bill Krieger waved at him from behind the main camera. He was watching his show take shape, standing by the coffee-and-donuts table alongside Paul Crater, a young studio executive. Krieger wore another linen suit, this one rust-colored. Crater was immaculately dressed in an Italian pinstripe. He smoked a menthol cigarette that smoldered at the end of an ornate cigarette holder carved from the tusk of an African elephant.

"You've seen the first episodes," Krieger said. "How do you like them?"

"Me? I love them. You know that. I've told you."

"I meant the network. What does the top brass say?"

"I just talked to them. They loved the dailies, just ate 'em up. There's only one little problem."

"Yeah? What's that?"

"Well, this Lee guy. What's his name?"

"Bruce."

"He seems, you know, awfully Oriental."

165

"What are you talking about? He *is* Oriental. Moreover, he's *supposed* to be. Kato's an Oriental. I don't see the problem here."

"Just make sure he keeps his mask on as much as possible."

"What are you saying? That the network hates Orientals?"

"No, but the American people sure are suspicious of them these days. And can you blame them? What with Vietnam and all?"

"Bruce is Chinese. The Chinese hate the Vietnamese. They've hated 'em for thousands of years. They don't even look alike, for God's sake."

"I can't tell them apart," Crater said. "Can you?"

"Actually, yes, I can. Not every time, but most of the time."

"Most of the American people can't."

"They should learn, dammit. The world is changing."

"Bill . . . I'm just relaying what the top brass says. They thought you should have cast an American as Kato."

"You got to be kidding," Krieger exclaimed. "And do what, tape his eyes back like they did with Charlie Chan? Paint his skin yellow and glue on funny eyebrows?"

"The network feels that an American playing an Oriental goes over better in Middle America than does an Oriental playing an Oriental."

Krieger was appalled. "Pursuing that argument further, maybe we should get a guy with a dress and a pair of coconuts to star in *The Marilyn Monroe Story*."

Crater laughed. "You're a character," he said.

They were interrupted by the first assistant director, who said, "Very quiet, please. First positions, everyone."

Contrary to its reputation, a TV shoot is low on glamour. On this one, apart from the stars, who typically only emerged from their dressing trailers for the actual filming, everyone else was pointedly blue-collar. The director wore khaki slacks, but everyone else was in jeans, including white jeans, made fashionable in 1966 by being worn by David Hemmings in *Blowup*. A few of the grips, who did carpentry and other hard labor, suspended their relentless construction work and stood around watching. The teamster captain, resplendent in black jeans and a beer-belly-stretched T-shirt emblazoned "Hell's Angels, Bakersfield" stuffed a frosted jelly donut into his mouth as he sat down in a folding chair.

Crouching near the camera, the director said, "And . . . action!"

The villain with the gun trained it on the Green Hornet, while his buddy slipped a pair of brass knuckles over his fingers.

"All right, Green Hornet," said the one with the brass knuckles, "where's the formula?"

"Where it belongs . . . safe from men like you," the Green Hornet replied.

"Okay, have it your way." The brass knuckles were raised up into the air, and were about to come crashing down on the Green Hornet's vulnerable chin when the door exploded open, slamming against the wall with a crack like a cannon shot. With a wild *kiai,* Bruce burst into the room.

"Kato!" exclaimed the Green Hornet gratefully.

Bruce kicked the breakaway table. It shattered into a thousand toothpicks, sending splinters flying over the camera and on top of all the onlookers. Then he spun in a wild flourish—about ten percent tae kwon do and ninety percent Hollywood—and kicked the pistol away. It flew across the room and landed in the fireplace.

Thinking the scene nearly over, the Green Hornet spoke his usual line, "Good work, Kato."

But Bruce wasn't done. He slid into the tiger position, extending his hands like claws in the direction of the villains. Then he screamed again and, launching himself high into the air, took out a hanging lamp that dangled over the conference table. It sputtered and spat electricity and sparks. Then Bruce came down hard on the conference table, his leg extended in a beautiful drop. The conference table buckled, then broke in two and collapsed along the centerline.

Scared half to death—for real—the villains ran off the set. The teamster captain dropped his donut. Two grips dropped hammers. Krieger felt his neck muscles tighten, and the studio executive in the Italian suit nearly swallowed his cigarette holder. The assistant director nudged his boss.

"Ah . . . cut! Cut! Cut!" the director said.

Bruce smiled and straightened his jacket. "How was that?" he asked, proud of himself.

"Very, ah, different," the director said.

The script supervisor disagreed. "It's not going to match," she said.

"I thought that might be a little more exciting," Bruce said.

"Does it match?" the director asked the cameraman.

"Perfectly," was the reply. The man offered a thumbs-up to augment his point.

"I think that's lunch," the director said. "Lunch, everyone. Let's set up for Scene 100 and restart in one hour."

As the grips began the arduous task of striking the set they had spent all morning building, the director put an arm around Bruce's shoulders and led him out of their way.

"You knew that would match, didn't you?" he said.

"Well, I thought it would."

"You have a lot more production experience than you let on."

168

"There's a lot of films being made in Hong Kong. I kind of grew up in that environment. I know I was wrong in improvising without checking with you first, but I knew what I did would make the shot better."

"And you were right. Check with me first before doing it again, though."

"Right."

"For one thing, I didn't know that was a breakaway table. When you came down on it I had visions of your leg in a cast. All I need is to lose my co-star in the middle of production."

At that moment the stunt coordinator came running up, looking weirdly at Bruce. "Are you okay?" he asked.

"Sure. Why?"

"I thought you'd break your leg."

"Me too," said the director.

"That wasn't a breakaway table," the stunt coordinator said.

"What?" the director exclaimed.

Bruce smiled mischievously.

"It was Formica. We borrowed it from the set of *Perry Mason*. Raymond Burr used to read his briefs on it."

"A real table," the director said, shaking his head.

Bill Krieger walked up, having shed the studio executive and inspected the remains of the set that Bruce had just demolished.

"Hi, killer," he said. "You ready for lunch?"

"Maybe I should be driving," Bruce said, looking down at his chauffeur's suit.

"When you get your own Rolls you can drive," Krieger said, steering his cream-yellow Corniche up to Pink's Hot Dog Stand, which was something of a Los Angeles institution. Parked outside it was an assortment of cars meant to display their owners' moods: '65 Mustang convertibles full of blonds and surfboards; 12-cylinder E-Jags, red of course, with willowy starlets behind the wheel; and 1956 Chevies, not quite collectors' items yet, merely old cars driven by San Fernando Valley teenagers. From one of them came the broadcast sound of the Beatles singing "Yellow Submarine."

Krieger double-parked the car next to another Rolls and led Bruce to the hot dog line, where Hollywood met the common man and everyone felt like a star. "The show is going great," he said, "and it's time to talk about the next project."

"The next project? We're just starting this one."

"Never figure that anything done for television will run more than thirteen episodes. We always look to the future. It's just a matter of survival. You *are* committed to Hollywood, aren't you?"

"We sure are. Linda and I are renting a house in Bel Air."

"That's great. You guys sure are moving up in the world. From living out behind the *kwoon* to having a house in Bel Air is quite a step."

"It's the American way."

"So let me bounce something off you. This is a project I'm really keen on, and I want your input."

"Let's hear it," Bruce said.

"Okay. It's the Wild West. A Chinese immigrant wanders the land."

"He's a good guy," Bruce said. "A hero."

"Of course he's a hero. He's the star of the show. He wanders the land solving problems. Every week he solves a problem."

"With no gun. Just his hands."

"Great! No gun, right. He uses his hands and feet.

170

He's . . . what's his background? Wasn't there this temple . . . ?''

"You've done your homework," Bruce said happily. "You're talking about the Shaolin Temple in Honan Province, in the north along the Songsham Mountains. It was at Shaolin that Chinese temple boxing—what Americans call kung fu—started. The monks had used it for training and discipline mainly, but also for self-defense. The place was always at the center of revolution activities, and emperors were always trying to destroy it. A few hundred years ago the monks began teaching their methods to outsiders, say in the seventeen and eighteen hundreds. *Wing chun* evolved from one of their students. That's the short version of Shaolin history.''

"It's perfect," Krieger said. "Let's say in the eighteen hundreds one of the students of the Shaolin Temple earned the anger of the emperor.''

"Which wouldn't have been hard," Bruce said.

"So he fled to America, maybe with the agents of the emperor in pursuit. Plus he was looking for something.''

"His father," Bruce said. "He lost his father, who came over ahead of him.''

"The father has been done to death. Every other show has a missing father. How about his brother? He wanders the land looking for his brother.''

They finally reached the counter, and to the counterman Krieger said, "Four with everything on 'em. Two Cokes. That okay with you, Bruce?''

"Great.''

"As for the brother . . .''

"He never finds him," Bruce said.

"At least not until the fifth year. A problem: Why do you suppose the brother is in America?''

"Gone to find the streets that are paved with gold? No, that wouldn't work for a Shaolin priest's brother."

"Why would our hero be a priest?" Krieger asked.

"It was the Shaolin priest monks who taught kung fu to their disciples, who also were priests, or became them. I think it changed from century to century. Anyway, you had to enter the monastery and stay there for a few years. I think sometimes it operated like an American military academy. A nobleman with some sort of trouble could drop his kid off to be raised. Occasionally a strange wanderer got taken in. There is the story of Bodhidharma, a Buddhist monk who crossed the Himalayas on foot and arrived at Shaolin when it was in terrible shape. One of the Chinese emperors had tried to destroy it. That happened often. Anyway, the monks were in bad shape healthwise. He developed a system of exercises based on yoga. He called his system the Eighteen Hands of Lo-Han. That came to be Shaolin temple boxing, which evolved into kung fu."

"You're really up on this, aren't you?" Krieger asked.

"I'm very proud of my heritage and don't want to see Mickey Rooney cast in the role of our kung fu cowboy, the way he played a Chinaman in *Breakfast at Tiffany's*."

"The part is yours, I assure you. So anyway, he was dropped off at the Shaolin Temple to be raised by the priests or monks or whatever. They teach him kung fu and a lot of Shaolin philosophy."

"Which is Taoism, for the most part, with a few Confucian and Buddhist influences."

"Which he brings to the United States to search for his long-lost brother. He lands in the Wild West . . ."

"And wanders the land, searching for his brother and solving problems without a gun," Bruce said. "But what sort of problems?"

172

"Oh, the usual ones. You saw *The Fugitive,* didn't you? David Jansen played a man on the run."

"I missed that one."

"*Route 66,* then," Krieger said. "Surely you saw that."

"Oh yeah, that was a hit back in Hong Kong. Two young men prowl Route 66 from Chicago to L.A. in a Corvette."

"Solving problems," Krieger said. "Our Shaolin priest could seek shelter at a ranch house, only to find the widow who lives there being threatened by one or another malevolent force. Let's say a nasty landowner who wants to annex her plot of land to use it as a corral for his horses."

"The Shaolin kicks the shit out of the bad guys, saves the widow, and lays a little tao on everyone in the process," Bruce said.

"Yes! That's it exactly. He solves problems using something no American has ever seen before . . ."

"Kung fu," the two men said at once.

"Starring Bruce Lee," Krieger said.

"He teaches what he was taught by his teacher in the old country, and passes it along to those he meets in the Old West. God, Yip Man would die if he knew about it."

"He's your guru, right?"

"Just my teacher, but there is a certain reverence that goes with the title. He's the *wing chun* grandmaster. He wouldn't approve of my teaching the system to Americans. There are others who agree with him. But I think I have them taken care of."

"And you now are perfectly capable of spreading tao among the people of the Old West."

"Yes, but only *after* I kick the shit out of them," Bruce said.

Krieger paid for the hot dogs and the two men walked back to the Corniche. A parking ticket had appeared on the windshield. Barely glancing at it, Krieger tossed it into the glove compartment. Sitting once again behind the wheel, he said, ''This is fantastic. We got action! We got culture! It's a Western!''

''But it's an Eastern,'' Bruce said.

''An Eastern! Yeah, an Eastern. They're gonna love it. God, man, the thing will run forever!''

''Kung fu,'' they said again simultaneously, as if it were a Shaolin temple chant.

✺ 21 ✺

1967

TO CELEBRATE THE SUCCESS OF *THE GREEN HORNET* AND, PERHAPS, the Summer of Love that was being widely proclaimed around California in 1967, Bruce came home with a spanking-new red Porsche. He roared up the driveway of the Lees' quaint ranch house, which was expensive and tasteful, though not at all as grand as so many other homes in Bel Air, that most expensive of communities where the stars lived.

He pulled to a halt, sending gravel flying, and leaned on the horn. Linda came flying out, wearing chic bell-bottoms, a silk blouse bought at one of the ritzy boutiques on Rodeo Drive, and a vest embroidered with Indian motifs. A string of love beads hung around her neck. A discreetly small lapel button read "U.S. Get Out of Vietnam."

"Did you steal Steve McQueen's car?" she asked.

"He stole mine. Come on, get in. We're late."

She leaped over the door and landed on his lap.

"How can I drive with you sitting on me?"

"I've heard a lot about Chinese traditions. Now let me tell you about an American tradition."

"Tell me quickly," he said.

"It's called 'watching the submarine races.'"

"That doesn't make sense. If submarines raced, they would be underwater. And if they were underwater, you wouldn't be able to see them, true?"

"So true."

"So, what are you trying to pull off?" he asked.

"Let's start with your belt," she said, squirming around and reaching for it. "You see, in America when you park with your honey by the seaside and climb into his lap—or better yet, into the backseat . . ."

"There is no backseat in a Porsche."

"So we use our imagination. Making love in a sports car prepares you for the life of an athlete."

"Or a contortionist," he said.

"The point is, when a policeman comes along and asks you what you're doing, what do you tell him?"

Bruce smiled and said, "But, Officer, we're only watching the submarine races."

"Got it!" she exclaimed.

"In Hong Kong we don't watch the submarine races, we dance the cha-cha. Let's do it later. Got to get to the party. Now either get off me or help drive."

"Okay. I'll work the stick. You work the clutch."

He clutched. She threw the car in reverse. The car bulleted backwards. There was a loud gear grind while they got their coordination down right, and then the Porsche speeded away.

With a few mistakes and an occasional gear grind, the Porsche survived the trip that led west on Sunset and then north on the Pacific Coast Highway to a knoll overlooking Trancas Beach, where Bill Krieger's grand Spanish house sat, behind a handful of expensive cars and the valets to park them. The house was a lot more grand than the Lees', with an interior atrium open to the sky and featuring a beautiful crystal-clear pool and Jacuzzi.

Stephen, the butler, led Bruce and Linda in, and escorted them through a tastefully done marble foyer decorated with paintings of the Southwest desert and pueblo scenes. The furniture, for the most part, was Southwest—all sand-color cushions and darker sand-color fake-stone chair frames and table legs. Entering the house was a bit like dropping in on a 1760s Franciscan monastery in Santa Fe, except that a band played and alcoholic beverages were everywhere.

On the second-story landing, late for his own party, Bill Krieger rushed from one room to another, in search of the ideal shirt. Spotting his star, he came to the railing and looked down on them.

"Hey, guys, glad you could make it. We'll be right down."

"Good to see you, Bill," Linda called out.

In the background Stephanie, Krieger's slinky blond wife, zipped by in search of the ideal earrings. "Hi, Bruce and Linda," she called down.

"This is some place," Linda said as they wandered into the dining room, where caterers were setting up the private dinner for *Green Hornet* executives and stars that would precede the larger cast and crew party. Laid out on the big table overlooking the Pacific Ocean were cold poached salmon, sliced cucumber in dill sauce, and asparagus vinaigrette, among other dishes.

"We're getting there," Bruce said, taking her arm and leading her out onto the deck.

It was a crystal-clear day with a light western wind blowing in off the ocean and gently tinkling the wind chimes that hung by the door. Low rollers were moving onto the sloping beach, producing waves barely adequate for surfing. Yet a number of surfers were out there, competing

177

for attention with sunbathers and strollers. A volleyball game raged on the surf side of the house to the north, and from a radio on a large beach blanket occupied by four hippies came the sound of "Sgt. Pepper's Lonely Hearts Club Band."

"Do you really think so?" Linda asked. "Do you think we'll ever have a house like this?"

"Sure. Why not? As soon as *Kung Fu* clicks we'll be set up for life."

"I mean, I love our Bel Air house, but *this* is fabulous."

"You can almost see Hong Kong from here," he said wistfully.

"Will you take me there someday? I'd love to go."

"Absolutely. We can go during the hiatus."

"The what?"

"You know, the break. When we're done shooting this year's episodes of *Green Hornet*."

"That's in two weeks."

"So? How long would it take you to pack?"

"But . . . who would look after the house? Who would look after Brandon?"

"We'll hire someone to watch the house, and Brandon can come with us."

"Honey, he's too young to travel."

"He can stay with Grandma, then."

"My mother can't handle him for that long. How long would we be away?"

"A month, I guess. We could see my father. We could visit Yip Man. He'd like to meet you." Bruce had no sooner said those words than he saw the pink blush in her cheeks and the way her blond hair blew in the sea breeze, and reconsidered. "Maybe not. God, why does life have to be so complicated? Why can't people just get along?"

Linda rested her head against his, and kept it there until

the Kriegers came downstairs and the party began. The "A" party was first, a private dinner for the producer, the director, the stars, and their wives. It was a brilliant Malibu day, and Van Williams was fired up about the beach house he'd just bought with his share of *Green Hornet* money.

Money was the talk of the day, money and projects. It was a true Hollywood dinner, all shop talk, which meant lots of high hopes and even higher dollar figures. The sky was no longer the limit. It was 1967 and everyone had a scheme for making money. Everyone had a script to be turned into a fabulous pot of gold. Everything was assured. For Bruce, *Kung Fu* was the pot of gold. Van Williams had his own version. So did the director. What great ideas they had and how much money they would make was the Hollywood version of playing Monopoly.

When the "A" party was over, the "B" party began. Suddenly the doors opened up to the minor players and studio hangers-on who were, in their unique way, an essential part of the Hollywood experience. Trainers, trainees, stuntmen, makeup women, wardrobe mistresses, press agents, grips, and technicians made up just part of the crowd. The caterers brought in more food, and a folk-rock band sang and played songs by the Beach Boys and the Mamas and the Papas. A handful of scantily dressed young men and women lounged in the Jacuzzi, the pungent smell of marijuana drifting from a joint they were passing around.

When the band swung into "California Dreaming," Bruce and Linda found themselves on the dance floor. They weren't quite dancing; more like hugging in tempo.

"Did I ever tell you I was the cha-cha champion of Hong Kong?" Bruce asked.

"At least a hundred times. Did I ever tell you I was the

submarine race-watching champion of San Francisco Bay?"

"Yeah. But you're a married woman now and I don't want to hear about it. When we get to Hong Kong, let's go dancing. I know this little dance hall where I used to rip it up."

"It sounds good, but honey, we can't go."

"Why not?"

"For one thing, we don't have the money. The house and the car cost us a fortune."

"Yeah, but *Green Hornet* is going great, and *Kung Fu* is just around the corner."

"Let's wait until we're caught up just the same. Besides . . ."

"Besides what?"

"You're not supposed to fly when you're pregnant," she said.

"You're kidding? I thought . . . I mean . . . Wow!"

"Hong Kong will have to wait until our daughter is born," Linda said.

"How do you know it will be a girl?"

"A feeling. Call it my *chi*."

He wrapped his arms more tightly around her and they swayed to the music, barely aware of their surroundings.

"We'll have a beautiful baby girl and, when she's big enough, take our whole family to Hong Kong."

"That's a deal."

The band segued from "California Dreaming" to "Light My Fire," and the tempo picked up. Bruce led Linda off the floor, saying, "Come on, Mamma, no shaking up the new baby."

It was then that Bill Krieger came in from his study. Angry and tense, he stepped to the bandstand and stopped the music. All eyes were on him; the veterans in the crew knew what was coming.

"I know the timing is lousy, but I wanted you to hear it from me first," he said to all at the party. "The show's been canceled."

The silence was as thick as a tomb.

"I just got the call. We'll finish out the last episode and that will be that. I'm sorry."

Van Williams and his wife, Vickie, looked at each other and then at Bruce and Linda. "I just paid sixty thousand bucks for a house in Malibu," Williams said, shocked.

The news hit the party like an iceberg. Linda looked deflated despite her own good news. How would they afford to feed a new mouth? Despite Bruce's optimism, they weren't doing *that* well. There were a lot of debts. It was expensive to live in Bel Air. For one thing, gas for the Porsche had just hit sixty-nine cents a gallon. They certainly wouldn't be going to Hong Kong *now*.

"What will we do?" she asked him.

He shrugged off the news of the show's cancelation. "There's nothing to worry about. Bill and I will just roll into *Kung Fu*."

He took her back in his arms and led her into a cha-cha, humming the music he remembered from that night at the Circle of Heaven Dance Hall.

The Summer of Love became the dismal fall of 1967, which hit the Lee household with all the joy of a long, cold drizzle. Bills piled up, unpaid. Linda put them into two piles—ones that had been turned over to credit agencies and ones that hadn't.

There was no way of paying them. Bruce had put aside teaching when he got *The Green Hornet*. His *kwoon* was little more than a memory, as was his teaching career. To be sure, he had private clients within the Hollywood community. Martial arts was becoming a novelty among the younger actors and those male stars who were likely to get parts in action movies. Steve McQueen, for one, had Bruce teach him a few things. So did Lew Alcindor, the basketball player who had yet to change his name to Kareem Abdul Jabbar. But the money Bruce made teaching didn't pay half the bills.

There were occasional rays of hope. Hollywood ran on hope in much the same way Las Vegas did. You personally might be broke but nearby, bells were ringing and someone was hitting the jackpot. The Hollywood Hills were thick with promises. Linda set aside her first-of-the-month bills one day when she heard Bruce talking on the phone from his study. His voice was proud and confident, with occasional glimpses of hope. The sound of it made her feel better, and she waddled in to join him.

When she reached the study door the conversation was over. He had replaced the phone on its cradle, but his hand lingered atop the receiver, as if something more could be wrung from it. His eyes were downcast; through the open window the neighbor's parrot was squawking. The bird sounded confident too.

When he heard Linda shuffling into the room, Bruce looked up at her and his familiar smile popped back on his face.

"Hi, hon."

"Who was that you were talking to?"

"Bill. The network still hasn't made a decision on *Kung Fu*."

"I'm sorry."

"But it still looks real good."

"Good," she said, "Good."

"Don't worry. Who else are they going to get to star in it? Mickey Rooney?"

"I'm not worried," she said.

He walked to her and they hugged. No matter what they said, both were very worried.

🈂22🈂

1969

EIGHTEEN MONTHS LATER, LITTLE HAD CHANGED. *KUNG FU* WAS
still on hold, having slipped into the sort of Hollywood
neverland where projects linger in suspended animation
awaiting some magical coming together of events.

A morning's worth of disappointing phone calls merci-
fully over with, Bruce dressed in old jeans and got ready to
do some yard work. It wasn't exactly exercise, but it was
better than sitting around watching the bills continue to pile
up. He first peeked in the bedroom to give himself a boost.
Linda slept peacefully, lost in a midday nap with Brandon
stretched out beside her. On the other side of her was
Shannon—born the year before and as beautiful a baby girl
as any he had seen.

A wonderful family, he thought; *how am I going to put
food on the table for them?* With no answer at hand, Bruce
went outside and took the lawn mower out of the garage. He
fired it up and began mowing the front lawn, moving back
and forth in measured strips and losing himself, for a time,
in the mindless work.

Down the street and without him noticing it, a red-and-
yellow tow truck cruised slowly, its driver reading license

plate numbers off the backs of the expensive foreign cars parked in driveways up and down the street. He was after Bruce's beloved Porsche, and pulled into the driveway and hooked it up while its owner was preoccupied with his problems.

When he saw what was going on, Bruce switched off the lawn mower. The driver looked over at him and saw not a homeowner or car owner but the Chinese gardener. Certainly he didn't recognize Bruce Lee, creator of *jeet kune do*.

"They home?" he called from behind the wheel.

Shocked and embarrassed, Bruce shook his head no.

"You see 'em, you tell 'em the car was repo'd."

Bruce made no reply. His Porsche, for so long the symbol of his success in Hollywood, was gone. Instead there was a repo man sitting behind the wheel of a tow truck admiring his lawn-mowing skills.

"You do good work," the driver said. "Got a card?"

Again Bruce said nothing.

"No speakee English, huh? Sorry I asked." With that, the man put the truck in gear and drove off.

Bruce watched his car disappear around the bend, too devastated even to get angry.

Another fall came to Southern California, and with it more bills and less money. Following the loss of his Porsche, Bruce retreated to what he knew best—martial arts. He spent more and more time in his home gym, pumping iron in a fury of anger and adrenaline. When he wasn't working out, he often could be found by his medicine cabinet, taking handfuls of vitamins. His back acted up frequently, the dull ache that sat permanently in the spot where Johnny Sun had damaged his spine occasionally sharpening into an agonizing pain.

Linda knew nothing of this, so on that autumn morning

when she set out for work for the first time, Bruce sat in the kitchen feeding the children and generally playing house-husband. He was, he thought, doing a fair job of pretending that he liked it.

Shannon sat in a booster chair while Bruce helped her cut her French toast. That done, she struggled to eat using a baby fork while he mindlessly did curls using an eighty-pound dumbbell and read the front page of the *Los Angeles Times*. The broadcast news played on a table radio: American troops were on the offensive in the Mekong Delta; scientists were analyzing the first Moon rocks brought back by the crew of Apollo 11; and sports fans were still talking about the unexpected World Series victory by the New York Mets.

Brandon busied himself turning his farina into something like a sand sculpture.

"C'mon, Brandon, eat it, don't play with it," Bruce said.

"I *am* eating it," the child said, stuffing some in his mouth and immediately making a face.

"You have to eat your breakfast if you're going to grow up to be big and strong," Bruce said.

"I *am* big and strong," the boy insisted.

"How's it going, Daddy?" Linda said, entering the kitchen dressed for her new job.

"The score is kids two, breakfast nothing," Bruce replied. "Can I get you something as long as I'm cooking?"

She shook her head. "It's my first day. I can't afford to be late."

"We can't afford anything. You should have breakfast. My God, I'm starting to sound like an old woman."

"No you're not. Did you make my lunch?"

He handed her a brown paper bag, which she stuffed into her handbag. "Tuna on whole wheat and an apple," he said.

"It sounds very healthy. Thank you, hon. How do I look?"

"Stunning."

She looked at him for any sign that he resented her going out to work to support the family. He showed no such thing, but smiled complacently. Then a taxi horn tooted out front.

"Got to go," she said, and gave him a lunging kiss.

"Good luck."

"Mind your sister and no TV," she said to Brandon.

"I *like* TV," Brandon said, piling his farina as high as it would possibly go.

"Are you sure you're okay?" Linda asked Bruce.

"I'm great." He smiled warmly; almost too warmly.

"You're still a teacher, you know."

"I know."

"The best teacher in the world. I mean, they all come to you: McQueen, Coburn, Alcindor. You know how they talk about you."

"Yeah, I can't wait to hear what they'll say when they find out you had to get a job."

"We got into this together. We'll get through it together. You're still my real-life hero."

He smiled again, a smile that wasn't quite as phony as before, but nearly so. Linda gave up. When he wanted to be unapproachable, there was no breaking through his barriers.

"Have a good day," he said. "And don't worry about me. I'll work out and make some calls. Maybe we'll get lucky."

"Our luck will change soon. I'm sure of it."

The taxi driver honked his horn again. Linda gave Bruce another kiss, and then was gone out the door.

Bruce finished feeding the children and cleaned up in the kitchen. Then, breaking Linda's rule, he switched on *Sesame Street* and parked the children in front of it. The show kept them transfixed for an hour, an hour that he desperately needed to get in touch with himself.

He went to his gym, stripped off his shirt, and bowed to Pete, the *wing chun* dummy that for several years had been Bruce's most visible connection to his martial arts past. He moved in and gave Pete a blistering shot to the head. In that instant, Pete flashed in the back of his mind as the Ming Warrior, the demon of his father's and his nightmares. Bruce saw his wooden peg arms as being the leather-sheathed arms of the monster, brandishing a sword.

"No! I'll kill you!" Bruce screamed, and gave Pete a brutal forearm to the chest. The dummy cracked.

"You're not getting me! You're not getting my family!" He dealt out a flurry of wicked chops to the arms, and they went flying. Sensing victory not over a wooden dummy but over the demon that had pursued him across the Pacific Ocean to America and that now appeared to threaten his son, Bruce exploded in fury. He unleased a *kiai* of power, destroying Pete in a terrifying fury of fists, elbows, and feet.

The dummy was a shambles on the floor. Bruce's anger was gone, and in its place was only exhaustion, frustration. Then he heard the crying, and whipped around to see Brandon. His son stood in the door, crying, terrified. He had been watching the whole thing. At that moment, Bruce felt like his father, Lee Hoi Chuen, watching over the frail body of the young Lee Jun Fan. In his son he saw himself as a child, and he knew that somehow, in the darkness, the demon lurked. It was as if America had never happened.

Later that day, as the sun crept toward the western horizon, setting on America but rising on Hong Kong, Linda came home from her first day of work. She carried a bag of groceries—the first reward of her new job. She left them on the table and flipped through the mail. As usual, the mail was a stack of bills and collection agency forms.

"Hi, honey, I'm home," she called out.

There was no reply.

"I picked up some stuff at Ralph's. Are you hungry? I'm starved."

Still there was nothing.

"Bruce? Bruce, where are you?" she asked.

There was a noise in the gym, and she put down the mail and walked in that direction. When she crossed through the dining room and into the workout area, she found Bruce and Brandon sitting cross-legged on the floor. They were putting Pete back together, using Elmer's Glue. Shannon played quietly nearby.

"What on earth happened?" she asked.

"Pete started it," Bruce said, offering an enigmatic smile.

1970

In September of 1970, *Kung Fu* finally had its premiere on network television. The show had been in the works for several years and was easily the most talked-about network presentation that year. It was the first American television "Eastern," one that featured Chinese culture against a backdrop of the Old American West.

Bruce and Linda watched the pilot with the lights off. On the set in their Bel Air living room, music swelled over the black of the screen. There were vaguely Oriental sounds—wind chimes or something, and wind. A lone coyote howled across the prairie. The opening credits faded up accompanied by an announcer:

"*Kung Fu*—starring David Carradine—is brought to you by Budweiser Beer. Budweiser, the king of beers . . ."

David Carradine walked on as Caine, the half-American, half-Chinese hero. His head was shaved and his eyes were made up to look Chinese. On his forearm was a tattoo

189

supposed to have been given him at the Shaolin Temple; the tattoo was of a dragon.

Bruce and Linda sat on the couch, shell-shocked. "Three years' work," Bruce said, devastated, and Linda took his hand and squeezed it.

The telephone started ringing. Neither made a move for a long time; then when Linda went to answer it, Bruce held her back.

"I don't want sympathy calls. It's probably Steve McQueen calling to tell me how I got screwed. I know how I got screwed and don't have to hear it again."

Linda said, "If that's what it is, I'll tell them you're not home."

She walked across the room and picked up the receiver. "Hello . . . What? . . . What? I can't understand you . . . One minute, please."

She put aside the receiver and turned to her husband. "It's long distance. They're speaking Chinese."

Bruce sighed and got up from the couch. He took the phone and answered the call. Linda returned to the couch, but when she saw her husband's mood get even darker, she went back to his side.

He rolled back against the wall and leaned there, slumping down a bit. Finally he hung up the phone and stared at her, desolation in his eyes. "My father's dead," he said.

Tsuen Wan Cemetery was set on the outskirts of Hong Kong at the beginning of the slope up Victoria Peak. The mountain was known in Chinese as Tai Ping Shan, "The Mountain of Great Peace." Lee Hoi Chuen was laid to rest in a Buddhist ceremony. Bruce stood impassively, dressed in white, the Chinese color of mourning, while a priest prayed over the grave and friends brought offerings of food to sustain the departed in his celestial journey.

Bruce's eyes were fixed on the color photograph of his father that had been laminated into the headstone. His eyes were very like Bruce's, an equal mixture of sincerity and strength. *Brandon has that same mixture of qualities,* Bruce thought; in fact, it was amazing to note for the first time just how much the boy resembled his grandfather. Bruce was so caught up in the moment of his father's funeral that he failed to notice the deference with which all others at the ceremony treated him. Had he been paying attention, he would have seen that all there were treating him like a star—a vast difference from the treatment he had been getting in Hollywood over the past few years.

A few hours later he found himself drawn to the brick alley not far from Tang City Hall. It was eerie, in a way, walking down the path his father first took him on as a child, the one that led to Yip Man's *kwoon.*

The *kwoon* was empty save for rising incense and the figure of the old man moving gracefully in the center of the room, doing a series of exercises with a ceremonial sword. Yip Man was painfully thin, his close-cropped hair now totally gray, but his movements were still beautiful to watch. Bruce waited until he was noticed, then exchanged greeting with his old teacher. They had had their differences, but all was forgotten in a moment of remembrance of that special bond between master and star pupil. Relieved, Bruce poured out his heart to the old man; told him everything: about Linda, about the Council of Elders and Johnny Sun, about Brandon and Shannon, and about the demon that had pursued him across the Pacific and, perhaps, back. Bruce recounted the most recent apparition.

"And then?" Yip Man asked, pouring *cha* into the same cups he had used so many years before.

"It comes, it goes," Bruce replied, in Cantonese.

"In your dreams?"

"No, I'm always awake. At first I thought I was sleeping, then I realized I was awake. It's not a dream, *Sifu*."

"No, it's not."

He sipped his tea and bade Bruce to do likewise. He continued: "When your father first brought you here, he told me everything. He too thought his visions were a dream at first. He wanted you to learn *wing chun* to protect yourself—from men and . . . from other forces."

"I thought that was all superstition," Bruce said.

"Superstition is a name the ignorant give to their ignorance. You were special then; you're special now. That's why the demon wants you."

"Maybe you should teach me to be more ordinary."

Yip Man gently touched Bruce's shoulder, the only time outside of sparring that he had ever made physical contact. "The gods are bored, Little Dragon," he said. "They make some of us special to test themselves. When they beat us, they know we are nothing and they are gods."

Bruce struggled to understand the reasoning.

Yip Man continued: "Put yourself in the demon's place. How many really good opponents are there?"

The old master reached out a bony hand and pulled his beloved chessboard closer. Bruce glanced at it, and his astonishment showed.

"That's the same game we were playing years ago," he said.

"When confronting the demon, you must think of the long term—like with this game. I have spent a long time preparing you for the fight."

"What if I refuse to fight him?" Bruce asked.

"You have no choice. You're fighting for more than yourself."

"What are you saying, *Sifu*?"

"This demon has a taste for first sons. It means you. It also means your son, Brandon."

The blood drained from Bruce's face. In an instant, he understood his fate. The fight with the demon was inevitable and had to be won, for the sake of Brandon. There was no choice, Bruce knew. Even if it meant his own death, the fight had to be won.

"When you are at your absolute peak he will come for you," the old man said. "When the monsoons blow, be prepared."

Yip Man spread his hands above the chessboard, as if seeking to divine the future. Then he made a move with a pawn. "This is where we left off a long time ago," he said. "Let's finish. It's good to finish. Especially because I'm ahead."

☒ 23 ☒

THERE WAS TIME TO KILL BEFORE THE FLIGHT BACK TO LOS Angeles. His father was gone and Yip Man, his *sifu,* his other father, had informed him of an inescapable fate. Bruce had to be alone with his thoughts for a while and, like many in Hong Kong, found no place better to be alone than in the anonymity of a crowd.

And so he prowled the old city, alone like never before. Hands jammed in jeans pockets, Bruce walked through the narrow streets in the direction of Kennedy Town. Fellow Chinese brushed by him on all sides, and he paused here and there in his rambling to peer at displays of clothing or food. He bought perfume and a scarf to take home to Linda, a toy for Brandon and a doll for Shannon.

One time he felt something at his back, a presence of some kind, and twisted around to look at it. He feared the demon, but found only a twelve-year-old boy who tried, unsuccessfully, to hide the fact he was staring. *It's him,* the boy thought, his eyes as big as saucers. *It's Bruce Lee; it's Kato.*

Oblivious to what the boy was up to, Bruce walked on, thoroughly immersed in memories of his childhood home. *It's not such a bad place,* he thought. For one thing, no policeman with a memory of that incident at the dance hall

194

had come to greet him at the airport when he arrived, and the event of which his father spoke so direly seemed to have been forgotten. Bruce hadn't been forgotten, however, by the thousands upon thousands of Hong Kong residents who watched *The Green Hornet*. As he walked through the streets seeking solitude, Bruce was increasingly being recognized as a star.

He strolled past the jade sellers, the mah-jongg tile makers, and the herbalists selling snake musk and powdered lizard. He heard chattering behind him, and turned to see the same small boy, this time joined by two friends. They stared at him openly, and nodded and chattered excitedly to one another.

Bruce walked down Man Wa Lane, past the rope makers and their storefronts and stalls. He glanced at the elaborate calligraphy of the stamp makers. When he turned around he found a dozen children on his trail. When he walked, they walked. When he stopped, they stopped. They stared and giggled. A few shyly averted their eyes. He was like the Pied Piper; wherever he went, they followed.

''What's going on here?'' Bruce asked at one point, but was met only by a chorus of giggles.

He shrugged and walked off down the street, trailed by a crowd of kids. It was beginning to dawn on him that they recognized him from television. His father had told him over the phone on several occasions that *The Green Hornet* was ''a big hit'' in Hong Kong. But the conversations were long ago, largely forgotten, and his father always exaggerated anyway. Whatever the kids saw in Bruce, it was beginning to cheer him up. And he desperately needed some good cheer in his life, even the little that could be brought by having a gang of urchins recognize him.

Bruce walked past the Hang Wen Restaurant, internationally famous as the ''bird place.'' Bird owners brought their pets there, many in ornate cages, for communal singing. The sight of that restaurant always gave Bruce a laugh, and walking past it made him feel even better. Soon he was walking briskly to his hotel, the sadness of his father's funeral set aside for a time, followed by his growing band of admirers.

He showered and put on fresh clothes, then went down to the lobby restaurant for dinner. Back in his room a few hours later, he watched local television until it was time to call Linda. A lot of coordinating went into finding a mutually good time to talk half a world away. When they finally did connect, he learned that she had spent the night curled up on the mat beside the reconstructed Pete—the closest thing she could find to Bruce. That touched him deeply, and after they said good-bye he made repeated calls to the airline trying to get his return flight moved up. There were no seats on earlier flights, so Bruce begrudgingly settled in for the night and what turned out to be the first decent sleep he had had since learning of his father's death.

The following morning he found himself, suitcase in hand, crossing the gangplank to the Star Ferry. The boat plied the waters of the harbor, sailing back and forth from Hong Kong Island to Kowloon, site of the airport. In addition to being a commuter link, the Star Ferry was also an important tourist attraction, and the boat was crowded with both local people and camera-toting Japanese, Indonesian, Indian, and American tourists.

Out on the street, a pudgy black English limousine screeched to a halt. Four well-dressed men jumped out, led by an especially well-tailored member of Hong Kong's growing executive corps. He wore a white turtleneck beneath his expensive suit, a sporting touch that, in 1970,

196

betrayed him as being connected in some way with the arts or entertainment. With him in the lead, they dashed through the columned terminal to the boat.

The gangplank began to lift, but they leaped aboard just in time. Bruce watched them from the rail near the stern with idle curiosity. His interest grew as they scurried around the ship, scrutinizing the passengers one by one. Before long he recognized in their eyes much the same look he saw on those children the day before: a touch of awe.

The man in the white turtleneck reached him first, and upon seeing Bruce let loose with a burst of relief. "Mr. Lee! Mr. Lee! Thank God we caught up with you. Can we talk?"

The man was so winded he could barely speak.

"I can if you can," Bruce said.

"I'm Phillip Tan," he said, pulling himself together well enough. He was a slightly built, somewhat elegant man. "I'm a producer and I want to make a movie with you."

"Like I said, I can if you can."

In Hong Kong as in Hollywood, talk is cheap. But there was something about Tan's enthusiasm that got Bruce interested.

"I'm serious. You're Kato and here Kato is a big star."

"I was kind of wondering about that," Bruce said, thinking of the children.

"Here they don't call your show *The Green Hornet*. It's *The Kato Show*. So when I heard Kato was in town, I considered it a good omen."

"You know why I am here," Bruce said.

"Yes, and I am deeply sorry about your father. My condolences."

"Thank you."

"I am a man who can spot a good omen a long way off."

"I have to get back to my family, Mr. Tan. I'm on my

197

way to the airport. If you don't mind riding with me, we can talk on the way.''

"Not at all. But listen to me. Leave tomorrow for America. Give us time to talk. There's a great deal to talk about.''

Bruce assessed him coolly. "I miss my family a great deal. The funeral was difficult for me.''

Tan was not about to be put off. "If you say no to my movie, I'll buy you a new ticket—first class.''

The ferry pulled away from the dock and out into the harbor. It was a brilliant fall day, with no monsoon in sight. Their meeting was indeed a good omen.

"Keep talking," Bruce said.

"The movie is called *The Big Boss*. It's an action film, with lots of kung fu.''

"Are you sure you wouldn't rather get David Carradine?'' Bruce asked bitterly.

"Who is David Carradine?'' Tan asked.

"Nobody," Bruce said with a smile. "Nobody at all.''

Tan said, "Making this film will be very good for both you and me. You will see.''

Bruce thought quickly. Talking to Tan would mean being kept away from his beloved family for another day. But it could also mean being able to support them for the first time in years. And perhaps support them in style. Bruce had made films in Hong Kong when he was a boy. He could make them as a man. This time he would be the star, however.

"When we get to the terminal in Kowloon I have to call my wife," he said. "But yes, I think that I will stay here overnight. You and I *do* have a lot to talk about.''

1971

The small Chinese film crew set up their antiquated camera and lights outside an ice house in Pak Chong, Thailand, which had mainly cheap rates to recommend it. The weather was humid and very hot and the air was thick with bugs. Even in the ice house, where blocks of ice were stored awaiting shipment, flies and assorted kinds of biting gnats swirled relentlessly through the air.

The Chinese director of *The Big Boss* was a horse-racing fan, and in the many minutes between takes liked to prowl around the set, using one hand to press a transistor radio to his ear and the other hand to swat bugs. Today, when his pacing brought him near to where Bruce sat reading a magazine, an English announcer could be heard calling the third race at the Happy Valley Race Track back in Hong Kong.

Speaking to Bruce in Chinese, the director said: "We'll do the scene where you fight the hit man for the big boss."

"Where's the guy?" Bruce asked. "Maybe we can rehearse."

"No rehearsing!" the director snapped. "I want it fresh. I want it real. Hold on . . ."

The third race was over and he lost. He unleashed a string of Chinese curses at the radio. When he turned his attention back to business, he said: "I got this great fighter from the States. If you beat him, the story ends one way. If you don't, I might change the ending. I might make him the star."

The director whipped a cigar out of a tobacco-stained shirt pocket and jammed it in his mouth. He laughed a cackling laugh.

"Idiot," Bruce thought, and walked away in disgust to take his place inside the ice house.

"Action! Action already!" the director yelled.

The scene called for Bruce to hide in the darkness inside the ice house waiting for the hit man to arrive. The hit man's approach was deliberately meant to recall those old Westerns where the bad guy, the evil gunslinger dressed in black, struts down the dusty main street aiming to gun down the sheriff.

As the camera rolled, Bruce stepped out of the ice house to meet his adversary. His eyes widened when he saw who it was who had come all the way from America. It was Luke Sun, Johnny Sun's younger brother. He had grown into the fullness of manhood, with muscles bigger than his brother's and an equally murderous determination in his eyes.

If Bruce was surprised, however, Luke clearly had been planning the move for some time: tracking Bruce down, getting cast in the role of the hit man, and probably working for nothing (not to mention bankrupting his family flying to Thailand). Hatred such as that knew no bounds.

"My brother can't talk right, he can't walk right," Luke hissed.

The director checked his script for that dialogue. He couldn't find it.

"You've dishonored my family," Luke went on. "I've sworn to kill you."

There was clearly no reasoning with the man. Bruce said: "Swearing is easy. Killing is hard."

"I've read your book. I've studied *jeet kune do*. I know all your tricks."

"Let's see how well you learned your lesson," Bruce said.

Luke went right onto the attack, and his onslaught was blistering. His moves were *jeet kune do,* all right, as far as they went. He had learned that the discipline drew moves from over two dozen martial arts, and had memorized all of them. But he performed them in sequence, like a mechanical man. Still, he was strong and charged like a bull, throwing fists and elbows.

Bruce blocked and countered as best he could, looking for an opening. Against that onslaught he backed up the stone steps leading to the ice house. Bruce sought higher ground, and when on the top step, lashed out with a wicked right roundhouse kick. But Luke intercepted it and lifted up mightily, flipping Bruce inside the door.

"Follow them! Follow them, you idiots!" the director yelled at his crew, who fumbled to hoist both camera and tripod and race with them into the ice house.

Inside the structure, the noise of the fight was overwhelmed by the clamor of machinery. A conveyer belt ground relentlessly, moving one-hundred-pound blocks of ice from the freezer room where they were formed to a loading dock for placement in the refrigerated bodies of trucks.

Luke forced Bruce into a corner where the conveyer passed the ice through a port in the brick wall. He had Bruce by the neck and was bending his head back down toward the belt. Bruce's shirt caught in the mechanism and was ripped to shreds, torn from his chest as if made of paper. The big man's eyes nearly bulged from his head from the strength of his fury and the power with which he clenched his teeth while trying to see Bruce's skull ripped apart like the shirt.

Bruce took a deep breath and brought his forehead up, butting Luke just above the bridge of the nose. Caught by the sharp and unexpected attack, the younger man's forehead was split and blood gushed down into his eyes. Bellowing in fury, he wiped his sight clear with the back of his hand.

That gave Bruce the chance to wiggle away, though, which he did while pounding Luke with a flurry of three-to-one punches and, before Luke could recover, a punishing right kick to the head. That blow, which would have killed a lesser man, barely fazed the kid. Luke charged back at Bruce, pushing him back with a furor of fists and elbows that were met and countered at near-stroboscopic speed.

Bruce lurched backward and, given a split-second opening, came at Luke with a flying kick that knocked the big man back against the conveyer belt. Luke snatched a block of ice, lifted it over his head, and hurled it at Bruce.

Unimpressed, Bruce stood his ground and demolished the block with a fore-fist punch from tae kwon do. The ice blew apart as surely as if someone had embedded a hand grenade in it. Splinters of ice flew everywhere, showering the camera crew and the director as he struggled to film the fight. The man had wanted a staged fight that looked realistic. What he got was a *real* fight that looked like World War III.

Then Luke charged through the cloud of ice and hit Bruce with a flying kick that sent him reeling backwards out of the ice house and back down the stairs. Bruce did a backwards somersault, and landed in a foot-deep puddle formed when waste water from the ice-making operation had collected in the dirt road in front of the building.

Luke charged in at him. With almost no good footing, both men went down wrestling in the mud. The director had just gotten set up inside and now the fight was back out in the daylight. Cursing the gods who also caused him to bet on losing horses, he pushed his crew after the fighters. "Hurry! Hurry! Get it all!" he screamed.

Luke Sun grabbed Bruce by the hair, slammed his face into the muddy water, and held him down. For sheer strength, muscle-to-muscle in a mud wrestle, there was no beating Luke. Still, Bruce managed to get his head above water, but then, using both hands, Luke pushed it back down.

As the camera rolled again, Bruce thrashed but was unable to find release. As seen by the cameraman, his actions became more and more frantic, then weaker. Then he stopped moving entirely, and lay perfectly still.

"My God," exclaimed the director.

Luke pulled Bruce's head up, lifting him by the hair. Bruce's face was covered with mud and dead leaves. His mouth lolled open, his eyes staring blankly. He looked like a drowned cat.

"You've killed him," said the director, finishing his sentence.

Luke said, "This man disgraced my family," and hurled his head contemptuously back down into the muddy water. The force of the impact splashed water onto the director's snakeskin boots.

Luke stood and walked in the direction of the camera crew. He faced them and was about to say something when Bruce rose from his premature grave, fury in his eyes. "Your family *is* a disgrace," he said, hurling himself into the air and hitting Luke in the back using the identical kick that Johnny used to put Bruce in the hospital so many years before.

Luke stumbled forward, his rock-hard body bowed but not broken. He turned to face Bruce, but it was too late to do anything but take the punishment. Bruce was inside his offenses now and working with both hands and elbows. In a flurry of punches that came too fast for even the camera to catch, Luke's nose exploded in a burst of blood, skin, and cartilage. His collarbone was shattered by twin elbow strikes. Bruce whirled and his flying feet connected with Luke's knees, kidneys, and temples.

The big man staggered. What was keeping him on his feet was beyond understanding. Bruce flipped through the air, his legs slamming onto Luke Sun's neck and catching it in a vicious scissor grip. The momentum sent the two of them crashing to the dirt road. With his steel-cable legs, Bruce could garrote Luke. Luke's tongue thrust out grotesquely, like that of a hanged man following his execution. There was a demonic quiver in Bruce's facial muscles, a berserk glow in his eyes. He thought, *I have had enough of these two guys.*

"Zoom in! Zoom in!" the director yelled. "Make sure you get the shot where he dies!"

Bruce then remembered where he was and who he was. He was an actor in a film, and even if Johnny Sun had once appeared to him as the demon, Luke was merely an avenging brother. Not too big in the brains department, perhaps. But was that a reason for him to die?

Bruce released his grip and jumped to his feet. Luke was battered and bleeding and gasping for air, but he was still alive. Bruce looked down at him and said, "It's done between you and me. If I ever see you again, I'll kill you."

"Now *that's* a movie," the director yelled, whipping a cigar out of his pocket.

"Wrong," Bruce said. "That's evidence in an attempted murder trial."

He went to the camera and popped open the magazine door. He unspooled the film in the harsh Thai sun. It was turned into so much worthless plastic spaghetti.

"What're you doing? No! No!" the director shouted, biting his cigar in half in astonishment.

"We'll shoot a better fight tomorrow," Bruce said. "But next time let's *script* it. I'm sick and tired of nearly getting killed for some trashy film."

"Asshole!" the director yelled. "Unprofessional asshole!"

Ignoring all, Bruce walked past the broken Luke Sun and right off the set. There was no joy in his victory—except for the fact that he was back in front of a camera at last. Most importantly, he had earned the money he needed to send Linda three plane tickets and a key to his newly rented apartment in Hong Kong.

☗ 24 ☗

At the end of shooting for *The Big Boss*, the cast and crew flew back to Hong Kong and were taken from the airport by mini-van. Bruce bade farewell to the people he had worked with those several months, and stepped out into the sweltering summer humidity to stand in front of the Waterloo Hill Apartments, an older but well-kept building.

He carried his bags up the staircase and dropped them on the landing outside his door. He slipped the key in the lock and turned it. The door swung open and the first sound he heard was "Daddy!"

The bedroom door swung open and Shannon toddled out, a beautiful blond baby girl with black, almond-shaped eyes.

"Shannon!" he exclaimed, dropping to his knees between his heavy leather suitcases.

Another shout of "Daddy!" heralded the arrival of Brandon, who rocketed into his father's arms next to his sister. The children covered him with kisses and hugs.

Brandon said, "Daddy! The flight took so long they gave me wings." He proudly displayed Pan American captain's wings, given to him on a tour of the cockpit.

"That's great, tiger. I always told you you could fly."

"Did you finish your movie, Daddy?"

"Yeah, it's all done. We finished it up this morning."

"Can I see it?"

"The second it's ready, I promise."

He picked the two of them up and pushed the bags in the door with his foot. Then he kicked the door shut and carried the kids into the apartment.

Linda came out of the bedroom, her eyes wild with joy and longing. "Mommy, Daddy's home," Shannon said.

Bruce put the kids down and held his arms open for Linda to fly into them. They hugged and kissed for a long time before the kids managed to separate them. Laughing, Bruce and Linda took the kids to the couch and sat with them there.

"How long have you been here?" he asked when he finally got the chance.

"Two hours."

"That's it?"

"Yeah, the plane landed at one-fifteen and it took me an hour to find our luggage. The kids were hungry, so we found a cute little place to eat by the terminal."

"Which one? I know every restaurant in Hong Kong."

"McDonald's," Linda said with a smile.

He laughed. "So then you came here? How did you find it?"

"The taxi driver found it. Actually, I was hoping to travel by ricksha, but was told they don't have them anymore. So we got here and let ourselves in and have spent the time since putting our stuff away. The kids drank all the soda you had in the fridge. Sorry, honey."

"I can afford lots of soda now," Bruce said.

"So we're in the money again?" she asked.

"Well, not exactly. But we have a toehold in the money. At least we can pay the bills and eat."

"And most important, we're together again," Linda said.

"Yeah," he said, and pulled her into another long kiss that soon had the kids restlessly tugging at them.

"Aren't you guys tired from the flight and wouldn't you like to lay down for a nap?" Linda asked.

"Hey Bruce," Linda yelled, balling up a white bedsheet and tossing it under the powerful stream of ice-cold water from the shower. "Can we skip refilling the refrigerator with soda and buy an air conditioner instead?"

"Yeah, baby, first thing tomorrow."

"Promise?" she asked, soaking the sheet with water and balling it up more.

"Yeah, I know where I can get a good one cheap. This is Hong Kong, remember?"

"If they're that cheap, buy two of them," she said. She unfurled the sopping-wet sheet and, holding it like a matador holds his cape, she charged—stark naked—into the bedroom, where Bruce lay drenched in the sweat of love-making. Linda flew onto him like Superwoman, her ice-cold cape wrapping about both lovers.

"Wooooo," he shouted in shock as the cold hit him. Then she was in his arms and they were entwined together, cooling off in the only way that seemed to work—short of air-conditioning—in that tropical city where the monsoons blew. It would soon, Bruce recalled, be monsoon season; he tried not to think about that or Yip Man's warning as to what could happen. His family was together again.

"That's better," Linda said.

"I missed you," Bruce said.

"Never again."

"Never."

They kissed, deeply and intimately.

"How long will we be living here?" Linda asked after a time.

"A while, I think."

"I can handle that. I didn't pack much."

"You won't need much," he said, rolling on top of her and pulling the sheet over them like a cowl.

As the sun went down on the Lees' first month in Hong Kong, the family sat on the deck of a Chinese junk, the sails flapping gently in the evening breeze. Hong Kong by junk was a sight to see, especially for someone who remembered just how badly the city was devastated by World War II.

By 1971 the city had become the economic masterpiece of the East. High-rise office towers were everywhere. Banks mingled with brokerage houses. Export firms made millions upon millions shipping the goods of the great Chinese mainland to cities around the world. In the retailing streets, the ragtag old wood and paper signs that reached from sidewalk to rooftop had been replaced by equally large neon signs. Like Las Vegas or Tokyo, nearly every square foot of the central city had become a neon wonderland.

Looking at the skyline from the deck of the junk, it was hard to imagine how age-old demons or even monsoons could intrude upon this gem of the 20th century. But it was monsoon season and, out to sea and over the horizon, storm clouds were brewing. Bruce could feel them coming and knew what they meant, but as was so often the case, could say nothing to his loved ones. It was a fate he would have to face alone.

And then, on one beautiful Hong Kong night in 1971, *The Big Boss* had its premiere. Outside the Movie Palace, gigantic banners announced the name of the movie and offered a billboard-sized likeness of Bruce in a fighting stance. Spotlights swept the sky and thousands of fans, unable to get inside for the premiere, milled in the street while paparazzi swarmed for photos.

Inside, the packed theater watched as Bruce, playing the hero, was led off bare-chested and in handcuffs by Thai police. The ending was daring by the standards of Chinese movies; the hero was hauled off in chains. As the scene closed the theater was stark silent. Bruce felt his tuxedo collar growing tight around his neck, like a noose.

He turned to Linda and said, "Remember in L.A. when we went to see *The Producers*?"

"Um, yeah."

"I think this is gonna be like *Springtime for Hitler*. Let's get out of here before they lynch us."

They pushed out of their seats, stepping over Phillip Tan and the director to get to the aisle.

"Where are you going?" Tan asked.

"Running for our lives," Bruce said, as the audience erupted in cheers and applause at the sight of his name in the credits.

"Honey!" Linda said, shocked and surprised.

The applause had become a standing ovation.

"They love it!" Tan shouted. "They love *you*."

Indeed they did. The film had turned the audience into one organism, a Chinese organism bursting with pride and identity. And this new communal feeling was focused on one man—Bruce Lee. He was a symbol of their aspirations, their traditions, and their hunger for real heroes.

They spotted him in the aisle and went nuts. It was pandemonium, a riot, mob worship, as they reached first to touch him, then to hoist him on their shoulders. The crowd snatched him from Linda and lifted him up above them, carrying him as if he were an ancient emperor.

"Bruce!" Linda called out as he was swept away from her and up the aisle and out of the theater.

"Linda!" he responded. "Linda!"

That did no good. He was their idol and they wanted to

celebrate him no matter what. Phillip Tan grabbed Linda by the hand and pulled her into the crowd. They tried to keep up, but could not. They swept out on the streets with everyone else, but by then the thousands outside and the paparazzi who were waiting for the end of the premiere had joined in. Bruce was being carried down the street at the head of his own parade.

Tan said, "He's gone. We'll never get him back again."

He was speaking symbolically, of course. Still, Linda's face clouded over. Something was definitely beginning— the ascendancy of Bruce's stardom. But something surely was ending too. As much as there was excitement that night when delirious crowds first carried him off and proclaimed him a star, Linda also felt a twinge of sadness. Maybe that part of their lives where they struggled to pay the bills was over. But maybe gone with it was the time of special intimacy, when they could do everything together without the whole world watching.

1972

The town house was in Kowloon, across the harbor from Hong Kong but with a spectacular view of it. The Lees had just moved in, so recently that most of their belongings were still in boxes. In the year since Linda joined Bruce in his native land, Bruce had gone from a nearly beaten man, unable to support his family, to a successful young film star. The fact that few in the United States knew him as anything more than the actor who used to play Kato in the short-lived *Green Hornet* series was beside the point. Fame in America and the rest of the world would come. As things stood, Bruce was happy to be making a living, and Linda was elated to have not only a new house but someone to help her run it.

Mrs. Ngan Ma was the housekeeper who, in the Chinese tradition, was known as "Aunt." On this particular day she had busied herself opening the moving company boxes and putting things in dressers and on shelves while Linda walked Brandon home from school. When Linda unlocked the front door and walked in with him, the boy looked like the picture of the private school boy, with his freshly pressed uniform, starched collar creased sharply over a red-and-blue striped tie, and armful of books.

"Good afternoon, Brandon," the old woman said, wiping her hands on her white-trimmed black apron.

"Hello, Aunt Ma," he said happily.

"No, just call me Aunt. Good afternoon, Mrs. Lee. How did things go at school?"

"Good," Linda said. "It's really wonderful there. All the kids are dressed up. They look so *neat*. And they're all so well behaved. It's nothing like American schools."

"The children aren't behaved in American schools?"

"Not exactly," Linda said with a laugh.

"Here we expect it. Did you enjoy yourself, Brandon?"

"Yes," he said, shrugging off his jacket and hurrying toward the stairs leading up to the bedrooms.

"Where are you going in such a hurry?" Aunt asked.

"Daddy's taking me to the circus," he said happily.

"Go upstairs and change, honey," Linda said. Then she added to Aunt, "He's really happy."

"He has a wonderful father," she agreed, taking an armful of dish towels out of a box and refolding them.

An hour later, Brandon and his mother sat on the front stoop, waiting for Bruce. The shadows were getting long as the afternoon waned. It was a neighborhood of young couples, and all of the many schoolchildren were home or out playing in the street. Some walked with their mothers or grandparents. A few enjoyed the company of fathers who'd had the good luck to get home early from their office jobs across the harbor in Hong Kong. From her vantage point on the stoop, Linda could see the Star Ferry approaching its Kowloon dock carrying yet another boatload of daddies home from their offices. Cars drove off it alongside pedestrians, and Linda smiled at her son.

"Daddy's car is on the ferry," she said. "I'm sure of it."

"What's Daddy doing today?" Brandon asked. "Is he having a fight?"

"No, not today, honey," she replied with a laugh.

"Does Daddy *like* fighting?"

"They're not real fights. They used to be, but now they're play fights."

Brandon held the circus tickets in his hand, clutching them for all they were worth. Linda looked down the street for Bruce's car.

"So what is Daddy doing? He's late."

"He's editing his new movie."

"What's the movie about?"

"Fights," Linda said, adding to herself, "like the one he's going to have if he forgot about the circus."

But that seemed to be what had happened. An hour later the sun had set and Aunt was moving around the house, turning on lights. There was no Bruce. Three phone calls to the studio had produced no results. No one knew where Bruce was. Phillip Tan's office was closed. The director was out of town on a shoot. Linda was livid; when she rejoined her son he was still sitting on the stoop, holding the tickets.

"Did you talk to Daddy?" he asked.

"No, honey. I couldn't find him. But I'm sure he'll be here soon. There must be traffic. There's lots of traffic in Hong Kong."

"I can't wait to see the circus."

"Chinese acrobats are the best in the world," Linda said.

Brandon nodded. He didn't want to believe that his daddy had forgotten him. But he squeezed the tickets so tightly the ink was nearly running. Aching for the boy, Linda said, "Come in and have some dinner while you're waiting."

Brandon shook his head.

"Aunt cooked for us. It's beef with oyster sauce . . . your favorite."

Again he shook his head.

"The circus is really long. He'll be here. You'll see the second half."

Brandon nodded. He was trying to believe, though it was hard.

Linda went back in the house to try the phone again. She had no more luck than she'd had the other times, and when she returned to her son, found that he had fallen asleep. It was night now and there was no longer any point in waiting. The circus was over. She picked up her son and carried him inside the house and up to his bed. As she tucked him in bed the tickets, now thoroughly crumpled, slipped from his tiny fingers.

Then she slipped on a jacket, told Aunt to watch the children, and went to the street to hail a cab.

☗25☗

It was the middle of the evening when Linda's cab pulled up to the main gate of the Pearl of the Orient Studios. "Wait here," she told the driver, and went across the sidewalk to the doorman. He was dressed in a red uniform, like the porters at some American hotels.

"May I help you, miss?" he asked, then recognized her. "Mrs. Lee . . . my apologies."

"Where is my husband?" she asked.

"I have not seen Mr. Lee since I came on duty."

"When was that?"

"Two hours ago. Perhaps he is in the east editing suite. Would you like me to call?" His hand reached for the wall phone.

"No," Linda said. "I want this to be a surprise."

When she got to the door of the suite that Bruce used as an office as well as for editing, she found it partly ajar. She stood in the door and watched. Bruce shuttled between two moviolas—editing machines—and two teams of editors. Production design sketches and shots of Rome, many of them depicting the Colosseum, were push-pinned to a corkboard wall. An unmade single bed was sandwiched in a corner amidst cabinets, film racks, and bins. Bruce's desk and research files occupied another wall. The sight of the room left Linda with the clear impression that it, not the Kowloon town house, was home.

Bruce was editing *Return of the Dragon,* a film he'd written, directed, and starred in. In the year since he completed *The Big Boss,* Bruce had turned *Return of the Dragon* into an all-consuming obsession.

He was staring into the view-piece of a moviola and dictating to his team. "Cut here," he said. "Pre-lap the punch sound here when his head rocks back. Make it quicker: ba-bum. Like that: ba-*bum.*"

"Can I talk to you for a moment?" Linda asked.

Her voice cut like a knife through the business-like atmosphere of the editing suite. All eyes turned to her. She stood at the door, her demeanor cold and controlled.

"Linda," Bruce said, surprised.

"Can I?"

"Unh . . . sure. Can you guys take a break?"

His staff looked relieved to be getting out of there. They were all family men and could spot a husband-wife tiff a mile off. It was bad policy to be hanging around when the boss was fighting with his wife—especially when the boss was capable of taking your head off for real. They slipped past Linda and down the hall toward the cafeteria.

When he was alone with his wife, Bruce asked, "What?"

She stared at him, saying nothing.

"What? You wanted to talk. What?"

She continued to stare at him. He racked his brain, reviewing the issues in his head. What *could* she have in mind? A sickening feeling flooded into his head along with realization.

"Oh, my God," he gasped.

"You should have seen his face," Linda said. "I guaranteed you'd never forget it."

"I . . . I thought it was tomorrow."

"Why didn't you answer the phone?"

"We were working. We turn the phone off."

"God forbid anything should interrupt your work."

"It's important, Linda," he insisted.

"It's a damn movie, Bruce. You're not deciding the fate of the Free World here. It wouldn't kill you to pick up the phone and talk to your wife."

"What're you trying to say, huh? What? I mess up once and I'm a lousy father?"

"I didn't say that. You said it. And it's not just once. This was just the worst."

"I'm *working*. I do that for my family. For you and for Brandon and Shannon."

"I wonder," Linda said.

"What do you mean?"

"I think you would do this if you lived alone on the moon. It's an obsession with you."

"Hey. Two years ago we were hiding from the bill collectors. Two years ago my wife had to go out to work for peanuts while I stayed home with the kids. Now we've got plenty of money. We have everything we wanted."

"Except I don't have a husband and my children don't have a father."

"That's not fair, Linda. This is my work time, and I *am* working for them too."

"But you never stop. For God's sake, Bruce, it's not a race."

"Yes, it is. It really is a race."

"But not a *sprint*. You have your whole life, and Brandon won't be a little boy forever."

Bruce rubbed his eyes. A headache was coming on, and it was going to be one of the bad ones. One of those he didn't talk about, the ones that started as a sharp pain behind his eyes and rolled backwards through the brain and down, finally settling at the base of the brain and throbbing with a severe pain that sometimes threatened to suffocate him. He fished a key from a pocket and unlocked the top drawer of a steel filing cabinet.

Curious, Linda walked to his side to see him rummaging through a veritable medicine chest of colorful boxes and bottles, all of them with Chinese labels. From this strange pharmacopeia he popped a few capsules.

"What's all this stuff?" she asked. "What are you taking?"

"Medicine."

"What kind of medicine? I can't read those labels."

"Chinese medicine," he said, washing down the capsules with several sips of tea.

"For what? Your back? You have American medicine for your back. What do you need this stuff for? Please tell me that it isn't powdered rhinoceros horn or something-or-another snake like they sell out in the street. What do you call those guys? The *feng shui* men? The fortune tellers."

"You wouldn't understand," he said, shaking his head to help clear away the headache.

"Where along the line did you decide that I don't understand?" she asked, her anger rising.

They stared at each other, anger mixing with the sort of desolation that creeps between lovers when an argument has gone beyond the point of reason.

"I didn't mean it the way it sounded," he said.

"You're something else. There's a secret! Is there something else you want to tell me?"

He shook his head.

"Is there another woman?"

Again he shook his head.

"Don't you love me anymore?" she asked.

Bruce ached to tell her the truth. But how could he

218

possibly tell his American wife about the demon and his dark purpose? How could Bruce ever tell her about Yip Man's prediction that Bruce was fated to fight the demon, certainly to the death? And that he would have to do it in order to protect Brandon, his firstborn son?

"Things are building in the right way for a change," he said, groping for a likely story. "I've got to make the most of it while it lasts. For all of us."

"That's a lie," Linda snapped. "We all tell ourselves lies. That's yours."

She walked out. This time he didn't follow her. But some of her words struck. Maybe there wasn't time to take Brandon to the circus, but there was time to protect him from the evil that was coming. So the next sunset he went alone and unnoticed to the roof of the Kowloon town house and lined the cornices with *pat kwa* mirrors. There were clouds out to sea. He could see them clearly, for the view went all the way to the horizon and there was something out there, blowing in with the monsoons, something very old and very evil. The mirrors would keep the residents of the house safe. The *feng shui* men said so. The mirrors had worked when his father used them, and they would work now that Brandon was the innocent firstborn child who needed protection.

Bruce was sure of it.

For the time being and no matter how Linda pleaded, however, there was business to be attended to. Matters of family would have to wait. So it was not long after he put the *pat kwa* mirrors on the roof of the town house, that Bruce sat shirtless in his editing suite at Pearl of the Orient Studios, writing the screenplay for *Game of Death*.

Attached to his pectoral muscles were fibrillator cups like those routinely used on electrocardiograph machines. Electrodes buried in black rubber suction cups were connected

219

to wires that led to a shiny black electronic generator. The gadget sent regular pulses to the electrodes, which stimulated Bruce's muscles to contract and twitch. It was a form of easy exercise that had been popular for a few years, mainly among harried executives and others too busy to pump iron.

On the wall next to the desk was a corkboard covered with file cards that had been pinned up in neat rows. The cards contained the outline for the new film. Bruce filled them out during his rare free moments at home; he was *always* working, as if in the belief that sheer momentum could keep the monsoons from arriving.

An eight-track stereo was playing Elton John's "Funeral for a Friend." A stack of tape cartridges, all of them American or English, littered the top of a filing cabinet. A small television, playing with the sound turned down, showed pictures of President Richard M. Nixon denying knowledge of the burglary at Washington's Watergate Hotel. A poster for *Return of the Dragon* looked down on the desk.

Bruce responded to a knock at the door by saying, "Come in," in Chinese.

"Hello?" someone replied in English.

"The door's unlocked," he said without looking up. The voice was distantly familiar; it belonged to someone from long ago.

Bill Krieger, the producer who had discovered Bruce at the Long Beach Karate Tournament and cast him in *The Green Hornet,* stuck his head in the door and looked around. He was particularly taken by the sight of Bruce Lee hooked up to an electronic toy that was supposed to make him strong.

"Somewhere there's gotta be a series in all this," he said.

Bruce turned around. He was surprised, to say the least,

to see that man. Coolly he snapped off the fibrillator cups and tossed the wires on top of the machine. He flicked the switch on the black box.

"Three minutes is like doing two hundred bench presses," Bruce said. "Wanna try it?"

Krieger stepped into the room and shook Bruce's hand. "No, thanks. You might turn it up and electrocute me."

"The thought crossed my mind."

"Justifiable homicide, some would say. You know, you really should be careful with that gadget. You could give yourself a stroke or something. I think they've been banned in the U.S. I haven't seen one in five years."

Bruce shrugged. "What are you doing in Hong Kong? How long have you been here?"

"I got in this morning."

"If it's for the circus, you're too late. It's over. I know that for a fact."

"Nothing like that. Look, Bruce, I'm sorry about *Kung Fu*."

"Me too. I would have been saved a lot of grief."

"I did what I could for you," Krieger insisted. "I went to bat for you with the network. You know that."

"I know you *told* me that."

"Well, it's true. I argued my head off but they wanted a name actor. David Carradine is a name actor."

"He is now, after you put him in the lead role on *my* show. Before that he was nobody." Bruce sighed. "He'll be nobody again."

"The network also wanted an American in the role. That's why I had to rewrite Caine to make him half-Chinese, half-American."

"A half-breed," Bruce said, thinking back to the time Linda's mother used that term to describe their children. He

221

wondered if Brandon would be considered a half-breed. In America, probably he would.

"The network is scared of putting Orientals on television. It's Vietnam. All Asians look like Viet Cong to the network."

Bruce laughed bitterly. "Vietnam," he said. "Vietnam is practically a stone's throw from here and yet I haven't thought about it since I moved back. No one in Hong Kong thinks about Vietnam. It's an American thing, along with the belief that all Asians are alike."

"What *do* they talk about in Hong Kong?" Krieger asked.

"Mao Tse-tung. Nixon. My movies. I don't know. Why don't you go out on the street and ask?"

"Maybe I will."

"I'll tell you the places to avoid. Look, Bill, you didn't come all this far to talk politics or discuss old times. How'd you find me?"

"Linda said you'd be here. She says you're *always* here. Still the hard worker."

"I guess so. Whaddya want?"

Krieger said, "I got someone downstairs I want you to meet. His name's Freddie Weintraub. We got a proposal for you."

"What happened? David Carradine turn you down?"

"Forget him. Fred's got a script. Warner Brothers is behind it. It's a Hollywood feature film with all the trimmings."

"I thought Hollywood was afraid of Asian actors."

"For television, yes. For theatrical release, anything goes. What do you say?"

Bruce thought for a moment, then said, "Let me think about it overnight. Bring your guy around for lunch tomorrow. Does he like Chinese food?"

"Would I have brought him to Hong Kong if he didn't?"

"Good. You can buy me lunch and we'll discuss his script."

Krieger sensed an easing up of Bruce's hard feelings. He said, "Hey, I thought it was the actor who's supposed to take the producer to lunch."

"My circumstances have changed," Bruce said, grinning back. "You're on *my* turf now."

🗿26🗿

WEINTRAUB WAS A FLESHY MAN WHO CLEARLY HAD SEEN TOO MANY
meals in Chinese, and all other, restaurants. He sported a
full, black beard that reached down to the second button of
his bush jacket. He was one of those Hollywood types who
are completely obsessed with their work. Weintraub was so
caught up in himself he could walk by the shooting of an
action scene in one of Pearl of the Orients' endless stream
of aerial ninja movies without appearing to notice the chaos
nearby. The back lot of the studio was alive with activity,
which was why Bruce wanted his American guests to see it.
The message was clear: There's a lot going on here and I
don't need you guys. If you make me an offer, make it a
good one.

"I'm talking about an action film," Weintraub said.
"Plenty of action."

"I have plenty of action here," Bruce said, looking over
as a black-hooded ninja went sailing through the air,
brandishing a sword and screaming. He was hooked up to a
wire that the director fervently hoped would remain invis-
ible. It didn't; nor did it remain intact. The wire broke,
sending the hapless actor crashing down into a fully laden
fruit wagon. As Bruce and his group strolled along through

the back lot, the normally controlled chaos of an action shoot became pandemonium.

"I'm talking about *big-budget* action," Weintraub went on. "In English too. First class all the way. It's called *Enter the Dragon*. Do you like that title?"

"It's okay."

"The film will make you another James Bond."

"I don't want to be another James Bond. There's only room for one. Several good actors have blown careers that way."

"Then another Steve McQueen," Weintraub said. "I know you like Steve McQueen. He's your friend, for God's sake, and he's number one in the world."

"I don't want to be him either. I'm pretty happy being Bruce Lee."

"Then we'll make Bruce Lee number one in the world."

"I've read the script," Krieger said. "And it's everything you ever wanted."

"I wanted *Kung Fu*."

"*Enter the Dragon* is much bigger than *Kung Fu*."

"I'll have to read the script and decide for myself. I need some time. You guys can entertain yourselves in Hong Kong for a few days while I think, can't you?"

"I suppose we'll find something to do," Krieger said.

"I don't know what arrangement you guys have, but one thing you need to know up front is that I've become partners with Phillip Tan. Anything I do, I do with him."

Krieger and Weintraub exchanged glances, then both nodded.

"That can be handled," Weintraub said. "*Anything* can be handled. I just want to make this goddamn film."

Bruce led the way to a pagoda that was part of an unused set overlooking the ocean. It had a splendid view and was a good place to sit to finish the conversation. Bruce hefted the script, which was rolled up, as if it were a football.

"So this is going to make me a star in America?" he asked.

"This is gonna make you a star around the world," Weintraub said.

"I have it pretty good here, you know. I have a good income. I have a Mercedes. My family is here with me."

"You don't have America," Weintraub said, waving his hand out to sea. "It's right over there, kid, waiting for you."

Bruce sat down under the roof of the pagoda and opened the script of *Enter the Dragon*.

When Bruce got home that night it was well past midnight, so he parked the car and snuck into the house, careful not to wake anyone. He made himself a cup of tea, then took it up onto the roof, where he checked to make sure that all of the *pat kwa* mirrors were in place. The sky was clear, but monsoons could blow in off the South China Sea at any time and with little warning. The mirrors were in place. He finished his tea and went down to the bedroom.

Bruce began to undress, pulling his belt off as soundlessly as possible and hanging it on the hook on the back of the door. Despite his silence, Linda stirred in bed. Moonlight bathed her face in a white, decidedly non-Chinese glow.

She said, "It's okay. I'm awake. You can turn the light on."

"I'm sorry."

"I said it's okay. What time is it?"

"I don't know. Between one and two, I guess."

"Where were you?" she asked, sitting up and drawing her knees to her chest, hugging them.

"Finishing writing the new version of *Game of Death*.

And I had another meeting with Krieger and his friend. I lost track of time. Are the kids okay?"

"Don't you ever get tired of asking that question?"

"We've been through this before, Linda. I don't have a choice. I have to make that movie."

"Which one? There have been so many I'm losing track."

"Enter the Dragon."

"Oh, the American one. Do you like it?"

"Yeah, it's great."

"And you trust these guys? Bill Krieger screwed you before."

"He won't do it again. I'm sure of it."

"And Weintraub? I never heard of him."

"I feel good about my decision," Bruce said, sitting on the edge of the bed near her.

"I'm glad for you," she said.

"You should be glad for *us*."

"I don't know what *us* means anymore. I'm taking the kids home for a while."

"Home is here for now," Bruce said, taken aback.

"No, this isn't home. This is where we watch you work."

"Success has got its problems like everything else," Bruce said. "This is no big surprise. When we struggled we had problems. Now that we're successful we have different problems. It's better than having your car repo'd. It's better than when we had nothing."

"We never had nothing," Linda argued. "We were a *family*."

Bruce was weary. He was stretching himself too thin, and the ache in his head that had become more or less his constant companion reminded him of just how thin he was stretched.

"What do you want me to do?" he asked.

227

"Come with us," she said.

"Where?"

"Home. San Francisco. I want to see my mother. I want to see my old neighborhood. I want to swim in the Pacific Ocean—*my* side of the ocean."

"Forget it," Bruce said. "I worked in America for ten years. What did it get me? It got me nothing."

"You got me," she said, more than a little irritated that he didn't think of that.

"Yeah, and they hate me for it," he snapped.

"Who hates you?"

"Them. Americans. America. Oh, boy, they got such a good line of bullshit: Come and get it. America, the mountain of gold. It's for everybody. Yeah, it's for *everybody white*! They don't tell you that before you get off the boat, though. You gotta read the small print . . . if you can read."

Linda argued: "You were gonna show them. You were gonna teach them. You were gonna be *sifu* to America. What happened to that?"

"I tried. It wasn't enough. Nobody learned anything from me."

"That's not true. What about all those kids beaming 'cause you showed them how to defend themselves from neighborhood bullies? What about Jerome? You gave him confidence as well as an appreciation for Chinese culture."

"They could have learned that from anybody. I'm telling you, America didn't want me."

"Well, I'm not America. The kids aren't America. We want you. Don't push us away."

Bruce rubbed his temples. The headache was roaring up again, and with it his temper. Already the veins in his temples were throbbing like the engine on a race car. He was losing it.

228

"We're going home to America," Linda pressed on. "I want you to come with us. I want the kids to have a father again."

"Is that some kind of guilt trip? I'm not taking any guilt trips."

"This place is eating us up. This *city* is eating us up. Can't you see that?"

"This place has given me a life," he said. "I'm somebody here. I'm special. Back there I'm just another gook, indistinguishable from the gooks they hate so much in Vietnam. I'm just another wetback Charlie Chan slopehead coolie dishwasher in a stinking chinky restaurant!"

Bruce launched into a poor imitation of Mickey Rooney in *Breakfast at Tiffany's*. He contorted his face until it was squinty-eyed and bucktoothed. He stumbled around the room, playing the role of an incompetent, bumbling Chinaman as seen in dozens of American movies.

"Starch you shirt, Mistah White Man? Please? No tickee, no shirtee. Orda one flum column A and one flum column B. Me happy to build de lail loads. Me happy to dig mines for you, Mistah White Man. Me no walk on sidewalk. Kiss you white ass . . ."

Bruce wound up and smashed his fist through a bureau drawer. The sound of crunching wood made Linda wince.

"You know why *Kung Fu* worked, David Carradine or no David Carridine? It worked because it showed a Chinaman—sort of a Chinaman anyway—*doing things right* for a change. Americans were so accustomed to seeing Chinamen bumbling around saying 'L' instead of 'R' and tripping over shit that they flipped out every time Caine turned, Superman-like, from a nobody into a hero. A hero, like I am here, in Hong Kong. I *like* being a hero, Linda, and I want to go on being a hero. Do you want me to go back to

229

San Francisco and go back to being a nobody? Is that what you think I am?''

There were wails in the other room. The children were crying in their bedroom, shrieking in fear at their father's outburst. It was like being back in Bel Air, the time Bruce took apart Pete and Brandon witnessed the performance. Linda got out of bed and started toward their door.

"I don't know who the hell you are anymore!" she shouted. "Do you?"

She pushed past him to reach the children. He covered his ears to block out their cries. He was coming apart and his whole family knew it now.

Bruce pulled his clothes back on and ran out the door, slamming it behind him. Soon he was behind the wheel of his Mercedes, the wheels squealing on the damp night pavement.

☗ 27 ☗

IT WAS A TENSE DAY IN DECEMBER OF 1972 WHEN PHILLIP TAN and Bruce Lee burst from the door of the studio commissary, leaving behind the usual gaggle of costumed actors, sweating laborers, on-the-make secretaries, and overdressed executives. Phillip and Bruce were not happy with each other; they were having a partners' spat.

"I thought we were partners," Phillip said.

"We *are* partners."

"Let's not forget that without me you would have gotten on the plane and gone back to America to baby-sit while your wife worked."

"And without me you wouldn't be driving a Rolls. Remember that Morris you used to putt around town in?"

"Krieger and Weintraub are Hollywood sharpies. I don't trust them."

"And you're a Hong Kong sharpie. They don't trust *you*. The way I see it, the three of you are on equal footing."

"And you get the best of both sides," Tan said.

"That's not fair," Bruce argued. "I told them without you it was no deal."

"A coproduction 'in association with Phillip Tan'? That's an insult."

"The film is big budget. Warner Brothers. In English with international distribution."

"Your films have international distribution now," Tan argued.

"Sure. They show in every Chinatown in the world. I want *more,* Phillip. I want worldwide distribution in mainstream cinemas."

"Don't sell me, Bruce," Tan said. "Don't sell a salesman."

They walked in silence through the Pearl of the Orient lot. Their problems were classic. Tan felt that he had discovered Bruce, who in turn believed that he had already been a hot property thanks to playing Kato. Tan felt that he had put money into Bruce, building him up into a star of Chinese martial arts movies. Bruce countered with all the money that Pearl of the Orients made off his kung fu ability. To top it off they were partners, and now two Americans—one of whom had screwed Bruce in the past—were moving in.

They walked through the executive parking area that lay just outside Tan's office. His Rolls was there, glistening in the bright Chinese sun following its regular washing at the hands of studio maintenance men. Bruce's Mercedes was there too, but in the process of being driven off for *its* regular washing. Bruce failed to notice that, he was so enmeshed in the pall of silence surrounding his partner and him.

Tan's office reflected the taste, power, and success Phillip and Bruce's joint efforts had made possible. The furnishings were expensive and British, reflecting Hong Kong's lingering heritage as a British Crown Colony. The desk was mammoth and mahogany, decorated with ornate Victorian silver picture frames and pen-and-pencil holders. A large oil portrait of Tan hung behind the plush leather swivel chair. Across the room was a soft brown leather couch; other furnishings included an antique brass spittoon, a bronze, table-height ashtray stand, and an Edwardian sideboard that served double duty as a bar. It was filled with various kinds of mineral waters and teas.

The two men were still tense when they walked in. Bruce had another migraine, one of those that seemed to reach up from the depths of hell to seize his brain in an iron grip. He massaged his temples, hoping for relief. It didn't help.

Tan noticed the discomfort. "What's the matter?" he asked.

"My head is killing me."

"Maybe you have the flu. I had it bad last year. My whole family was sick like dogs."

"It's just a headache. Do you have any aspirin?"

"Sure. One?"

"Four. Okay, it's a really bad headache."

Tan nodded to his well-tailored executive secretary, who left.

"Forget the headache and think about the deal," Bruce said, trying to shake off the pain. "It's an opportunity."

"Sure it is. For them, for you."

"You're a salesman. You know how it works. They made an offer. You can get more. Make a counteroffer."

"We don't need them," Tan argued.

"Yes, we do. We have to grow. America is the largest market in the world."

The secretary returned with the aspirin. She poured a glass of Perrier and brought the medicine and water to Bruce. He downed the tablets, following them with a gulp of water. Then he collapsed on Tan's plush couch, suddenly more exhausted than he had ever been in his life. Few of the important bouts of his life had made him quite so tired.

Seeing this, Tan motioned for his secretary to leave.

When she was gone, he said, "This is more than a headache. More than the flu."

"I don't know, Phillip. I don't know how much longer I can keep this up."

Noticing his partner's pain, Tan softened. "You want it so bad, don't you? You want their love so bad. Our love's not good enough."

"I set out with a dream," Bruce said. "I wanted to show the world the beauty of our culture. I wanted to give them a hero, a Chinese hero."

"We're on our way. Don't you see that?"

"You and I can't distribute films around the world by ourselves. We can't crack the American market alone. We *need* them. Do you think they could do a good job of distributing a film in Asia?"

Tan laughed. "Of course not."

"It's the same thing if we try to go into America without them. Besides, let them spend *their* money opening up America for us. What's the cardinal rule of business expansion?"

"Never play with your own money," Tan repeated, as if by rote.

"So? Let's do it."

"I guess you do have an argument," Tan sighed.

"You'll make an agreement with Krieger and Weintraub?"

"Sure. *If* they sweeten the pot a little."

"Good. I want one other thing too."

"Name it."

"I want to stop breaking my wife's heart. I want to play with my kids and not look at the clock. You know what Brandon's saying? He's saying he wants to learn kung fu. He wants to be like his daddy, can you imagine that?"

"Boys should want to grow up like their fathers," Tan said. "You should be proud."

"And I am. The trouble is—I don't have time to teach him. Can you imagine that? Bruce Lee's son may have to go to some second-rate *sifu* because his dad is never home anymore."

Hearing this, Tan walked to the large picture window that looked out over the ocean. Bruce got off the couch and joined him there.

"They're American, Phillip. I need to get back to America with my family—or I'll lose them."

"Are Linda and you having problems?"

"Some, yes."

"Why didn't you tell me?"

"It's not the sort of thing a man brags about. Especially a man who's a hero to his people. Bruce Lee can't make his *wife* happy? Can you imagine if that got in the newspapers?"

"I see."

"I love them, Phillip, and if I lose them nothing means anything."

Just then Tan's executive secretary came back in, looking distressed. "I'm sorry to interrupt you. But Mr. Lee's housekeeper is on the phone. She sounds very upset."

Bruce's eyes went as wide as saucers and the headache was forgotten. He crossed to Tan's desk and punched a button on the phone.

"What's wrong?" he asked in Cantonese. "Put Linda on . . . What? I'll be right there."

He hung up and turned to Tan. "They're leaving me," he said. "They're on the way to the airport."

Bruce ran out the door and to the executive parking lot. He stood in bewilderment in his empty parking space. The sign read "Bruce Lee" but the Mercedes was gone.

"Where's my car?" he yelled at the attendant.

"It's Thursday, Mr. Lee. We always have it washed and gassed on Thursday."

Bruce eyed Tan's Rolls, and had started back inside to get the keys when he spotted a motorcycle messenger on a slick Kawasaki circling around the parking lot, looking for a place to stash the bike while dropping off a package. As the motorcycle swung by him, the driver taking sideways glances as it registered that he was looking at Bruce Lee, Bruce made a diving leap and landed behind the startled driver, tossing him off as if he were a feather.

Bruce throttled up the cycle and streaked off. The messenger got to his feet and brushed the dirt off. He said to the parking attendant, "That was Bruce Lee."

"It sure was," the attendant replied.

"Bruce Lee stole my motorcycle," exclaimed the messenger, who was thrilled. He might have lost his cycle, but the day was still the best one of his life.

Lying low on the handlebars like a racer, Bruce vaulted the barricade at the studio gate, looking very much like his friend Steve McQueen in *The Great Escape*. The tires squealed as he turned the corner and cut through downtown Hong Kong on his way to the Cross-Harbour Tunnel, which was much faster than either the Star or Wanchai ferries.

He roared down the narrow shopping streets, dodging pedestrians and peddlers alike, and through the wider, modern business boulevards. Soon he was in the harbor area whizzing by loading cranes and container ships. He turned onto Gloucester Road, and opened up the throttle to roar through the Wanchai and Causeway Bay districts to find the entrance to the tunnel.

Soon he was in Kowloon taking at sixty a corner that was designed for twenty-five. It was a blind corner, and he didn't see until too late the taxi that was pulling away from the town house, taking his family to the airport. The cab was packed with people and luggage, and the driver couldn't see too well either. Bruce jammed on the brakes, but it was too late. He collided with the taxi head-on, flipping over the handlebars, landing on the hood. The driver jammed on the brakes.

"It's Daddy!" Brandon yelled.

Bruce rolled off the hood and ripped open the rear door, half diving into Linda's arms.

"I'm sorry . . . I'm so sorry," he said.

"Bruce! Are you okay! Where did you get that bike?"

"I stole it. I'll pay the guy back."

"Are you hurt?"

"Only by the chance of losing you."

He buried his head against her breast.

"Shhh . . . it's okay," she said, rubbing his head and smoothing his hair where it had gone wild from the race through Hong Kong and Kowloon.

"Let me just make this American movie. One more, and we'll go home. We'll be respected in America then. It won't be like before at all."

"Can we see a little more of you while you're making this movie?"

"Sure. I promise. I swear it."

"How many times does this make that we've broken up? Almost broken up."

"I don't know. Three . . . four. Let's make this the last one. Don't ever leave me. Don't ever leave me again," he pleaded.

"No," she said. "No, never."

⌘ 28 ⌘

1973

FATE HUNG HEAVILY OVER HONG KONG AS THE SKIES DARKENED and a gigantic storm system moved inexorably in from the sea, bringing God-knows-what. The boat people, who for generations had lived on thrown-together boats lashed together in the harbor and out-islands, moved quickly to the several typhoon anchorages that provided relative safety. Even as they were tying up in their temporary homes, the skies darkened more and even the water of the harbor roiled with tossing waves and feathery whitecaps. A monsoon was coming, and it was a bad one.

The back lot of Pearl of the Orient Studios was racked by the newly arisen wind. The American film crew had taken over the studio, and all available spots were given over to sets for *Enter the Dragon*. Grips struggled to nail and tie them down against the storm, but one movie facade blew over anyway, sending workers scurrying to get out of the way.

Standing alone at the window of Tan's office, Bruce looked out to sea and watched the storm blow in from off the South China Sea. Yip Man's words weighed heavily on his mind. The old man had said, "When you are at your absolute peak he will come to you. When the monsoons blow, be prepared.''

Bruce was surely at his peak, both physically and in terms of popularity. After ten years of rejection in America, America was now at his doorstep. A mammoth film production crew had migrated from Hollywood to Hong Kong and promised to make him an international star. Surely Bruce could not be more powerful. Yet he remembered well the warning of his old *sifu,* and stared at the growing storm with the realization that it could mean the end of his life. It could mean the time had come to fight the demon once and for all, with Brandon's life hanging in the balance.

Bruce pressed his fingertips against his temples. Another migraine was coming in with the storm.

''You should see a doctor,'' Tan said.

''Or a *feng shui* man,'' Bruce replied.

''Don't be ridiculous. Do you want some more aspirin?''

Bruce nodded, so Tan pulled a bottle from his desk drawer and tossed it across the room to his partner. Bruce popped off the cap and downed a mouthful without bothering to count them.

''You're going to give yourself an ulcer with all those pills,'' Tan said.

Outside the window, the rain began to fall in sheets and pound against the glass, driven by the fierce sea winds. ''It looks like we may drown first,'' Bruce said.

''Or blow away. They're calling Tropical Storm Dot a typhoon now. It was supposed to come yesterday, but it waited until today when we're shooting the final scene. The gods must be angry.''

''The final scene of *Enter the Dragon* is indoors. We'll survive. The movie will get done.''

There was a knock on the door. An assistant director—a

239

very California-looking one, with blond hair and a surfer's tan—stuck his head inside.

"Sorry, Bruce. Sorry, Mr. Tan. We're ready when you are."

"I'll be right there," Bruce replied.

"Americans," Tan said. "They're very efficient."

"That's what they say about us," Bruce replied.

He turned away from the window just as the monsoon was whipping Hong Kong to a frenzy. He knew that the final battle with the demon was coming soon.

"Are you ready?" Tan asked, thinking, of course, only of the movie.

"Are you scared of anything, Phillip?"

"Yes. A few things, like bankruptcy. You?"

Bruce shrugged.

"You've got a right to be scared," Tan said. "You're the one in front of the camera. Me, I'm just a smart man . . ."

"Who can spot a good omen a long way off," Bruce said.

"Did I really say that?"

"A long time ago, when you chased me on the ferry."

"When it's all over, you'll be the great Bruce Lee and I'll be remembered as—Bruce Lee's friend."

"Don't sell yourself short."

"We changed many things, you and me," Tan said. "I never sell that short."

Bruce threw a fake jab at him. "I better go," he said. "I gotta finish the scene before your whole studio blows away."

Indeed, even as Bruce spoke the monsoon winds whipped across the harbor to Kowloon and blew the *pat kwa* mirrors off the roof of Bruce's town house as if they were so many dry leaves. Bruce and his son were now unprotected, and the demon was loose in the city.

The mammoth sound stage at Pearl of the Orients was fairly well insulated from the weather, with backup generators to

240

provide electricity in case the power lines went down. The climactic fight scene of *Enter the Dragon* was set in a hall of mirrors. Cameras were everywhere, along with members of the American crew. Unlike the shoot in Thailand, this production was indeed full scale. But even with all the trappings of a Hollywood film shoot, once Bruce went into character and stepped through the revolving door into the hall of mirrors he was alone with images of himself, seemingly thousands of them.

He crept intensely through the images of himself, prowling like a cat, ready for anything. Behind the cameras, Krieger, Weintraub, and Tan watched. Bruce was ready to fight. In the script, he was ready to bring down Han, the villain. But in his own mind Bruce was ready to fight the devil, who he knew now was coming.

Abruptly the sound stage began to shake and vibrate like it was riding the spine of a killer earthquake. Bruce looked behind the cameras to the crew, but they were all gone. They had disappeared as if yanked from Earth by a gigantic hand. Moreover, the back wall of the set was closing, moving toward him as if to seal him in from the real world. Bruce lost his footing then and crashed to the floor. The stage went black then, and the spectral white lightning that had heralded the demon's other appearances filled the room. It came down from high above, truly a judgment from the gods.

The shaking stopped, and only the far-off and furious sounds of the monsoon could be heard. The fourth wall of set closed in trapping Bruce and a numbing cold that came up from a graveyard somewhere. Bruce stood up, then dropped lower, into a fluid defensive position, waiting for the demon that he knew was nearby, hiding in the spectral light.

There was a high piercing sound, more than a whistling, less than a shriek. The razor-sharp blade of the *kwan-do,* the knife of General Kwan, a fearsome saber at the end of a long pike, whizzed through the air. Bruce ducked and the blade seared overhead, missing taking his head off by a micromillimeter. Bruce twisted and faced the demon.

The Ming Warrior seemed taller than before and smelled worse. The stench of the graveyard oozed from his flaring nostrils, and the muscles that bulged beneath his leather arm guards were stained with the blood of centuries.

The demon charged, swinging his terrifying weapon with superhuman speed. In a pas de deux of death, Bruce parried and leaped, ducked and sidestepped as the *kwan-do* cut at him from every angle. He got in one high kick to the demon's chest, but the blow seemed puny and hardly fazed the dark god. Bruce leaped back, away from another slashing blow, ducking behind one of two mirrored pillars. The demon slashed it in two with one swipe, as if it were wax. The thick mirrored pillar crumbled to the floor, shattering in a thousand razor-sharp fragments.

Reversing his motion, the warrior delivered a similar strike to the other pillar, collapsing it in on the first. Whoever the warrior was and whatever hell he came from, he clearly had Bruce in his sights. Using the *kwan-do* like a spear, he threw the weapon with all his might. It was aimed right at Bruce's chest. Using his lightning reflexes, Bruce grabbed it in mid-flight. But the power with which it had been thrown was truly superhuman. So hard was the *kwan-do* thrown that once he grabbed it, Bruce was jerked backwards by the momentum of the weapon. It impacted in the door.

Using all his might, Bruce yanked it out of the door and twirled it around. It was his turn to be armed. Moving slowly, he stalked the demon, whose eyes, glowing green like those of a lizard, stared at the weapon.

Bruce raised it and cocked his arm to throw. But the

demon's eyes blazed angrily, and the *kwan-do* burst into flame. Stunned, Bruce dropped the blazing shaft. It clattered to the ground, burning brightly like the tail of a comet. Then the shaft detached from the blade and, before Bruce's disbelieving eyes, turned into a cobra, its malevolent eyes looking around from its flaming head. A serpent from hell, it slithered off into a dark corner of the set, a sinuous cord of flame.

Bruce gaped at it for a second or more. When he looked up, the demon was gone. Bruce quickly scanned all possible directions, but his adversary was nowhere to be seen. So he crept toward the mirrored cubicle that grips had built at the far end of the set. Bruce crept inside, and his image was reflected on all sides, as if by a kaleidoscope. There was no demon, however.

As he peeked around a corner, he was suddenly grabbed by a gigantic pair of hands that lifted him off the floor and shook him as if he were a rag doll. Spiked bracelets rattled on either side of Bruce's shoulders and his arms were pinned to his sides. Then he was pulled toward the demon's leather-sheathed, foul-smelling chest, and just as quickly tossed away.

Bruce was sent flying backwards through a glass wall that exploded with the impact. Tiny razor blades of glass filled the air. The explosion propelled Bruce back into the fog-shrouded hollow where he had previously fought the warrior. The same thigh-deep fog was there, sucking at his legs, smelling sickly sweet like funeral flowers.

The dead tree that rose far overhead had attracted an even deadlier-looking buzzard. The devil's disciples Bruce remembered from before were there, but frozen stiff like mummies. He scrambled to his feet and looked around for the demon. There was no sight of the monster. So he began picking his way through the fog, edging around the tree, always on guard for the overwhelming attack that he knew would come sooner or later.

There appeared a horizon of sorts, a sky in the distance, but from it came the threatening clouds of the monsoon. The storm moved rapidly toward him, much faster than any earthly storm, and with it came driving rain that drove off the ground fog. As Bruce fought his way forward, moving toward the eye of the storm, the landscape changed.

He found himself in a terraced concrete world that was studded with trees, some dead, some coniferous and whipping in the growing wind. As the fury of the monsoon mounted, the earth began to tremble as it had at the start of the attack, back on the set.

From all sides, headstones wrenched up through the concrete like granite flowers. In an instant, the world was transformed into a half-cemetery, half-amphitheater, a cross between his father's resting place and a martial arts battle-ground. It was the colosseum from hell.

Then the earth was torn beneath Bruce's feet and he had to leap out of the way to keep from being knocked over. A monolith grew out of the stinking, rain-soaked ground, all gray and ominous. It rose larger and larger, looming above Bruce. As he looked up at it, his face became etched with horror. The monolith was a gigantic tombstone. The inscription read:

BRUCE LEE
1940–1973
Founder of *jeet kune do*

His picture was embedded in the granite, laminated just like his father's was. Bruce was frozen in place, horrified by it all, by the correctness of Yip Man's prediction. Suddenly he was grabbed from behind like before, held by the shoulders by gigantic hands that were sheathed in chain-mail gloves. Before he could react, he was lifted off the ground and smashed against his own tombstone. Bruce's own blood smeared his portrait as his head was banged repeatedly into the granite monolith.

The demon had Bruce completely at his mercy. He bashed Bruce's face against the tombstone until it was as raw as hamburger and blood flowed in rivers down the face of the stone and thoroughly soaked the laminated picture. Bruce tried to rebound, to find that extra bit of energy that had saved him so many times in the past.

It wasn't there. Bruce was nearly finished. He was limp in the brutal arms of the giant. The warrior turned Bruce and held him propped up against the headstone with one hand, then cocked his other fist to administer the coup de grace. Then he stopped. His blazing green eyes were fixed on something else, something that had appeared nearby.

It was Brandon playing on the lawn with a yellow Tonka Toy truck. The vision appeared in the wall of the terraced amphitheater. Yip Man's direst prediction had come true—it was Brandon who the demon really wanted.

The warrior flung Bruce aside like so much trash. He set off toward the helpless child. Bruce cleared his head, looked up, and yelled, "No. *No-o-o-o!*"

Bruce found his reservoir of strength. He flung himself onto the demon's back, but was thrown off like a mere annoyance. The monster kept stalking the child, smashing through headstones as if they were made of papier-maché.

Bruce scrambled into the path of the demon and assumed a protective stance. He used what moves he could, but no martial art seemed to work against the warrior's fiendish determination and superhuman strength.

Fueled by a fear more primal than self-preservation, Bruce sprang back. He screamed a *kiai* from the depths and launched himself into a twisting high kick that caught the demon full force in the windpipe—his one vulnerable spot. The sickening crunch of cartilage being destroyed filled the heavy air.

The giant was stunned and, clutching at his crushed throat, faltered. Bruce realized that he had found the vulnerable spot and began to home in on it. But not before the demon's eyes glowed with molten hatred. Suddenly, the giant's whole face exploded with spikes and his lizard eyes dimmed back to darkness. Undeterred, Bruce moved in for the kill. Over and over, his fists, elbows, and kicks found their mark with lethal accuracy. The demon was rocked back, blow after blow, away from Brandon and back toward Bruce's grave.

The warrior tried to grapple with Bruce, but had lost the advantage and was having trouble breathing. Each breath was ragged and wet with blood and sputum, like that of a war-horse that had been shot in the gut. The giant was weakening. Seeing his advantage, Bruce leaped onto the demon's shoulders and slammed his forearms around his head and neck. Choking, the demon went down on one knee.

Leveraging for all he was worth, his *chi* burning like a supernova, Bruce wrenched the head, twisting it around like one uncorks a bottle of old wine. With one final *kiai,* Bruce snapped the demon's neck. The giant collapsed and Bruce rode him down, like a lumberjack riding a falling redwood.

The monster was a beaten hulk in black armor, lying bleeding and gasping on the ground, half dead. Bruce leaped into the air then, bringing his lethal foot down on the giant's neck, one more blow to end it.

The demon's eyes milked over. He would haunt no further dreams.

Bruce looked over to Brandon. His son was safe, blissfully unaware of all that had been done to protect him. The vision faded away then. Bloody but triumphant and feeling a thousand feet tall, Bruce leaped into the air and, in a final act of rage, delivered a double kick to his massive gravestone. It exploded and the flash enveloped him.

Bruce was back in the hall of mirrors. He was okay, life itself was okay. The set was intact and the crew was there as before. Tan, Krieger, and Weintraub stared at him with deep concern in their eyes. Bruce looked down at himself and saw no difference from before the battle. There was no blood, no bruises, and his clothes were intact. Something had happened, though; the crew stared at him with concern and disbelief in their eyes.

Krieger said, "You okay, Bruce? We kind of lost you for a minute."

🜲29🜲

BRANDON AND SHANNON SAT ON THE LIVING ROOM FLOOR OF THE Kowloon town house playing with a model train set. A freight train was being loaded with blocks hauled there on Brandon's Tonka Toy truck. Linda was in the kitchen, making dinner with the help of Ngan Ma.

Like a spirit, Bruce stood in the doorway watching his family. Success, real success, the kind you get by being a good husband, father, and lover, not by making money or becoming famous, was within his grasp. And it was so easy; all he'd had to do was kill the demon.

Like it was the most natural thing in the world, Bruce Lee sat down on the floor to play with his kids.

"Hey, Dad! Mommy, it's Dad! What are you doing here?"

"I live here," Bruce said.

"I mean, it's still daytime," Brandon said. "Wanna play trains?"

"Yeah, I love trains," he said, and he meant it.

He kissed his son and pulled his daughter close. Linda came from the kitchen, happy to see her husband *acting* like a husband. She paused in the doorway, leaning against the jamb. He looked up at her.

"Hi, honey, I'm home," he said.

She smiled. "Welcome home, sailor," she said. "How was your day?"

"Terrific. Couldn't have been better."

"What did you shoot?"

"The fight scene in the hall of mirrors."

"How did it go?"

"I won," he said proudly. "I beat the demon."

She gave him a quizzical look. "I thought the script called for you to fight some guy named Han or something."

He shrugged. "Every opponent is the demon," he said.

He got to his feet and started toward her. She expected a kiss, but when Bruce got close enough he spun and kicked the wall clock off its mounting. It spun in midair and he caught it in his hands. He laid it face down on the end table.

"That's better," he said.

With that he gave his wife a kiss, the kiss of an eternal lover.

Holding hands, Bruce and Linda walked across the back lot of Pearl of the Orient Studios. *Enter the Dragon* was done, all but one shot. And for that climactic moment, Linda wanted to be there. It not only was Bruce's crowning achievement; it meant that finally they could return to the States, and do it in style. The last shot of *Enter the Dragon* was both a beginning and an ending. Both Bruce and Linda found a certain symmetry in that, considering the fact that Chinese culture was filled with examples of yin and yang, black and white, beginning and end. Perhaps they *were* bringing something of Chinese culture back to America.

As they walked across the set they exchanged greetings with hundreds of crew members and extras, and Linda got yet another reminder of just how much of a star her husband was. And there was a sense of destiny about the film. Everyone associated with the project *knew* that it would catapult Bruce to international stardom. Everyone he saw that last day wanted to be a part of history by shaking his hand or just saying hello.

At last Bruce and Linda reached their destination: a scaffolding built behind a mammoth set. An assistant director with a walkie-talkie waited at the base of a ladder. He brought the radio to his lips and said happily, "He's here."

The man then jogged around to the front of the set. Bruce turned to Linda.

He said, "Well, this is it. The final shot."

"Make it great," Linda replied.

He started to climb the ladder up the scaffold. Halfway up he stopped, turned, and smiled back down at his wife.

"Hey, Linda," he called out.

She returned the smile.

"I forgot something. I forgot to tell you I love you."

She looked startled. "You know, I don't think you ever said that to me before."

"Yeah, but I meant it every day," he replied with a grin as wide as the horizon.

He climbed the final rungs and disappeared over the wall.

Bruce stood on a catwalk above the Han's Island set. Below him, a hundred martial artists stood in rows, as proper as soldiers in a full-dress parade, ready to salute the triumphant hero. The cameras rolled, taking in the whole vista. A hundred martial artists looked up at their hero and, uncued, bowed.

He returned the bow. As he stood back up, fully erect, Linda saw his head haloed in the setting sun, saw her husband and lover and the father of her children standing like a golden idol with the flaming orange-red sun setting behind him. And in that moment even she too wanted to bow.

• • •

Three weeks before the opening of *Enter the Dragon*, Bruce Lee died in Hong Kong of what the authorities said was a cerebral edema, a swelling of the brain. Twenty-five thousand people attended his funeral.

Linda brought his body back to the United States for burial.

He was thirty-two.